SHADOW
CATCHER

Books by Charles Fergus

FICTION
Shadow Catcher

NONFICTION
The Wingless Crow
A Rough-Shooting Dog

SHADOW CATCHER

A Novel

CHARLES FERGUS

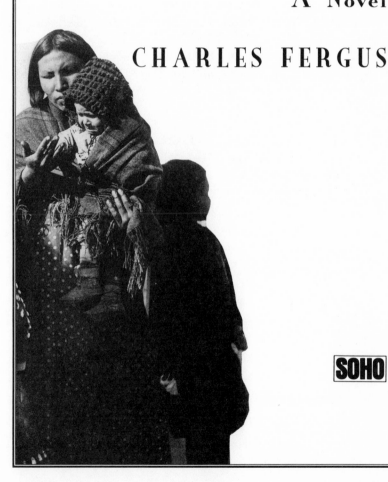

SOHO

ACKNOWLEDGMENTS

I thank the following people for their help in the making of this book: Manfred Keune, Susan Applegate Krouse, Ed Leos, Elaine Gaul, Dot Anderson, the staff of the William Hammond Mathers Museum at the University of Indiana, Bob Bell, Terry Dunkle, David Sleeper, Leonard Rubinstein, Brian Fergus, Ruth Fergus, Nancy Marie Brown, Art Brown, and Upton Brady. Also Barbara Mathe and the archives staff at the American Museum of Natural History in New York, Todd Strand and the archivists at Historical Society of North Dakota, and the University of Oklahoma Library.

Several books were especially valuable:

James McLaughlin, The Man With an Indian Heart, by Louis L. Pfaller, O.S.B., Vantage Press, 1978.

Moon of Popping Trees, by Rex Alan Smith, University of Nebraska Press, 1975.

My Friend, the Indian, by James McLaughlin, Houghton Mifflin, 1910.

Other Summers, by Edward Leos, The Pennsylvania State University Press, 1980.

Library of Congress Cataloging-in-Publication Data

Fergus, Charles.
Shadow Catcher/Charles Fergus
p. cm.
ISBN 0-939149-55-9
1. Indians of North America—Fiction. I. Title
PS3556.E65S51991   91-20079
813'.54—dc20   CIP

Published by
Soho Press Inc.
853 Broadway
New York, NY 10003

Book design and composition by The Sarabande Press

First Edition

to NMB

There is something on people's faces when they don't know they are being observed that never appears when they do.

Susan Sontag
On Photography

The photographs appearing on pages 2, 23, 61, 69, 82, 92, 107, 124, 130, 157, 178, 184, 194, 206, 222, 257, 266, 280, 290, and 301 are from the Wanamaker Collection, courtesy of the Department of Library Services, Photographic Collection, American Museum of Natural History.

The photographs on pages 18, 87, 141, 170, 236 and 305 appear courtesy of the Wanamaker Collection, William Hammond Mathers Museum, Indiana University.

Photographs on pages 28, 34, 54, 129, and 251 appear courtesy of the State Historical Society of North Dakota.

The picture on page 40 is from the Phillips Collection and appears courtesy of Western History Collections, University of Oklahoma Library.

SHADOW
CATCHER

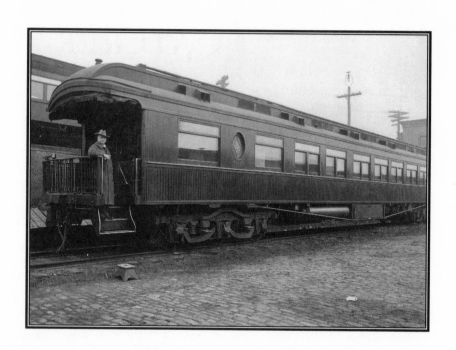

1

I'll be go to hell.

James McLaughlin pressed the paper flat. It was the center two pages of the Roto section of the Sunday Washington *Dispatch*.

I'll be jumped up and calf-kicked. . . .

He straightened his pince-nez, blinked.

The layout formed a large oval: eight round photographs orbiting a block of type. Strange photographs. He glanced at the type, at the comments the Commissioner had scribbled in red and then underlined, but the photographs drew him back.

The one that caught his eye was of a girl. Clean-limbed, slim, with splendid raven hair. She reminded him, suddenly and with a pang, of the Indian girl he and his wife had raised: a trying young woman, gone west. No doubt they would meet her when the Expedition curled back around to Idaho.

The girl in the picture was also an Indian. Cherokee, maybe Choctaw; pretty girl, elegant if she could exchange that dowdy wool uniform for a dress. Cherokee—he was sure of it now; he remembered them in uniforms like that, and wasn't it blazing that day? Lord how those girls must have suffered— schoolgirls who had sung "America the Beautiful" to open the ceremony in Tahlequah.

In the photograph the girl stood straining forward, neck arched, face aglow. Her lips, generous, were parted in a smile . . . signifying surprise? Interest? Attraction? One shoulder

3

tipped slightly upward, one hand rested lightly at her waist while the other hung frozen in midair, all set to reach out and touch a companion's arm, or point, or wave. The longer he stared at the photograph the surer he was that, yes, she *was* alive, if he but waited a moment longer she would actually move.

He frowned and gave his head a curt shake. Something about the picture made him uneasy. He scratched at the corner of his eye with a fingernail. Finally he figured it out. He was seeing something he hadn't any right to. The photograph wasn't a proper portrait, the girl hadn't been posed head-on and sober and direct, she paid no attention to the photographer at all. And that was what made it wrong. As if she'd had no idea someone was pointing a camera.

His frown deepened. And his eyes, gray behind the glass panes, slid inexorably to the next photograph—also an Indian, this one an old man. Seminole? McLaughlin prided himself on being able to look at an Indian and identify the tribe. He had worked among them for so long that even with their hair cropped, and wearing white man's clothes, more often than not he could tell Hopi from Navaho, Mohave from Apache, even Yankton Sioux from Hunkpapa Sioux. Here an old Seminole farmer, touch of Negro blood, see it in the nose; he wore tattered bib overalls, a plaid shirt buttoned to the neck, and a battered hat. Seemed to be talking to somebody out of the frame, a wry, expectant look on his dark, broad face, as if gauging a reaction to something he had just said, or bantering like they did. Everyone said Indians were stoic. Some could be as sociable as an ulcerated tooth, but stoic? Damn few he'd met. And again: no idea, no notion at all that he was being photographed.

Two half-breeds in slick ill-fitting suits, ties undone, collars open. Now he understood why the Commissioner had sent the paper, had circled this and other photographs, and bled his red ink all over the margins, because the half-breeds were

4

passing a bottle. The one who had just gulped had his face all screwed up; the other, reaching for the flask, slobbered like a sick calf.

The next picture, also circled, showed a shack with a splintered door and broken windows. Could be anywhere, Sac and Fox, Kiowa, Apache—shacks like that all over the West. A small dark boy sat out in front, bloated belly, dull eyes, dirt-streaked face, playing with the severed foreleg of a deer. A pile of cans, garbage heaped against a fence—McLaughlin could almost hear the flies buzzing, catch the stench.

No wonder Cribbs's bowels are in an uproar. He read the copy in the center of the page:

CANDID PHOTOGRAPHY FROM THE AMERICAN WEST

The camera as a tool for capturing life as it is lived has heretofore gone unexploited. With these photographs, the world is introduced to a new way of seeing. The photographs are unposed and unretouched, taken by an expert operating in the West. The *Dispatch* plans to print more of these remarkable images in future editions.

That was all. No captions, no credit line. *An expert operating in the West.*

He read the Commissioner's comments, folded the newspaper, and took off his pince-nez, attached to a short black ribbon; he polished the lenses absently and ineffectively and returned them to his vest. He creaked up out of the chair, a short, squared-off man with big hands and arms that filled the sleeves of his suit. His full head of hair was white. His mustache hung like snow ledges above his mouth. His eyebrows flared whitely in a curve opposite to his mustache. His fresh celluloid collar stood straight up all around his neck, except in the front, where it bent down like stunted white wings on either side of the neatly knotted red four-in-hand.

In the passageway he walked legs straddled and arms outspread, like a man negotiating a field of grass at night. The Santa Fe had a good roadbed but you never knew—a hidden sag, a crooked mating of rails, and you slipped and banged a knee or cracked an elbow, and there you were. At his age the last thing he needed was another ache or pain.

He knocked at the next door. The stateroom was identical to his: a gently arched ceiling of polished butternut, dark mahogany walls, green baize curtains, brass bed, steel sink, wardrobe, chair, and desk, the furnishings clean and shipshape. Joseph Dixon looked up from his writing. He was younger than James McLaughlin by fifteen years. He had a clipped gray mustache and gray hair with a ruler-straight part. His blue protuberant eyes were hooded by their lids. Dixon was Wanamaker's man, and this "Expedition of Citizenship" was Wanamaker's show, and McLaughlin had resolved to get along with the pompous fool because six months in the confines of a private railcar was a very long time.

"Evening, Doctor Dixon. I wonder if you've seen these. Apparently they're causing a stir back east."

McLaughlin opened the newspaper and passed it to Dixon, who spread it on the desk. Dixon's eyes bulged wider, then narrowed. "How odd," he said. "How very odd." Looking at the photographs, his head described minutely the oval in which they were arranged. His face, a most facile instrument, took on an expression of disgust. "Trash. I'm surprised a newspaper would print this."

"Any idea who the photographer might be?"

"No idea." Dixon took a handkerchief from his pocket and dusted the newsprint from his hands. "A fad. Faddists every-where these days. It's like these futurists or cubists, whatever they call themselves. Modern art—nothing romantic or fine or uplifting about it at all." He had taken note of Cribbs's scribbling. "I can see why the Indian Bureau wouldn't want these published."

McLaughlin sucked on his teeth and nodded slowly. "You're sure you don't know . . . ?"

"Haven't a clue."

McLaughlin thanked Dixon, took up the paper, and left.

The hall passage ended in the observation room, with purple velvet chairs, a matching settee, bookcase, map file, desk, and a berth like a shiny black cocoon tucked into the joint between wall and ceiling.

Ansel Fry sat at the desk, staring out the window. The Bureau stenographer assigned to McLaughlin for the trip, he was young, trained in the new Pitman shorthand, and very sure and quick. It was dark outside; the train was passing across a great empty stretch, and the solidly black window cast back an image of Fry's face: unlined, smooth-shaven, with a long thin-bridged nose and a smallish mouth, mouse brown hair already thinning at the temples. An unremarkable face, McLaughlin thought. These clerks—so interchangeable, so bland.

"Let's do a telegram," he said.

Fry looked up, startled. "Yessir." He got out a pad and a fountain pen as McLaughlin settled into a chair.

"To the Honorable E. J. Cribbs, Commish Indian Affairs, et cetera, et cetera. Date it today"—McLaughlin brought out his watch, pressed the little stud in its side to pop open the lid—"and get it out tonight." He shut and pocketed the watch, propped his feet on an ottoman, and rested his head against an antimacassar. "Received Washington *Dispatch* Roto section. Stop. So-called candid photographer unknown to Doctor Dixon and myself. Stop." He paused. "Photographs without artistic merit and injurious to Indian Bureau. Stop. Will inquire regarding suspicious persons on reservations and report as needed. Stop." The thick white eyebrows bobbed once, settled. "That's all."

He handed Fry the newspaper. "File it, please."

File it, Fry did. And got it out again after all had gone to

7

bed. He flipped through the pages hurriedly to the center spread. He stared at the photographs, drawing deep and ragged breaths.

The sky was a high, washed-out blue. No clouds, but little millings of pestiferous gnats. Pink dust rose and hung. The Indians—four tribes: the Shawnees, Potawatomies, Sac and Foxes, and Kickapoos—had arrived on horseback and in wagons. Ansel Fry smelled horse sweat and manure and fragrant flowers in the grass.

He looked over one shoulder, then the other. Took a deep breath, traced a shoe toe through the dust. Unbuttoned his suit coat and let the lapels part. Touching the vest, he felt the hard disk beneath. The lens peered out through a buttonhole. The hidden eye let him see with his whole body, a cone of vision circling as he turned.

Sticklike planted trees. Whitewashed agency buildings. Listing, rusting water tower. People, dozens of them, faces the color of old pennies. The men wore high-crowned flat-brimmed hats and ragged suspendered pants; the women had on billowy calico dresses, a style he remembered his grandmother wearing. They looked civilized enough, he thought, but they were—what?—a generation or less removed from savagery.

There were whites in the crowd, spectators and agency personnel, so he figured he wouldn't stick out. He worked his way slowly between the knots of people. Out of the corner of one eye he watched a fat woman herding a flock of eager yet cautious children. An old man lighting a pipe, his seamed cheeks sucking in, puffing out. A girl: She wore a dark skirt, a white blouse budded with small upturned breasts. She was still young enough to be wearing her hair down, its twin black cascades framing her pretty oval face.

Closer. Olive skin taut across high cheekbones. Fine downy hair that rose in front of an ear to join a rich black mass.

He assumed what he hoped was a nonchalant pose. He pressed his left forearm across the bottom of his vest, flattening the fabric, stabilizing the lens. His right hand, pocketed, found the string and drew up the slack.

He waited for the right moment.

It came, when three boys set up a taunt, and she whirled and stuck out her tongue, then caught herself and laughed.

The quiet click was lost in the drone of the crowd.

He felt something hot and bright surge from the pit of his stomach to his face. He slipped a hand up under his vest, found the knurled knob and turned it. From inside came a faint tinny ratcheting and a soft tick as the plate advanced and the shutter cocked.

A hand fell upon his shoulder. He jerked up straight, his breath whistling in his throat. Turning, he stared into Benny Booth's face.

Close-set eyes, apple-red cheeks, head practically the size of a medicine ball and a body to match. Booth was thick and quick. From a strap around his neck dangled a 3A Kodak. His smile delivered itself from above black pebbled metal and staring lens. "Chop-chop, Small Fry, ceremony's about to start. Your boss is looking all over for you."

Fry followed the bulging shoulders through the crowd. He slid the back of his hand across his mouth, and felt sweat trickling between his shoulder blades.

"It is a great joy," the voice rang out, "to bring you tidings from Rodman Wanamaker, who has sent forth this Expedition of Citizenship to the North American Indian." Dixon paused for the interpreter, and Fry, his pen leaving squiggles and loops, quickly caught up. He shot a look at the crowd.

Shirtless boys in too-big overalls, their shoulders a prop for dark hands; beyond, a sea of copper-brown faces, neutral, perhaps a bit suspicious, definitely rapt.

"My friends, your welfare is uppermost in Rodman Wanamaker's mind. He is a great man, a busy man, a captain of finance and an international figure, but he has not turned his back on his Indian friends. . . ."

Dixon was an orator, no doubt about it, master of inflection, rising inflection, falling inflection, master of the whispered word, the pregnant pause—the startling outcry: "Now, in this bold new century! In this stirring modern age!"

He's making history, Fry thought, and knows it.

The voice settled to a friendly, informative tone. "On February twenty-second last, thirty-two chiefs from eleven different tribes helped break ground for a mammoth Indian memorial that Mr. Wanamaker plans to build in the harbor of New York."

Someone in the crowd called out, "Where's New York?" A few people laughed.

Dixon paused, smiling, then forged ahead. "On that historic day, the President of the United States dug the first shovelful of earth. He was followed by Chief Wooden Leg of the Northern Cheyenne, who continued digging, using the thighbone of a buffalo."

The same voice, louder, more sarcastic: "Buffalo bones? Sweet Jesus."

Dixon sent his words out over the crowd. "The dominant feature of the memorial will be a tremendous, a colossal statue of an American Indian. A bow and arrow in his lowered left hand will show that he is through with war . . ."

"Hell we are!"

". . . while his uplifted right hand"—Dixon raised his hand and spread two fingers—"will present the universal peace sign of the red man. Thus the Indian will give in bronze a perpetual welcome to the nations of the world, just as he welcomed the white man when first he came to this shore."

A loud raspberry—then, from different parts of the audience, flaring like wildfire, scoffs and catcalls and jeers.

Fry looked up from his pad. Dixon's smile was set, his ears red. It hadn't gone this way at the other ceremonies. Not at all: The Cherokees, Creeks, Seminoles, Chickasaws, and Choctaws—the ones that were called the "Five Civilized Tribes"—had all welcomed the expedition with bunting and barbecues and bands. Their leaders, solid-looking men in business suits, had hoisted the expedition's huge flag (the selfsame one that the thirty-two chiefs had raised at the groundbreaking in New York) and had accepted smaller flags as gifts for their tribes. They had made appreciative speeches and willingly signed the "Declaration of Allegiance," a document hand-lettered in fine calligraphy on leather-bound parchment, destined for display in the promised memorial's museum.

Dixon's face assumed an expression of patient benevolence. "My brother Indians, the purpose of my visit is friendly. It is one of sympathy and deepest interest in the welfare of the red man. I am accompanied on this expedition by Major James McLaughlin, the ablest and most famous inspector in the Bureau of Indian Affairs, stalwart friend of the Indian, known in every wigwam in the land, a man who has spent forty years among the tribes.

"We have brought with us a phonograph donated to the expedition by the Wizard of Menlo Park, Mr. Thomas Edison himself. It is with great honor that I present to you a message, especially prepared in the White House for every tribe in the United States, from President . . . *Woodrow* . . . *Wilson!*"

Sam Giannetti, expert mechanic and photo finisher, had been winding a key in the side of a burl-walnut box. He flipped a switch and a thick black Bakelite platter began to revolve. He lowered a silvery tone arm, carefully removed his hand, and stepped back. Everyone stared at the walnut box. A crackling sound, as of a twig fire, issued from its cloth-covered front.

"My brothers"—the voice emerged strong and pure—"one hundred years ago, President Jefferson said to the Cherokees, 'My children, I shall rejoice to see the day when the red men, our neighbors, become truly one with us.'"

A rushing sound swept through the crowd, and people in back craned their necks. Most of the Indians had never seen a phonograph. Some thought that perhaps the president himself resided inside the polished wooden box.

"There are dark pages in the history of the white man's dealings with the Indian, and many parts of the record are stained by greed and avarice, but it is also true that the purposes and motives of this great government and of our nation as a whole toward the red man have been wise, just, and beneficent. . . ."

Fry, having heard the stock speech before, let his mind wander. Stood there with arms crossed, pen in one hand and pad in the other, feeling the disk like a plate of armor hidden beneath his vest—he had always thought whimsically that if anyone ever took a shot at him, the camera might stop the slug. But what about these redskins? Weren't there still tribesmen out here who believed that if you took their picture, you were stealing their soul? Sure. They had called those photographers, the early ones at least—the bold blue-eyed men with their magic black boxes—"Shadow Catchers." He tapped the hidden camera with his pen. Well, he didn't figure they would take a potshot at him, or even scalp him, but what else might they do? Maybe thump the bejesus out of him.

". . . government has given you education and industrial training, enabling you to take your places in civilization alongside your white neighbors . . ."

He checked the crowd. A little looking and he figured he had the rabble-rouser pegged: a pock-faced man with lank hair across his forehead, a cigarette dangling from his mouth. The Major had said the Kickapoos might be trouble, the "Kicking Kickapoos" he called them, driven out of Illinois into the Indian Territory, squeezed out of their new home when it was found to be the roof over a vault of oil, half the tribe gone over like jackrabbits into Mexico.

". . . Great White Father now calls you his brothers, not his children. . . ." The pock-faced man conferred with a gray-headed elder in dungarees patched with flour sacking. ". . . will usher in the day when the red men become truly one people with us, enjoying all the rights and privileges we do, and living in peace and plenty."

Then came the last line of the speech, which Fry had heard at seven ceremonies already and whose meaning he had yet to fathom (and if he couldn't puzzle it out, what about the Indians?): "It gives me great pleasure as President of the United States to send to you this greeting and to commend to you the lessons in industry, patriotism, and devotion to our common country that participation in this ceremony brings you."

The canned voice stopped and was replaced by a mechanical hum.

A moment of silence.

"Bullshit!" The pock-faced man flicked his cigarette onto the speaker's stand. The gray elder gave a nod, and, in a matter of seconds, the crowd thinned by half. By turning only slightly, Fry managed a quick surreptitious shot of Dixon's rage-twisted face, backed by Indians mounting horses and climbing into wagons.

He held onto the sink against the swaying of the car, leaned back, and inspected the arrangement in the mirror. The suit was gray, of an ordinary quality, its cut several years out of style. The vest had five black buttons. Unless a person were sharply observant, he would never notice that the middle button was different: It had a face of glass.

He shrugged off the coat, freed the string from its hole through the lining of the pocket, and unbuttoned the vest.

The camera was round, nickel-plated, six inches in diameter by three-quarters of an inch thick. On its face were the advancing knob and the button-aping lens. The string was knotted onto the spring release for the shutter. A ribbon, looped over his neck, hung the device in the hollow below his sternum. He slipped the camera off. A plate on its back was inscribed: PHOTOGRAPHIC SECRET CAMERA, PATENTED BY C. P. STIRN, NEW YORK, PATENT NO. 9655.

He cradled it in his hands. It seemed almost weightless. Yet it could hold so much.

Working quickly, he opened a small satchel resting on the commode tank and took out the changing bag, into which he placed the camera and a fresh, paper-wrapped plate. He rolled a towel thin and toed it into the gap below the door. He pulled the chain on the bulb above the mirror, and the room went black.

The rails clack-clacked beneath his feet. The car hit a sag, the sudden sharp drop releasing butterflies in his stomach. Fitting his hands into the changing bag's black linen sleeves, he groped for the fresh plate, found and unwrapped it. The camera was still warm from his body's heat; he opened the back, replaced the exposed plate with the fresh one, and clicked the camera shut. Withdrawing the exposed plate, he wrapped it and placed it in a separate light-proof box. He stowed everything in the leather satchel he used for his toilet kit, yanked the towel out from under the door, and stripped for the shower. He drew the rubberized curtain, twisted the porcelain knobs, and the chrome sunflower head shot water onto his face, his chest, his slat ribs and lank, paste-white legs; he soaped and scrubbed.

Kravitz was the only one who knew. Ira Kravitz was a photographer himself. He had set it all up, had shown Fry's pictures to his editor, arranged for payment, arranged for the plates to be developed and printed in a string of processing labs across the country—Muskogee, Gallup, Phoenix, Los Angeles, cities in which the expedition would lay over: Fry had a list a foot long locked in his trunk.

Kravitz lived in Fry's building, an elf of a man who lugged around a Graflex almost as big as he was, to photograph ward men and bill signings and people placing flags on graves for Decoration Day and train wrecks (not tonight, thanks) and fires and football heroes and Harry Houdini in chains.

It had all started with a botch-up. One Sunday, Fry, on his way out to photograph, had encountered Kravitz on the porch. The light had been excellent. Kravitz started talking about something, waving his hands in the way he had, cigarette between two knuckles. Fry found the string in his pocket, gave the secret little tug.

Kravitz stopped in midsentence. His forehead crinkled, and he reached out his finger and touched the faint bulge in the center of Fry's coat. "Camera?" he whispered. "Show it to me."

Even now, months later, hot water drumming on his head and cascading down his neck and sluicing between his shoulder blades, Fry got the chills remembering. As if he'd been caught stealing. Or fondling himself. Or peering in through a bedroom window at night.

It had mortified him. Kravitz had stood there waiting, an expectant look on his face. Fry fumbled with the buttons and, when the vest swung open, steeled himself. "Tasteless" was a word he expected, or "outrage" and "invasion of privacy." His father, Fry knew, would have reddened and drawn his head back on the scrawny cords of his neck, saying, "Such things are not *done*." Kravitz? He whistled softly. Asked how it worked.

Upstairs, Fry took off the camera and let him have a look. He got out boxes of plates and stacks of prints. Kravitz sat on the davenport going through the pictures: a man standing in front of a brick warehouse, preoccupied look on his face, unlit cigar between his teeth, hands patting his coat pockets for a match; a youth crossing a rain-wet street, collar turned up, face in a frown, feet blurred; a hat salesman with four hats stacked on top of his head; odd swatches of sleeves and trousers, eyes and mouths.

Kravitz shook another Mecca out of the pack and lit it, muttering to himself. A small boy in a sailor's suit, wandering through a field of granite markers with a flag in his hand. Man with a cardboard sign on his chest, BLIND, standing like a rock in a stream of passersby. Kravitz came to one of Fry's favorites: a dapper couple strolling, he carrying a suitcase in one hand and scratching his chin with the other, she watching her feet and smilingly saying something.

Women. He loved to photograph women. A lady on the street—ample bust, wasp waist, unguarded face, casual walk, no notion he had a camera. Two of them, carrying packages and parasols, stopped at a fountain to drink. Abigail Edwards, an unobtainable beauty from his hometown, she of the frosty stare and impeccable manners. He had caught her with one hand on her hip and her face opening in a playful, come-hither smile—for someone else, not for him.

He shifted on the chair, gnawed at a hangnail. These were not real photographs, of course. In real photographs the subjects stared fixedly at the lens. Their expressions were pleasant but guarded. They gave to the world their outward appearances, carefully composed, and surrendered nothing else.

Kravitz looked up, his eyes round and bright. "Only thing I've seen anything like this is Lew Hine's stuff. Know it?" Fry shook his head. "Steelworkers, breaker boys, immigrants on Ellis Island, kids in the sweatshops . . ." Kravitz held up a print of a bowler-hatted man in a sunken doorway, leering up at a skirt going past. "Hine uses a five by seven," he babbled on, "hell of a big box, has to be tripoded, see him coming a mile away. His pictures aren't posed, exactly, but they're static, he has to pull the slide, dust the pan, get his subjects' attention so they'll hold still, and *then* shoot." Kravitz looked at the photograph of the leering man, then back at Fry, awe suffusing his dark bony face. "With all of that, he can never make a truly candid shot."

A week later, Fry gave Kravitz his print. The enlargement was full frame and, like the negative, round. Kravitz's head and shoulders filled the frame, cigarette hand blurred, face mostly teeth and nose, glance veering to one side. Kravitz had studied the picture, then grinned, a tad ruefully, Fry thought. "So that's what I look like," he said.

The locomotive whistled at the front of the train, drawing Fry back to the present. He shut off the water and toweled himself dry. He was a photographer. A *candid* photographer. He hadn't really expected the newspaper to run his pictures, certainly hadn't thought they would cause a flap—much less that the Commissioner would see them and get mad. He would have to be careful. The chills came flooding back. If McLaughlin ever found out . . .

He recalled, just then, the review in the photo tabloid that had led him to the Stirn: "This ingenious little device can do more mischief than its weight in dynamite, or more good than its weight in gold, according to the disposition and will of the person who pulls the string."

2

On a May evening in 1909, four years before he sent forth his Expedition of Citizenship to the North American Indian, Rodman Wanamaker threw a party for Buffalo Bill. It was in the gilded banquet hall at Sherry's, on Fifth Avenue. Wanamaker—the son of John Wanamaker, the "Merchant Prince"—managed the firm's gargantuan Manhattan store. He sat at the center of the speakers' table, a slight, balding man with a mustache whose ends, waxed, indicated ten and two o'clock. On Wanamaker's right was the legendary scout, plainsman, and entertainer, Colonel William F. Cody— Buffalo Bill. Cody's flowing silver locks were gathered behind his head in a bun. He had been accompanied by Chief Weasel Tail and his son Charles, performers in Cody's "Wild West," then appearing in the city. The Weasel Tails wore buckskins and feather headdresses, and their faces were streaked with paint.

A newsman braced his Graflex, stared down through the pyramidal leather viewfinder into the shadowy, inverted depths, signaled to the men at the speakers' table, waited until all were set, then tripped the shutter. The men blinked at the flash and relaxed, shedding their faint, self-conscious smiles.

Two hundred guests in evening dress—politicians, clergy, leaders of industry and finance—dined on Potage Renaissance, Filet Mignon, Suprême de Volaille. Dr. Joseph Dixon, educational director for the Wanamaker Department Stores, entertained with hand-colored lantern slides of noted Indian chiefs. A champagne toast was proposed to Colonel Cody, and all drank, the Weasel Tails lifting their glasses with a stern and formal grace. Cries of "Speech! Speech!" resounded through the hall.

Buffalo Bill elevated his bulk in a manner uncharacteristically steady. He had kept away from spirits all evening: He would be on horseback before cheering thousands within the hour. He cleared his throat, winked at the audience, smiled.

"Mr. Wanamaker, Doctor Dixon, my friends: In my long career with the United States Army, I have served under thirty-two different officers and generals in my campaigns on the plains, and never have I led troops against the red men, never have I pointed my gun at an Indian, that I did not know a feeling of regret. Yet someone had to stand between civilization and savagery, and it seemed to be my lot to do so."

Cody acknowledged the applause with a two-handed wave. He clasped his hands behind his back, and a ruminative look came to his face. "It is a great satisfaction to know that a man here tonight is sending expeditions into the West—not to fight the Indians, but to study them; not to take away more of their land, but to help them achieve citizenship. Why is this man doing it? I have learned he intends to build a great monument"—Cody turned to Wanamaker—"with an Indian on top, showing him as he was when the whites first landed in America, with hands extended, welcoming us to this shore."

Applause, like the hollow wingbeats of pigeons between buildings. Wanamaker dabbed his lips with his napkin, smiled faintly, and gave a slow, fastidious nod of his head.

"A magnificent and . . . magnanimous"—Cody stumbled over the word only slightly, wouldn't even have tried it had he been the slightest bit drunk—"memorial to a vanishing race, right here, b'God, in the harbor of New York!"

More applause. Cody picked up an immaculate gray Stetson and placed it on his head. "My friends, I regret that I must leave you and go on down to the Garden, and shoot a few Indians. I believe they intend to rob the Deadwood Stage, and will want to know where little Willie is." Another wink, answered by jovial laughter. Cody made his exit, the colorful forms of the Weasel Tails following. The diners rose as one and cheered. Buffalo Bill answered with a wave of his hat; the Indians shrilled out war whoops.

A colossal Indian in the harbor of New York, of a size and grandeur to rival the Goddess of Liberty.

The Paterson, New Jersey, *Sentinel* likened the burst of sentiment that swept the nation to "a conflagration on the prairies." The Pennsylvania Council of the Improved Order of Red Men, a white fraternal organization, volunteered two pennies for each of its members—$1,500. President William Howard Taft endorsed the project, suggesting with Republican pragmatism that the statue be designed to function as a lighthouse.

Rodman Wanamaker was pleased. He had not felt such gratification since the time when, as buyer for the chain in Paris, he had purchased a Bleriot monoplane, shipped it back to the home store in Philadelphia, hung it from the rafters, and sold it to a customer, thereby making Wanamaker's the first dry-goods establishment ever to sell an aeroplane. Aviation fascinated Rodman Wanamaker. So did Indians. Their rites fascinated him, their customs and practices, the pathos that had accompanied their decline. He liked Indians, out there in the West. He liked to have Indians (chiefs, preferably, since he himself was a kind of chief) stop by his office when they were in town. Through such meetings he imagined that he had come to understand the Indian, to divine the red man's weaknesses and strengths.

In a rare moment of extroversion, Wanamaker granted an interview to the Brooklyn *Standard Union*. The reporter trailed him about the store on Broadway and Tenth, until Wanamaker stopped on "The Bridge of Progress," a causeway linking the two separate buildings that formed the huge store.

Wanamaker looked down on wagons and motorcars and pedestrians scurrying below. "The Indian in his history," he said, "showed great strength of character. He was dignified and honest, loyal and brave. Doesn't such a man deserve to be remembered by his successors to the wealth and resources of America?" The reporter raised his eyebrows, wondering if he should answer. Wanamaker waved his hand in dismissal. "The Indian was lazy. He was content to take what fortune gave him. He had no ambition, no thought beyond tomorrow. The march of civilization has trodden him under, and now he is gone."

Congress set aside land for the memorial. The architect Thomas Hastings, who had designed the New York Public Library, drew up plans for a three-story museum. Daniel Chester French—who would later sculpt Lincoln in the Lincoln Memorial—designed the surmounting statue. The robed and feather-bonneted Indian would stand sixty feet. His pedestal, seventy feet. The museum building, thirty-five feet. Total, one hundred sixty-five feet. The size of the memorial had been tempered by financial realities. The Statue of Liberty towered three hundred feet from the bay to the tip of her torch. The Indian would be a runt by comparison. However, he would occupy the heights of Fort Wadsworth, above the Narrows at the harbor's mouth, and thus would be the first landmark visible to a person, on shipboard, approaching New York. A returning traveler, a yachtsman, a visiting head of state, an immigrant German farmer booked clear through from Bremen to Bismarck, North Dakota: The shining bronze Indian would be the first sign of America that he would see.

3

Fry had worked for the Bureau a scant six months when the assignment came down. Sykes, his supervisor, delivered it like a sentence: six months in the field with Major McLaughlin, six months shuttling from one dreary reservation to the next across the deserts of the West.

To Fry, it was a peach. His face lit, his nostrils went in and out with his breathing.

"Don't look so keen," Sykes intoned. "And don't say McLocklin—it's McLofflin." Why "Major"? Sykes peered over his half-glasses and sighed condescendingly. "That's what the Indian agents all used to be called. Courtesy rank. Now they're 'superintendents.' Sounds more modern, I guess. Although"—he leaned close, whispering a cloud of medicine breath—"it's a whitewash. Few years back they were the scandal of the Bureau. It's some better now, but still a pack of grafters and thieves." He took off and folded his spectacles, pointed them at Fry. "Frank Frantz, late Territorial Governor of Oklahoma, late agent for the Osage, a top-roller if ever there was one, he skimmed thousands, maybe millions, from leases on Osage oil." He stiffened his back and sat up in the chair. "McLaughlin?" Fry had not said a word. "Good God, boy, he's the one went down and pinched Frantz. He's so straight they never dared dump him—the only agent I know of survived the spoils system, one administration after another." Sykes chuckled without mirth. "A tough

24

cookie. Someday I'll give you the lowdown on how he handled Sitting Bull."

Sykes waved his glasses nearly in Fry's face. "Listen. This is a big job. I'd go myself, but the wife isn't well. And we can't send Tuttle, he being newly married and all, and half off his clock with it. Poor Swenson"—Sykes shook his head confidentially—"too much of a man for the bottle." The brandished spectacles approached Fry's nose; focusing on them, he felt his eyes start to cross. He blinked back to the bloodless, lumpy face. Sykes said: "Which leaves you. You're green as grass, but you're all we've got.

"Don't stick your neck out. Just do your job. And don't bother making friends with McLaughlin, he's about as personable as a rock. And keep your mouth shut. Don't embarrass me. See you again in six months."

McLaughlin, James, No Middle Initial
He pulled the heavy green-paper card out of the file.

Date of birth: February 12, 1842
Place of birth: Avonmore, Ontario
First employment USID: Fort Totten Res., D. T., 1871, blacksmith
   Agent, Fort Totten Res., D. T., 1876–1881
   Agent, Standing Rock Res., D. T., 1881–1895
   Traveling Inspector, 1895–
Wife: Marie Louise Buisson
Children: Thomas James (dec.)
       Marie Imelda (dec.)
       Charles Cyprian
       William Russell (dec.)
       Arthur Sibley
       Annie Owns the Fire (adopted)
Religion: R. C.

Below, a mounting pay history, nothing else.

He went down the hall. The building was all polished-floor glare and chipped yellow walls. Fire hoses tapewormed inside glass-paneled boxes. Machines could be heard clacking, figures moved behind frosted glass. He unlocked a windowless room, punched the light button. The cabinet drawer opened with a screech. Under *McLaughlin, James* he found a thin folder.

The first photograph showed six men on wooden chairs in front of a low stone building. Immediately he recognized McLaughlin, from whom he had once taken dictation: the Major holding his hat in his hands, eyes stern and level, mouth masked by a mustache and a salt-and-pepper Imperial beard. A lot younger then, he looked tough, decisive, and wiry—he hadn't yet begun to assume the stoutness of three score and ten years. Fry turned the picture over. *Standing Rock Agency Staff,* 1890.

In the second photograph several dozen pale-faced soldiers, no weapons visible, stood with an equal number of dark-faced Indians wearing coats and spanking new hats; in the center of the gathering, behind a table with a hefty book on it, McLaughlin sat. His bowler hat perched too small on his head. He was frowning at, or at least regarding very sternly, an Indian standing with his back to the camera, his head turned to one side, apparently addressing the crowd. Fry brought the photo closer. Had to be. Mastermind of the Custer massacre, the most intractable, belligerent presence in the West—here in beaded moccasins, dark blanket wrapped around blocky hips, white shirt, long flowing hair, the profiled face slightly blurred by motion (one black eye, hooked nose, mouth a lipless gash) but still completely, frighteningly recognizable—the biggest of the big chiefs, whose savage exploits Fry had shuddered over in many a dime novel: Sitting Bull.

The third and final photograph showed a squad of perhaps forty Indian men wearing tall black hats and dark uniforms with star-shaped badges on their breasts. Bristling with rifles and pistols, they stood at attention, in ranks. Behind them and off to one side, mounted on a horse, faintly out of focus, sat a man with a bowler hat and a salt-and-pepper Imperial beard. Fry flipped it: *Survivors, Sitting Bull Fight.*

4

In the rosy light the landscape was an endless crazy quilt: farms and pastures, Holstein cows, huddled bungalows, pale faces peering from porches, sheds and snarled cables and jumbled rusty drums. McLaughlin recognized a fine turreted house, a thicket of derricks, a grimy mill. Oklahoma: the old Indian Territory, now more whites here than Indians, a state these past six years. *Oklahoma* was a Choctaw word meaning "red people," and Oklahoma had been the nation's dumping ground. It held the remnants of sixty-some tribes including Mohawks from New York, Modocs from California, Shawnees from Ohio, Choctaws from Mississippi, Kickapoos from Illinois. He had done business with all of these and more.

He sat in the dining room of the private car, an all-steel Pullman with the name SIGNET in white serif letters on its sleek, green-painted sides. The napkin on the table was a green, winged pyramid; as he unfolded it, the steward was at his side.

"Coffee, sir?"

"Please."

The steaming brown arc descended from a silver urn.

The track curved, and the sun crept across McLaughlin's hands. Broad hands, age-spotted, callused, thick fingers ending in hard yellow nails. He drummed his nails on the table. The girl. He couldn't get her out of his mind. He straightened, pinched the ornate handle of the coffee cup, drank.

It was that damnable picture had let her in. The day after
he'd had Fry file it, he made him dig the newspaper back out.
He took it to his room, sat and stared at that one especially
evocative image, finally got his penknife and cut the picture
out; slid it into the corner of the wardrobe mirror behind the
bracket.

He swallowed the coffee and felt its harsh warmth sinking
through his chest. What a peck of trouble she had been—still
was. Smart as a whip, but lacking in common sense. And such
a mind of her own. As much a daughter as if she'd been his
own flesh and blood. Lately they hadn't kept in close touch,
letters now and then, most of them going through Louise,
who kept up the family correspondence. A Christmas visit a
few years back, then the time he had gone to Lapwai, ostensi-
bly to inspect the sanitarium, when they had spent a good
couple of days together, driving, chatting, looking at the
Idaho hills, wrangling only a little.

Now this blasted picture. He set the cup down, rubbed his
eyes with the heels of his hands until green and blue sunbursts
flared. Seeing her like that—but it was not her, just some girl
who looked like her—imagining her so vividly, it was as if she
had broken into the office of his mind. Broken in to snoop
around in drawers, paw through waste bins, lift paper-
weights: leaning forward like the girl in the photograph, long
neck arched, full lips parted as if consumed in looking,
searching, hunting . . . she (or the thought of her) rifling the
files he had categorized, set in order, put away—files of
thoughts worn dog-eared, files he wished never to open
again.

The sun, flashing red behind telegraph poles, made him
blink. The door opened and Joseph K. Dixon came in.
McLaughlin started to rise, but Dixon waved him back down
and took the chair opposite.

Dixon had a dyspeptic, put-upon look on his face.
"George." He snapped his fingers at the steward, and the man

(whose name, Grover Jefferson, Dixon had never bothered to learn) hustled over with the urn.

"Well, sir," McLaughlin addressed Dixon. "What do you make of these Oklahoma Indians?"

"The Kickapoos are the most insulting, ungrateful, obstinate people I have ever met. The Osages run a close second."

McLaughlin smiled. "And you wanted to give them a flag. Just try getting something from them."

Dixon shook his head. "Now the Cherokees, they impressed me. Schools, industry, prosperous farms, far more advanced than I'd imagined. They make the immigrants, the Italians and the Eastern Europeans"—here a quick conspiratorial grin, cheeks bunching and teeth flashing in a demonstration that the eyes refrained from joining—"look like utter savages themselves."

McLaughlin, who hated a smile like that, kept his face sober. "The Cherokees were pretty well advanced"—he paused, searching for a way to distribute any blame—"before the necessities of national expansion caused their removal to the west."

"Mark my words," Dixon said. "All the red men will be like those Cherokees within a generation. So thoroughly assimilated that, in effect, they will have ceased to exist."

McLaughlin nodded. "The weaker race has gone to the wall before the stronger. It is in the natural order of things."

The photographer, Booth, came in, followed by Giannetti, redolent of darkroom chemicals. Minutes later, in walked Fry: That boy is always late, McLaughlin thought. The steward brought chafing dishes heaped with pork chops and potatoes, steaming peas, hard rolls, balls of butter in ice-filled trays. Dixon offered the blessing; cutlery clinked against china. As McLaughlin ate, he kept his eyes on the window, on the flowing, changing land.

He had doubts about this "Expedition of Citizenship," as it was so grandly named. If all went as planned, they would perform the ceremony before ninety tribes on more than sixty reservations and it might indeed inspire some Indians to become citizens, although many were already enfranchised. It would persuade others, quite incorrectly, that they were being granted citizenship on the spot, at which point he would have to explain. And another problem: Some of the tribes would no doubt view the hoopla as just one more trick to relieve them of land.

From the start he had judged Dixon a confidence man and a fake. When the Commissioner dumped the Wanamaker Expedition in his lap, he had set a senior clerk to ferreting out facts. Dixon was fifty-six years of age. He had received a Bachelor of Divinity degree from Rochester Theological Seminary and had gone on to preach, a Baptist. Although he used the title "Doctor," there was no evidence he had ever earned an advanced degree. In his ministry he had passed from one church to another, always under a cloud: One congregation built a costly church, bringing several members to financial ruin; at another the deacons barred the doors against him, and his wife sued for divorce, adultery the grounds. By 1904 Dixon had absconded to England, where he lectured for the Eastman Kodak Company on "The Call of the Kodak," "The Fruit of the Lens," "The Camera: A Moral Force."

Then he had latched onto the Wanamakers.

McLaughlin, in Philadelphia on other business, had attended one of Dixon's programs, "The Last Great Indian Council—The Farewell of the Chiefs." He had filed into Egyptian Auditorium with four hundred shoppers off the floors of the department store. The audience fell silent as the curtain rose. On the stage stood a shirtless man in moccasins, leggings, and a floor-length eagle-feather headdress. The man stood with his back to the audience, his arms upraised; the footlights dimmed and a red-tinted spotlight came angling in, throwing one side of the man into brilliant outline, while his other side and all of the scenery—

pine trees, cliffs, snowy peaks—fell into mysterious shadow. The man (a white actor turned coppery by the light?) sang a mournful song whose theme was the extinction of the Indian race.

Three reels of motion pictures followed, to the accompaniment of a pipe organ. Ancient Indian chiefs—he recognized some from the land negotiations—arrived on horseback at a tipi village; a great council was held, full of pipe smoking and sign language and solemn wrinkled faces. Then the Indians left the council and rode across the prairie, forded streams, climbed mountains, descended into a mist-filled valley. A chant began from a hidden Victrola, an eerie sound that swelled, peaked, then grew fainter as the aged chiefs rode into the sunset, the chant finally dying away to a sob as the last man on horseback faded into the dusk.

The audience had erupted in applause, and he had joined in, filled with a sense of tragedy, of pathos (he who had seen people starve, and die of whooping cough, and measles, and bullet wounds, and the bloody flux). He noted tears lining the cheeks of women, strong emotions contorting the faces of men. And when it was done, and he left the bustling store and stood on the sidewalk in the bright daylight and heard the clip-clopping of dray horses and the blatting of automobile exhaust, he knew he'd been conned.

McLaughlin finished his pork chop, laid down his knife and fork, and regarded Dixon, still shoveling food into his mouth.

The Last Great Indian Council. The Rodman Wanamaker Expedition of Citizenship to the North American Indian.

He had little use for show and pomp. His was a slower and a surer means to assimilation. Take a child and strip him of the old pernicious ways. Free him from his native tongue. Educate him, give him a trade and a true religion, spend toward schools, plows, forges, sawmills, infirmaries, irrigation canals—not on a fancy memorial with an ungainly cigar-store Indian perched on top.

5

It was a place of boxes. The rearing, green-painted school was a box. The classroom—with its *Table of Elements* and row of dead presidents, its tacked-flat American flag—was a box. Under each pupil's slightly uptilted desktop lay a storage box. What you were supposed to teach them, she imagined, should fit into their minds as neatly and perfectly as small boxes pack away into larger ones.

When she herself had been a student at Carlisle, the school had farmed them out every summer, determined not to let them return to the reservations where all that they had learned might be undone. For two of her summer outings she had been sent to Wanamaker's Department Store in Philadelphia. There she had worked at restocking shelves, slipping small, uniform, unmarked boxes out of the big battered cardboard ones that came up on the lift. That was the first summer; the next year she put in for Camping, but they gave her Ladies' Necessities, hidden decorously in the bowels of the store. More boxes. Breast pumps in boxes. Red rubber syringes for cleansing the vaginal passages, in boxes. Special soaps and sanitary pads. She had wanted Camping, with the hatchets and knives and canteens and rucksacks, the memory-tickling smells of canvas and leather. She would have taken Hardware, but had longed for Camping.

It was rest time now, and Annie Owns the Fire looked out over the twenty dark heads lying on the forty coppery hands on the tops of the slightly uptilted desks. A buzzer on the wall rasped loudly. The dark heads popped up, and the children leaned back in their seats, turning to look out the windows. It was high summer out there, birds chirping, bees buzzing, the sun beating down. Inside, within the blackboard-clad walls, you could almost hear the dust fall. School went on year-round at Lapwai: No telling how long these children would be present, no telling how many days remained to get the boxes at least partially filled.

"Class," she said, as all settled and looked at her, "this afternoon we're going to learn about the sun. The sun is a star, the nearest star in the heavens. Compared to other stars, it's sort of a medium-sized one." She went on about the gas helium, whose combustion threw off the blazing light, and about how the process had been going on for a billion years, and would continue for at least a billion more.

Ike Catches raised his hand.

"Ike?"

"How much a billion?"

She went to the board, picked up a piece of chalk. She wrote a 1 and a long string of zeros. Zero following zero, circles marching to the edge of the slate. It meant nothing to them. But you couldn't make a billion chalk marks on a blackboard, there wasn't room enough, and anyway, it would probably take you twenty lifetimes. Feeling thwarted, she turned. "Remember, class, it's dangerous to look directly at the sun. Use a piece of smoked glass or an old film negative to protect your eyes."

She stopped, set down the chalk, dusted her hands.

"I went to a Sun Dance once," she said. "Ike, you know what it is."

He looked up quizzically.

"Wiwanyag wachipi."

He smiled with instant recognition, his face as radiant as any sun. Then it darkened, went dead.

"Class, Ike is Lakota. I am Lakota, what everybody calls

'Sioux.'" She paused. "Wiwanyag wachipi—it means 'To see the sun, we dance.' On the reservation where Ike and I come from, the Sun Dance is forbidden." As it was forbidden, here and now, in this school, in this room, to "talk Indian." She said it again: "Wiwanyag wachipi." The children fidgeted, a few giggling nervously behind their hands.

"Now is the time of year when the Plains Indians hold the Sun Dance. Many tribes have the Sun Dance as part of their religion—the Sioux, Cheyenne, Crow, Ute, Blackfoot, Arapaho, many others."

The children were perking up now, listening: Paul Dodd was a Blackfoot, Susan One Fireplace a Crow, Ollie Bluelegs a Cheyenne.

"The dance goes on for days. Sometimes the people sacrifice their bodies—cut themselves, feel a little pain so they can clean out their minds, get rid of the extra baggage, the useless thoughts. . . ." How to explain it? She turned and swept the eraser across the board.

She looked back, scanning the eager, upraised faces. And noticed that the door was open a crack. She waited, and after a minute the door opened the rest of the way. In the frame stood Miss Granke, the boys' matron. The children, seeing who it was, sank down in their chairs.

"As I was saying, I went to a Sun Dance once." She said it directly, and clearly, to the woman in the doorway. A tall, slope-shouldered woman with a saggy bottom and a flat chest, a face that always looked as if she'd just starched and ironed it.

"Wiwanyag wachipi: 'To see the sun, we dance.' The people put up an ash tree in the center of a circle and danced around it. I wasn't supposed to be there, mind you, because I was raised white, and not very many white people see the need for Indians to hold onto their own religion. Father"—she looked around at the children, smiled at them—"well, he would have tanned my hide if he'd known I was there.

"Wiwanyag wachipi," she went on. Damning herself, and

not caring. "The Sun Dance is a way of remembering, of reminding ourselves we're a part of the earth. All of us are part of the earth, like the rocks and the deer and the trees, like the birds singing. We must always—"

"*Miss Owns the Fire.*" The voice cut through the air like the wall buzzer. "Please go to Mr. Siebert's office. *At once.*" Miss Granke came in, black high-collared dress, hissing skirts. "I will take over this class now."

She stood, her mouth working but no words coming out, staring at the dried-up, stiff old maid. The futility of it all: this school, these wasted faces, the lessons that seemed a remote and vacant ritual, the soul-numbing accretion of boxes inside more boxes inside more square-cornered, light-vanquishing boxes—her arm rose, and she hurled the eraser, which struck the black flat chest and rebounded, leaving a smudge. Miss Granke gasped and stepped back; her mouth fell open, then tightened in a grin.

She looked from Miss Granke's triumphant face to the children's frightened ones, lowered her own face and walked down the aisle between the desks. From the hall she heard the strident voice demanding attention. She passed down a long, narrow box with other boxes branching off it, with windows that admitted boxes of light to lie bent out of square on the floor.

She might have told them the rest of the story. How old Foam had spirited her there on the back of his pony. How she had felt ashamed when the people, her people, turned aside at the sight of her face. How the dancers circled the ash tree, young men and old, leaning back on the cords attached to the sharpened sticks piercing their flesh, staring at the sun through the wind-flickering leaves. The heyoka, squirming like a snake, half his face painted blue, half red. The smell of burning sage: It carried you up and away, emptying you and filling you at the same time. The thin piping of whistles. The white clouds mounding in the sky. The way the clouds fought

with the sun, covered it, held it away from the dance. The
shower of rain that came drumming down on the brush arbor
where the spectators knelt. An old woman had come up to her
then, kicked her roughly to the ground. "If it rains during the
dance," the old woman said, "it means somebody is impure."

6

"Little old hopper." Booth had caught one. His thick
fingers pinched the dun-colored insect across the back.
He moved it closer to Fry's hand, resting on the spring seat
between them. Fry resisted the urge to draw his hand back.
Booth said, "He's chewin' plug." The grasshopper had hard
bulbous eyes, smooth curving plates with black pinpricks in
the center; it wriggled its yellow legs and twitched its anten-
nae as the sticky brown bubble expanded at its chin.

At the last moment Fry pulled his hand back.

Booth grinned. The seat canted toward his greater weight.
On the wagon's front bench slouched a raggedy Indian, driving the team, while in back Giannetti sat cross-legged on the
bed, whistling opera tunes, steadying the Edison, which was
lashed to cleats and covered with a tarp.

They were on the road to Darlington. Another hot day. The
land was rolling, trees were few, and sage interrupted the pale
thin grass. In the distance, cowboys could be seen on horseback among white-faced cattle. Perched on fence posts, mead-
owlarks sang their bubbling, lilting songs, and the
grasshoppers whirred up scarlet-winged to land on harness,
manes, hands—when one lit on his skin and sprang away
again, its hooked feet made Fry flinch.

Booth held up the hopper, flicked its head off with a finger.
He dropped the decapitated insect over the side. He looked at
the lead wagon, another green-painted Studebaker, in which

41

McLaughlin rode. "Your boss," Booth said, "killed

all."

odded. "So I've heard."

e wild, wild West."

"Happened ages ago."

"Not so very goddamn long." Booth nudged him with a blunt elbow. "We'll be out there in a couple of months. There's Indians out there, Sioux Indians, still mad enough to take scalps. Better watch your topknot, Small Fry." Adroitly he lifted Fry's hat and pretended to inspect his scalp. "Getting kind of thin. Maybe they'll let you be."

Fry retrieved his hat—flat-crowned, black, thoroughly a greenhorn's lid—and resettled it. "No, Booth," he said, "it's you who'd better watch your step. They see you pointing that camera, they'll be after you with the skinning knives." Booth flashed his ready grin, but Fry figured the notion discomfited him just the same. Booth was city-born, and, like Fry, this was his first trip west.

Before the ceremony there was time to inspect the school. The superintendent was a thickset man with galluses and a bow tie. He sat in his office beneath a wall map of Oklahoma, the counties pink, yellow, orange, and blue, the state poised like a giant cleaver above his head. McLaughlin jotted in a small black book. Fry, present in case a statement needed taking down, struggled to stay awake. Estimated dollar value of vegetables grown during the school year. Planned expansion of the physical plant. Condition of the lathes and planer, the drill presses and brakes.

When the superintendent finished, McLaughlin opened his valise and took out the Roto section of the Sunday Washington *Dispatch*. Fry noted with surprise that one of the photographs—he couldn't remember which—had been clipped out. The superintendent stared at the spread with a mystified expression; then, reading the Commissioner's comments, dutifully clucked his tongue. "Has anyone applied to photograph the Indians?" McLaughlin asked. "Have any strangers visited the agency? Have you noticed any suspicious persons loitering about the grounds?" The superintendent's replies, all negative, McLaughlin entered in his book.

They walked to a dormitory, empty at this hour, long ranks of metal bedsteads, blue-and-white-striped pillows resting on blankets uniformly turned down. The room was hot and smelled of disinfectant. Flies butted at the window screens.

"We instill cleanliness of environment, cleanliness of body, cleanliness of mind." The superintendent stooped, grunting, and ran a finger across the floor beneath a bed. He smiled and held it up clean.

At the far end of the room Fry saw a figure.

"We do not permit the students to speak their native tongue. When they slip, they are punished firmly but fairly."

The figure sat on a bed backed against the wall. Fry caught a glint of black eyes, which swiftly averted themselves. A young face. Burr-cut hair. A small child, thin, wearing a dress.

"Academic subjects are taught in the forenoon. After dinner the boys learn agricultural and industrial trades, while the girls receive instruction in home economics. Many find employment in the laundry or bakery."

Fry caught his breath. The child, he realized, was a boy. The dress reached nearly to his feet, which were clad in brogans. Around one of the boy's legs, above the shoe top, circled a thick iron band. From the band, a chain led to a heavy ball resting beneath the bed.

McLaughlin had stopped and was looking. "You have a problem with runaways?"

"As at all boarding schools, there is a small percentage of students who persist in running home to their parents every chance they get." The superintendent sounded as if he was reading from a manual. "Such intransigence is dealt with firmly but fairly."

McLaughlin walked over to the boy and slowly went to one knee. The superintendent placed a hand on the bed and leaned down.

"Amos, this is Major McLaughlin." The superintendent enunciated slowly and loudly, as if addressing an idiot. "Major McLaughlin is from Washington. Major, this is Amos Brown. Amos has not come to terms with our rules yet."

The boy's eyes showed white all around. They shifted from James McLaughlin to the superintendent and back again. McLaughlin took the small hand in his and shook it. "Pleased to meet you."

The reply, if the boy made one, was inaudible to Fry. McLaughlin hauled himself up and patted the small dark head.

The light was adequate. McLaughlin and the superintendent strolled on ahead. Soon they were far enough away that, even in the stillness of the room, they did not hear the click.

From the hill, everywhere he looked, grass waved: grass with whiplike stems, grass with twinkling purple flowers, grass whose seedheads looked like the fletching of tiny arrows shot by the thousands into the ground.

Two hundred Cheyenne and Arapaho surrounded the flagpole. Most of the men wore denim and drill, but some had put on feather headdresses and garments of fine soft buckskin. Their moccasins sank into the powdery dust. They leaned on lances and held shields trimmed with eagle feathers and painted with moons, stars, and birds. They were the first Plains Indians the expedition had met with, and Booth and Dixon were lapping it up, running in every direction shouting instructions and grouping the Indians for photographs.

The superintendent introduced the expedition, and Dixon

stated Wanamaker's grand purpose and plan. The phonograph was energized. At the sound of the disembodied voice, the Indians began jabbering. A bare-chested old man with noodle arms stole forward and prepared to poke the Edison with the butt of his lance, but Giannetti rushed in and shooed the fellow away. (Some picture! Giannetti probably a blur, arms flapping, the Indian raising dust as he scampers off.)

Dixon resumed, his voice slippery with emotion: "There is no banner in all the world more beautiful than the Stars and Stripes. You find in the red stripes a tinge of your own color; in the white stripes a symbol of the purest thought that lifts from your hearts to the Great Mystery above; in the blue field with its white stars, the great starry sky that stretches above the prairie at night."

What garbage, Fry thought, the man's stuffed full of it. His pen scratched on in shameless complicity. Occasionally McLaughlin had lent him to Dixon to take dictation: flowery, overblown letters to Wanamaker, to Eastern newspapers, boosting the expedition. At all other times Dixon ignored him, made him feel like a piece of equipment. Which was okay, a steno got used to it. And a candid photographer—who wished above all else to be beneath notice—positively relished the invisibility.

"I do not know how you Indians act when you wish to express a great sentiment," Dixon was saying, "but the white man bows his head in reverence and kisses the thing he loves. I ask you now to step forward, take hold of this flag, bow your heads to it, and kiss its holy hem."

The Indians stretched the flag—a huge rectangle, eighteen by twenty-four feet—and bowed to it, icicle-like ermine skins dangling, vests embroidered with dyed porcupine quills falling away from naked chests. At Dixon's signal, they planted a kiss.

Booth clicked off the photograph.

"Get it?" Dixon called.

"Yeah."

"Get another, be sure."

Fry took his own picture then. He looked on, mildly astonished that these wild red Indians made no protest over all the shutterbugging. The bloody Cheyenne, the feared Arapaho, maybe they'd advanced to the point where they no longer believed the box would steal their souls. Maybe they'd been photographed dozens, even hundreds of times. He had read somewhere that the most famous Shadow Catcher of them all, Edward S. Curtis—bankrolled by none other than J. P. Morgan, who just that spring had kicked the bucket in his villa in Rome—was having trouble finding the "children of nature" he needed for his romantic, evocative shots. Curtis had taken to carrying a wardrobe of warbonnets and buckskins, tins of face paint, long-haired wigs for his subjects to wear.

McLaughlin's voice carried out over the crowd: "I shake hands with each and every one of you. I am the oldest inspector in the Indian service. I have negotiated almost every agreement made with the different tribes for the past eighteen years. My agreements have generally been for the cession of Indian land. Today, however, we are here to appeal to you not from the land side, but from the flag side. We want you to take this flag for your own, and love it, and cherish it."

How could you love and cherish a flag, Fry wondered, if you were a small boy who had risen in class to pledge allegiance, the words rote, your classmates tittering at the dress you wore, your leg fettered—what was it?—*firmly but fairly* to a cast-iron ball.

The Indian leaders signed the Declaration of Allegiance by giving their hands to McLaughlin, who pressed their thumbs against an ink blotter, placed them on the parchment, and rolled them from side to side.

And now Dixon added a new wrinkle to the ceremony. He

got out a heavy canvas sack filled with nickels. Brand-new mirror-bright five-cent pieces, of the type just now going into circulation. Tails, a buffalo; heads, an Indian.

Booth scrunched down over his Kodak as Dixon had the interpreter call the children forward. And did he give each eager boy and girl a nickel? Did he place in each upturned palm a coin, a shining 1913 minting of a near-extinct beast and, if you could believe the popular sentiment, a near-extinct, hook-nosed, feather-in-his-coif Indian? No. He stuck his hand into the sack, brought out a dripping fist, and threw the nickels above the children's heads. They hung there shiny as rain in the sun, until like a silvery shower they fell, thunking off hands, shoulders, skulls. The coins fell in the dust, and the children scrabbled after them, and there was yelling and laughter and glee.

The nickel stunt left a bad taste in Fry's mouth. And when Dixon pulled it, Fry had looked across at McLaughlin and caught a flash of disgust on the normally impassive face. That evening as Fry walked down the passageway, without thinking he stopped and knocked on McLaughlin's door.

After a time the door cracked. "Yes?"

"Major McLaughlin," he said, "I wonder if we might have a word."

McLaughlin stared at him in silence.

Fry looked up the hall, then down it. "It's about the Expedition."

McLaughlin said gruffly, "Come in." He wore carpet slippers and a navy dressing gown; he stood in the center of the stateroom with his arms crossed.

Fry glanced around. He was startled to spot the photograph—*his* photograph, the one of the Cherokee girl, the one removed from the newspaper—stuck behind the mirror frame.

Fry touched its curling edge. "One of the candid photos. What do you think of it?"

McLaughlin said sharply, "You wished to make some point about the Expedition."

Fry turned away from the photograph. The Major, still standing, did not offer a chair. "Only . . . it seems so theatrical," Fry said. "As if it's all for publicity, for show."

"Doesn't take much to figure that out."

"Isn't the whole point of the Expedition to interest the Indians in becoming citizens?"

"That's what they say."

"Then why all the picture-taking? This business with the nickels, and kissing the flag."

"You tell me."

Fry could feel his palms moistening, his face heating up. "I was also wondering, sir, why the Indians aren't citizens in the first place."

"Didn't they tell you anything when you came on with us?" McLaughlin's tone was impatient. "To become eligible for citizenship an Indian must first take his allotment in severalty, his individual parcel of land. So that the reservations can be opened for homesteading, so that ultimate assimilation can take place."

Fry nodded, watching his hands. What was it Sykes had said? As personable as a rock?

"It was something, seeing them today." Fry glanced up meekly. "The feathers and paint, the spears. Are they really dangerous?"

McLaughlin's eyes softened slightly. "They're pretty well tamed, son," he said. "Treat an Indian like you would anybody else, you'll get along just fine."

"Never lie, right?" Fry said. "Never speak with a forked tongue." He knew he sounded like a greenhorn, which embarrassed him, but sensed it was the way to approach

McLaughlin. "You were with the Sioux, Major, they told me in the office. With Sitting Bull. I guess he was the worst."

McLaughlin's face shut. There was no other way to describe it. The lips pursed and the eyes went flat. They glanced at the door, as if willing Fry to go through it. The Major tugged at an ear, veined and hairy as a mullein leaf. At length he said curtly, "Sitting Bull was under my charge."

"What was he like?"

"An arrogant, puffed-up man. A personal coward. A mischief-maker. *Much* overrated by the press." He fixed his stare on Fry. "Why do you ask?"

Fry shrugged. "Just curious."

"Plainly, you've been told that I was responsible for his death."

Fry felt the blush go general on his face.

McLaughlin turned, showing Fry his back. "Sir, if you will excuse me," he said. "I'm going to bed."

The darkroom door swung open and there stood Booth, grinning ferociously, his coat reeking of smoke, a newspaper tubed in one meaty hand.

Fry and Giannetti exchanged glances. Giannetti was a sallow, swaybacked man with black hair and a beard that could have stood shaving twice a day; he sat bent over, a loupe in one eye and a brush in his hand. He had spent the last hour retouching photographs, sighing to Fry about his wife and little girl, while Fry, to be helpful, ran prints through a dryer.

"Joke time," Booth said. The door, on a pneumatic closer, bumped him on the backside, making him turn and look. He chuckled, stepped inside. "You first, Sam."

"I'm busy." Giannetti inclined his head toward the print he was working on.

"Come on." Booth placed his large hand on Giannetti's

shoulder. He did that a lot. "Everyone will tell a joke," he said. "And to be one hundred percent authentic, and appropriate to the spirit of the Rodman Wanamaker Expedition of Citizenship to the North American Indian, it will be an Indian joke. Sam?"

Giannetti sighed and put down the brush. With the loupe strapped to his head, and under the yellow darkroom light, he looked like some kind of mechanical man. He thought for a moment. "Okay. There's this Indian, wanted to set a world's record. Drank a thousand cups of tea. Drowned that night in his tea-pee."

Booth roared. Head nodding, eyes blinking, shoulders quaking, he let go of Giannetti's shoulder. "Sam, you're a regular wheeze." He reached out his red-knuckled hand and found Fry. "Small Fry."

"Don't know any Indian jokes."

Booth's grin collapsed, he looked hurt. "You can't mean it. Why, Indian jokes are the staple of American humor. We told 'em all the time at William and Mary. On the gridiron, we were the Indians. Where, case I haven't told you, I anchored the line."

"I don't hear many jokes."

"No? Don't secretaries tell jokes? Not even male secretaries?"

"I'm a stenographer," Fry said. "There's a large difference."

"Sure." Booth winked at Giannetti. "But tell us a joke anyway. And let it be an Indian joke." He tightened his grip, and it was as if the handle of a vise had advanced a quarter turn.

Fry tried to concentrate, but drew a blank. "They don't like Indian jokes at the Indian Bureau."

The vise tightened another quarter turn. Fry winced. Thought of poking Booth in the nose. Thought better of it.

"C'mon, Benny," Giannetti said.

Booth smiled beatifically. "Tell you what." His pliant red

mouth moved like a rubber band. "Make it easy. Just give us a nice jig joke and change it to a redskin."

Fry struggled to remember a story he'd heard. And felt the pressure on his shoulder increase again, crossing the threshold from discomfort into pain. "There's this Indian," he blurted. "He wants to go home, wants to see where he comes from. He goes down to the steamship office to buy a ticket, but comes up a nickel short. They won't let him go unless he pays the whole fare. So he runs outside and stops the first white man he sees: 'Hey, lend me a nickel to go home.' The white man gives him two bits and says, 'Here, take four more of you bastards with you.'" Fry grinned hopefully; Giannetti laughed and shook his head.

Booth released his grip. "That is a cheeky joke." He reached out and pinched Fry's cheek hard. "An Indian can't go home. He's already home."

Booth tossed the newspaper onto the counter between the enlargers. He got a cigar out of his coat pocket, slit the paper band, bit off the end, and licked the leaf. "Just heard this one up in the smoker. Little Injun boy goes up to his daddy, who's a heap big chief." Booth scraped a match on his boot sole, held it to the cigar and puffed heavily. "He says, 'Father, how do the people of our tribe get their names?'" Booth's tone deepened. "'It this way, my son. When squaw has papoose, father goes to door of wigwam, pulls back flap, and first thing he sees, that is name of child.'

"'How 'bout my sister?' the kid says.

"'When your sister born I look out of wigwam and see bird perched in tree. Call her Pretty Bird.'

"'And my brother?'

"'When I hear your brother cry, I look out and there goes wolf running past. I call him Wolf Runs.'" The smoke from Booth's cigar paled against the ceiling light. "The little boy gets this look on his face. So the big chief bends down and says, 'Why do you ask, Two Dogs Fucking?'"

Booth whooped, and elbowed Fry in the ribs, and Fry realized he had better laugh. Giannetti laughed; the tears ran down Booth's cheeks. He nudged Fry off the stool like he wasn't really there, sat, rubbed his eyes, and collected himself. "Here." He swiveled the stool to face the counter and opened the newspaper to the center spread.

Fry's heart hammered up in his chest.

"Clipping service sent it," Booth said. "Must've thought we'd be interested. Hell, maybe they thought we took 'em."

Unlikely. Booth did flags being hitched up poles, dignitaries shaking hands, speakers orating, chiefs thumbprint-signing the parchment, kissing the flag's hem. Dixon took photographs too: portraits, glass plate eight-by-tens, each subject posed in a chair between camera and wall, the indirect light of a window glinting a box in each dark level eye, people Dixon referred to as "types," people in traditional costume who looked very Indian.

Giannetti took off the loupe and studied the page, the round pictures like planets in orbit about a fourteen-point Times Roman sun that read, "Candid Photography from the American West."

"Holy Toledo," Giannetti said softly. He slid the page into better light.

Fry leaned in. The issue was new. Looking at them like this, it was as if he'd never seen them before. They really were portals through which the world could be viewed: an Indian in buckskins munching on an apple; greasy grinning trainmen yelling at each other; a big pursy man with a watch fob and cane, swaggering down the street; an Indian woman, her eyes narrowed and her head tilted, vigorously scolding a young woman whose back was to the camera. They showed not the faintest indication that they *knew*.

Giannetti read in a wondering tone: "'. . . camera as a tool for capturing life as it is lived . . . unposed, unretouched . . .

taken by an expert operating in the West.'" He looked at the photographs. He looked at Booth. "I'm bowled over."

Booth frowned. "Dixon doesn't like 'em. I don't either. I mean, the quality's not there. Look at that, background's out of focus. Look at all the grain."

Giannetti touched the page. "This is what the camera was invented for. Not for portraits or landscapes or grip-and-grins."

Booth tapped ash on the floor. "The good doctor is not amused. Thinks they're stealing our thunder. He wants to know how they're made."

Giannetti scratched behind his ear.

"Number two Kodak?" Booth said. "The round neg?"

"No, a smaller format, I think."

"Little European job. A Zeiss."

Giannetti shrugged. "You know how it is, Benny. Every time you point that black box, what does the person do? Stiffens up. You look through the viewfinder and there he is, stiff as a board. You go ahead and make the shot and put the box away, and the person goes back to being himself, being alive, and you say, 'Damn, *that's* the picture I wanted.' What I'm getting at, this is a hidden camera."

"Yeah? In a briefcase, like, or a book?"

"Something like that."

Fry had pulled back. As usual, he was wearing the disk. Which now felt broad and thick as a manhole cover.

"Anyway," Booth said, rising, "if you're done with 'em, Dixon would like his latest batch."

Fry quickly fetched the stack of portraits.

"Thanks, Small Fry." Booth took the photos and folded the newspaper around them. He grinned and shook his bearish head. "'Why do you ask, Two Dogs Fucking?'"

7

She did not dare telephone home. The telephone was re-
served for the direst of emergencies, for illness and death.
Besides, there was no telephone in the McLaughlin house-
hold, and Mother would have to go down the block to the
Pettingills', and it would become public knowledge then; and
while Mother could deal with it, and Annie could deal with it,
Father—away now on this strange-sounding Expedition of
Citizenship—certainly would rather not.

So she was stuck with paper and pen. Nita—Nita Wheeler,
another young unmarried teacher—had gone out for a stroll,
maybe to give the gossip a good airing, maybe to afford her
roommate a little peace and quiet. No, she knew Nita. By now
it would be all over the school.

She could tell Mother—what? That she was coming home?
That much was probably true. She was pretty sure she wasn't
in so much trouble that she couldn't get the Antelope Creek
School. Hadn't it been vacant for almost a year? Ever since the
couple from Indiana, the white couple so full of idealism and
Methodist zeal, had found themselves unable to adjust? The
twentieth (or the fiftieth, or the two hundredth) time an
Indian face had loomed at the window at night, as the couple
were sitting down to sup, or reading by kerosene light, or,
heaven forbid, as the woman crouched in the tub for a bath,
had finally proven one time too many. And so (Sib said) they
had fled. Left the place pretty well stocked too, so he and
Bennie Looking Elk and Arch Fye had hunted out of the

school for a week last fall, killing a couple of deer there before moving on down to the Hills for elk.

She dipped the steel nib in the ink. She wrote quickly, keeping her forearm and hand rigid and moving her arm only at the elbow, tracking her copperplate neatly across the page; recording, simply, the fact of her suspension from teaching. She stopped. To go on, she needed some familiar faces, if only paper ones. She fetched the photographs from the nightstand in their matching brass frames. The portrait of Mother McLaughlin was forty years old: She had been about thirty when it was taken, well before Annie had come into her life; although, Annie reflected, she did not look all that different today. The half-Indian woman in the sepia print was round of face, her eyes neutral in their confrontation with the lens. Mother McLaughlin wore a plain dark dress with a lace collar and a pale cameo brooch. The photographer had seen fit to brush out the background, so it appeared that the round-faced dark-eyed woman was staring from a nimbus; as if she were some sort of airborne aboriginal saint viewing the earth from a passing cloud. Some fine old name hidden in that notion: Cloud Woman, Sees the Earth From Above.

The other brass frame enclosed a newer photograph. Two photographs, actually; the most recent one, which had come at Christmas, covering an older one. The buried portrait she did not bother to get out, knowing it so well: the official photograph made by the Bureau in 1895 when it promoted James McLaughlin to Inspector. The photograph coincided with the period of her strongest memories of the man. She had been six years old when it was taken, when he had come home from Washington that time, obviously excited and proud, in his luggage a framed copy of the portrait, which Mother McLaughlin had placed on the mantel—and soon after that Father left, and kept on coming back and leaving again, until she herself finally left for Carlisle. The old photograph depicted a stern man with a face whose determination expressed itself not in the jaw, which was covered with crinkly salt-and-pepper beard, but in the eyes, pale and forthright, cinched down by sun-dried, weather-hardened flesh, and, oddly enough, in the nose, which was Grecian and noble and direct. From the new picture, the Christmas one, the white-haired senior Inspector inspected her—stiffly, reproachfully it seemed—inspected his adopted daughter, whom he had seen schooled and trained and bettered. His last child and his only all-Indian one, who, to his ongoing chagrin, had not yet married (though many said she was lovely, and some did not say much at all, notably the other young women, which perhaps spoke more eloquently of her beauty than did words; but then she always figured physical beauty was no more than a deceitful temporary husk). But she was otherwise quite successful, a teacher at the new sanitarium in Lapwai, destined for promotion and other grand things.

Until now.

The door opened and Nita leaned in. Yakima Nita, yackety-yack. Whose all-consuming desire was to shuck her Indian-ness like an outgrown set of clothes, and get hitched to a certain young Nez Perce man who worked as an insurance salesman in Lewiston, drove a Model T, and was said to be "up and coming."

"Busy?" Nita asked.

"Not really." She laid the pen down, pushed the half-written letter aside.

Nita came in. She lit a cigarette, an act forbidden to women teachers at the school, and tilted her head to puff, practically striking a pose. "So, what will you do?"

"I don't know. Wait, I suppose, until Siebert decides what to do with me."

"You want to stay?"

"I don't think so," said Annie. "I need some time to myself. I have some vacation built up. Maybe I'll go camping or something."

Nita snorted. She abhorred doing anything outdoors.

Annie squared the letter with the corners of her desk. Decided she didn't like the gesture. Too controlled. Too much—she smiled at herself—too much like Father. "Actually, I'll probably end up going home."

Nita arched her eyebrows, plucked and then redrawn to a slightly more astonished contour with a reddish brown grease pencil, which color did not complement her Indian-black hair. The surprise in Nita's tone failed to conceal the mockery. "Annie Owns the Fire going home?"

Annie spun the page awry. Didn't bother answering.

Nita blew smoke from the corners of her mouth. "A man."

"No."

"Now that I could understand. I could understand it if Miss Owns the Whole Goddamn Fire finally picked herself out a man. Lord knows there are enough out there who follow her around just trying to get a sniff. But she wants to go back to the reservation."

"I think so. Yes."

"Why?"

"It's not easy to explain."

"Try."

"A lot of things happened back there . . ."

"Nothing happens back there."

". . . when I was little. Things maybe I should go back and find out about and try to understand."

Nita's laugh was a harsh bray. "Never go back," she said. "Burn your bridges. Life is today, and tomorrow, and the tomorrow after that. Piss on that old reservation life. Piss on being an Indian. And if you can get yourself a man . . ."

"I don't suppose I need one just now."

"No." Nita shook her head and pointed with her cigarette.

"That's your problem. You don't need a man or anybody else."

At that moment, a thousand miles south and east, James McLaughlin coughed angrily, stood up from his chair, and turned away from the flowing, parched, train-window plain-scape. The boy had done it. His blasted curiosity about Sitting Bull, though also of course the clipped-out picture, and likely the swirl of Indian faces and tongues, and the running empty land.

Sometimes if you walked the whole way through a memory you could leave it behind.

But how many times had he done precisely that? How many times had he doggedly trudged just once more through the whole bitter affair? Was it actually possible to leave a memory in the dust? Maybe, just maybe, it would never quit clinging. He was an old man, a weary man, his balls hung down on strings, and at the tag end of the day, no matter if all he'd done was sit on the train and ride, his legs ached and cramped, he was tired as hell, too sadly tired to think straight but always tired enough to remember. He clenched one fist and softly smote his hip, turned and shuffled out the stateroom door. He stopped in the hallway, having forgotten where he was going—until, standing there in irritated puzzlement, his blad-der reminded him.

Returning to the room, he took the newspaper photograph from behind the mirror frame. He laid it on the desk. The girl looked so much like Annie it scared him. It was too close, and she was too close to the event, and even though it had hap-pened twenty-three years ago, almost a quarter of a century, it was still vivid and shocking and bright. His blunt-fingered hands twitched. Of their own volition, it seemed, they picked up the photograph—almost clenched to crumple it, then stopped. He couldn't. Some faint superstition: She was his daughter, he would no more destroy a picture of her, even a picture that just looked like her, than stand and curse his God. And besides, crumpling this flake of newsprint would not change what had happened or the way he now felt.

But maybe there was a way. Go through it one final time. Record it, set it down in black and white. Hadn't he a stenographer, and more time on his hands than he knew what to do with? Maybe it would change some minds, destroy some misconceptions. Maybe it would never see the light of day, would be just for him. Sitting Bull, the Ghost Dance, the bloody killing dawn. Maybe it would cleanse him of them, once and for all.

8

In the baking heat the car occupied a siding of the Chicago, Rock Island & Pacific Railroad, better known as the Rock Island Line.

Fry sat slouched in the chair. The fine hair behind his ears stuck to his scalp. He was typing, transcribing in triplicate his shorthand record of the latest ceremony. The spidery black bars of the typewriter leaped in a blur to strike. Finished, he cranked the platen, separated the original and carbons and onion skins, filed the copies, and closed his pad.

He repaired to the bathroom. Strapping the camera on, he wondered what, truly, would happen if he got caught. The Major went strictly by the book: He finds out, it's all over. Send me back to Washington so fast my head would swim. Have me called on the carpet before Cribbs—Jesus, that shark. Lucky to keep my job. Would I even want it? The whispering secretaries, the sniggering clerks.

He smiled theatrically, mugging for the mirror. The smile fled and he became a gray man in a gray suit. He could do it. He could keep them from finding out. And Kravitz said they were good, and Giannetti said they were good, and in his heart he knew they were honest and true.

Out the door and onto the observation deck, where the heat brought him up short. The brass rail dazzled and the green canvas awning smelled of dust. The town spread out—dirt streets, wind-battered buildings, then, like a lapping sea, the flat dry land.

He found a drugstore with a Cream Soda sign and a screen door on a spring. Thick glass jars filled with colored liquids occupied the front window; inside, the air was heavy with drugs and fruit syrup, Coca-Cola and green soap. Soda fountain, magazine rack, shelves crowded with dusty vials. He looked through a display of postal cards and selected two. "A Pioneer Home" showed a man, woman, and two children in front of a small sod house. Deer antlers sat whitening on the dugout's roof, and a washbasin hung on the wall. The man and woman stared at the camera like stuffed groundhogs; the children's faces were set in sun frowns. They all looked about as lively as the men on the second card, who, although their eyes were wide open, were dead. Supine, shirtless, with dark blotches the size of half-dollars adorning their torsos, the men gazed up tranquilly, their heads cocked to one side as if they were listening to pleasant, ethereal sounds.

He paid for the cards and sat in a booth. He flipped the homesteaders over. "Dear Ira," he printed in a crabbed hand. "There are Indians all over the place, many other notables as well. I am pleased with the first two installments. You will be receiving my next package soon. Your friend, Ansel." He switched to the card of the dead: "Dear Mother and Father." He thought, with a certain mild malice, of his father, a pale man who worked half-hidden behind a teller's grille, a green visor shading his face, a flesh-colored rubber thimble on one thumb. Father was afraid of bank robbers, of poison sumac and floods and snakes, of intimacy with family and friends, of anything suggesting impropriety. He had bequeathed to Fry his high forehead and thin-bridged nose, the slight parrot's beak to his upper lip, his reedy chest. And, of course, his name. Originally "Frei"—that was how Grandfather had spelled it—Father had changed it, to look less German, and lately, with the trouble brewing in Europe, he had talked of changing it again, anglicizing it completely to "Free." The man, thought Fry, was anything but free. He was indentured to rent payments on a squat brick row house in Shi'poke, a glum section of Harrisburg where the river exhaled its rank breath through every crumbling mortar joint into every cramped room. Edwin Fry liked nothing better, of a summer evening, than to cloister himself in his postage-stamp back-yard, plucking the hated Japanese beetles from his roses, his zinnias, his mums, and baptizing their copper-plated souls in a can of coal oil.

Fry's pen hovered. His mother was more substantial to him: a thickset woman whose heavy Dutch accent kept her silent most of the time. He found himself visualizing her not as she was, but as she had been, in a photograph he had happened onto in the attic. She had been young then, and the photographer—a relative? a boyfriend?—had said the right words to make her lower, for an instant, the poser's mask. She looked at once shy and coquettish, with a tilt to her head he had never seen. He had flushed with lust, which quickly fizzled to shame. Father too would have burned to see that girl. And there it was. His parents had been young once, young and full of possibility.

He pursed his lips and wrote, "Thought you would enjoy this 'still life.'" He smiled at his low wit. "Justice remains swift in the West." He addressed the card, waved the ink dry, and turned it over. The legend was handprinted in white: *Moses Harper. William Curtis, alias Bill Kirk. Shot by Sheriff Posse near Anadarko, Okla.* 10–7–1911.

"Knowed those two."

A man stood, holding his hat. Loose-limbed and thin, his face all angles, the skin dead white above the mark of his hatband, deep brown below. He slid into the seat across from Fry and pointed a grimy finger. "Harper's place and mine are side by each. Curtis, he come from over t' Busheyville. Had this urge to rob a bank. Must of thought they was the next Dalton gang." He cackled shrilly. "Hid in the hills, but the posse wiped 'em out clean as a nigger eatin' a saucer of lick. Bloody? Like beef day at the Indin agency."

The man grinned a tangle of teeth. He was freshly shaven and had an Adam's apple whose terrain had defeated the razor. He stuck out his hand. "Harvey P. Deemer."

"Ansel Fry." The hand felt like hide wrapping brittle sticks.

Deemer turned and addressed two women. "Git on over here."

They approached, a short formless woman in a blue dress, a thin young one whose neck was disfigured by a goiter.

"My wife Inez and daughter Etta. This here is Ansel Fry."

"You wouldn't be related to the Frys from over t' Guthrie, would you?" the woman asked.

"No, ma'am."

"I farm," Deemer said. "South of here. Homesteaded in ought-one, when they opened the reservation. Proved up in ought-six and still goin' strong. Ain't that so, sugar?"

Mrs. Deemer nodded. "We grow wheat and alfalfa and raise turkeys."

The girl stood as if tethered to her mother. She looked perhaps eighteen; her brown hair was streaked with blonde, and her freckled arms looked strong. She seemed to be trying to hide behind a small patent leather purse.

"Y'all ever raise turkeys?" Deemer asked. "Stupidest critters on God's green earth. Come up a storm, with a little lightnin', and them birds'll trample each other in the dust."

"If it rains," the girl said in an astonished tone, "why, the turkeys just stand there lookin' up"—she raised her head, exposing the goiter, smooth and round, a misplaced breast— "and their mouths fall open and their lungs fill with water and they drownd."

Deemer asked, "Where d' y'all hail from?"

"Washington, D.C."

"Gov'ment man?"

"I work in the Indian Bureau."

A slight pause. "Is that so? We seen that private varnish at the depot, and commented on it."

"The car is hired out to the Rodman Wanamaker Expedition of Citizenship to the North American Indian."

"Citizenship? North American Indin?"

"We don't have the power to grant citizenship." The pronoun felt inaccurate, and faintly damning. Fry changed it: "*They* try to impress the Indians to strive for citizenship on their own. There's this ceremony they go through."

"Why do you want to put citizenship on the Indins?"

It seemed an easy enough question, but Fry had to think. "So they can vote. Have a say in how the country's run."

"Ask me, it's a waste of time. An Indin's got no git-up-and-go."

Deemer's wife nodded.

"They had all that land"—Deemer made a vague wave— "and never done a thing with it, never developed it, just left it lay fallow." His drawl had found an edge, and one eyelid quivered. "They deserve to have it taken away. Now today, gov'ment hands 'em plows, seed, wagons—citizenship. They don't hand me a thing. Know how I feel about Indins? 'Proximately 'bout the same way I feel about niggers."

Fry looked at the table. "I don't know," he began cautiously. "Some of the Indians are very industrious. There are Indian schoolteachers and nurses, Indian doctors and dentists."

"I'd never let my wife go to one," Deemer said, "nor let one stick his filthy hands in my mouth. As for industrious, what they work best at is drink. Gov'ment hands 'em a paycheck for land they never owned, builds 'em a house with an indoor pump, what do they do but knock a hole in the wall so's their ponies can snuffle water out of the sink." He shook his head scornfully. "Where's this expedition of yours been?"

"So far, only Oklahoma. Next is New Mexico, Arizona, California, the Northwest—"

"You'll see Indins all right." The man pecked at the tabletop with his finger. "Y'all come back here once you're done, and set down with Harvey P. Deemer and tell him what you learned. I'll lay odds your eyes is opened."

I'll lay odds too, Fry thought.

When Deemer got up, Fry rose and followed the family out of the store. They stood on the board sidewalk. The clouds had thickened, making the sun a white disk; the heat was stifling. Deemer set an unraveling straw hat on his head and raised his face. "Maybe rain," he said. The daughter smiled shyly, touching the tips of her fingers to her distended throat. "Etta Deemer," she said, "RFD, Anadarko. I collect postal cards, Mr. Fry. Got me a album. Think you might could send me one from California?"

He held the girl's smile with his own. Slipped the two cards he'd bought into his pocket, found the shutter string there. "I'll send you one of the ocean," he said.

The track was straight. He could keep the window cracked without worrying about smoke. There was a slight incline to the grade; the land was red, with a few scrubby trees huddled along dry streambeds. Now and then a town would rise up, wooden grain elevator, shorter church steeple, double row of stores, yellow station with brown gingerbread trim, always a boy or two on the platform to wave at the train. The locomotive would bark its whistle for the crossing, and slow; occasionally the train would stop to take on or discharge a passenger, or to deliver the mail.

He played a game with himself. *I am the next person I see.*

He searched out the window. A jackrabbit raced away through the tumbleweeds. The sight of a cactus filled him with exultation. The telegraph lines rose and fell, rose and fell. A dust devil whisked across a dry wash, leaning forward as if bound on some important errand. Scars and cracks were eroded into the land. A windmill whirled above a dry, bullet-riddled tank.

I am the next person I see.

He dozed, the dream fragments tumbling: the placid Susquehanna coming broad through the water gap—ridges receding, blue and paler still, wrapped in woolen haze—an aeroplane sparkling above the city, crowds of people shading their eyes to watch—the morning glory painted inside the Victrola horn, the lonely odd little boy who would lug it down to the river in the dusk, to lie in the rank grass, direct the belled end toward City Island and put his ear to the tapered end—guitar chords, the singing of revelers, sometimes only the gabbling of ducks and the sad, hollow croaking of herons.

He opened his eyes. Caught a ruddy, sun-dazzled butte attempting to sneak past. *The next person I see.* His eyelids drooped again. Later, he opened them.

There.

The old woman was taking in wash. Faded dress and sunbonnet. She stopped to watch the train and was drawn briskly past, growing smaller in successive window panes. House and leaning barn, red chickens, windmill with AEROMOTOR in red script on the tail, shelterbelt of stunted trees. The farm passed swiftly and he closed his eyes to hold it. House weathered the color of hickory bark, rust-stained roof, pink spray of hollyhocks beside the porch. *I am an old woman.* The picture completed itself. *I am an old woman who talks to the mule, who searches for eggs in the weeds behind the barn. The wind sharpens its teeth on the roof. It sets its shoulder to the corner and shoves. It lifts the rug of sod and shakes it, blows the dust under the door and through the cracks in the walls. I could sweep three-four times a day, if I had the git-up-and-go.*

Children?

One, the train took her to California, where grapefruits grow on trees. Husband? *Gone. I'll follow within the year. Attached to the dead, you wither. The wind is never still.*

9

A rooster was crowing somewhere when he came awake to find the rails silent, the car still. He dropped down from the berth and pulled on his clothes.

On the observation deck the air was chilly. A long range of mountains toothed the east, naked and cobalt blue; behind them the sky glowed red. The station was dark and deserted. Beyond the siding, adobe huts sat like lumps of melted cheese. Horses hung their heads in brush corrals. He smelled the delicious tickling of sage, woodsmoke sweeter than incense, earthy undertones of garlic and manure.

The West: At last there could be no doubting it. He was not sure what it would be like, certainly not provincial and staid like Harrisburg, or full of itself like Washington. When he walked along city streets, sometimes he would imagine the West looming over his shoulder like a great glowing cloud, brooding in the place where the sun set and the wind gathered. Most of Fry's particulars on the West came from yellow-backed dime novels and newspaper stories that read like dime novels; from flickering silent movies (cowboys, Indians, bad men who pointed their guns right in your face, and didn't the ladies scream *then*); and, finally and most emphatically, from Buffalo Bill's Wild West—"The Grassy Sward Our Carpet, Heaven's Azure Canopy Our Canvas, No Gilding, No Humbug, No Freaks." At the age of eight he had first witnessed Buffalo Bill. The Plainsman had been luminescent in a white sombrero, white buckskin jacket and pants, riding on a white

70

stallion. He circled the arena, long locks trailing his hat, coolly gunning down the ki-yipping Sioux. Soon after, Fry composed a letter suggesting that he, Ansel Fry, should join the great scout in the West. He addressed it to "Buffalo Bill Cody, Way Out West." His mother did not refuse a stamp. He stood on tiptoe and shoved the letter across the counter at the post office. He went home and waited. Months passed, and no answer came. He tried to fathom what might have happened. The Pony Express rider who carried the mail across the Staked Plain had been waylaid; a Comanche had burned the envelope, or ripped it open and stared at the letter upside down. Or Buffalo Bill had been bushwhacked: Rain-in-the-Face had finally shot him down, hacked off the coveted scalp. But then he had spied a fresh poster covering a barn wall, and had known that the King of the Bordermen was not dead.

When next he saw the Wild West, he climbed onto his seat and shouted, "Didn't you get my letter?" But Buffalo Bill never heard, and the people sitting round turned and chuckled, and his father grabbed him by the back of his pants and sat him back down.

The Mescalero Agency lay in a grassy bowl among pine mountains. Stake-and-rider fences converged on the two-story office, a schoolhouse with bell tower, weather-beaten barns, and sheds. A quarter mile away stood a hamlet of tipis and brush shelters.

The Apaches were tattered skinny men hunkered down, cigarettes pinched between forefingers and thumbs. Their hair was clipped, and some wore faded Army coats. White ladies, wives of the agency employees, sang "America the Beautiful" to begin the ceremony; one woman, black gloves buttoned to her elbows, accompanied on a small pump organ. The Apache leaders raised the flags and signed the Declaration of Allegiance, Booth made his snaps, and the ceremony

71

was history. Dixon set up his portrait camera in a classroom, and the interpreter lined up people for him to photograph; McLaughlin and the superintendent went to look at a vegetable garden; and Fry, seeing a prime chance for picture-taking, followed the Apaches home.

Panting dogs of no particular lineage trotted at his heels; their coats were mostly white, with bluish spots like huckleberries. Hummingbirds visited pink fireweed and red paintbrush. Gopher tunnels crisscrossed the ground in long brown welts.

Before he reached the camp he smelled it, a thick raw fetor of excrement. Trash lay in the grass, broken bottles, splintered boards, blackened cans. Flies lifted in murmuring swells. A naked toddler with a vacant face dribbled his urine in the dust.

From among the tents, a drone of women's voices. He walked down a path to where an old man lay snoring before a hovel of boards and brush, his face puffy as an apple left out through too many frosts. Fry let his coat fall open. Placing his hand in his pocket, he set himself and took the picture. He turned toward a group of women regarding him suspiciously and took their picture too.

The Apaches! In grade school he had written a report on them, using as his source a book that his neighbor, Mr. Hippensteel, lent him. The frontispiece was an engraving of an Apache warrior, a lean, bandy-legged man in a floppy pale shirt, with a breechclout—like a long diaper—tucked into his belt front and back, and with supple leather moccasins that could be worn unrolled to the knees to fend off thorns and brush, or folded down to the ankles in extreme heat. A headband kept the warrior's hair out of his eyes; a carbine and crossed bandoliers completed the outfit. The Apache glared evilly from the page. The toughest, most merciless fighters in the world: White women, the book said, preferred death to capture by these savages, and Fry had duly noted this fact in his report, not fully appreciating why.

He kicked a can out of his path and detoured around a rusted bedspring. Finding himself on the edge of the camp, he maneuvered to get a shot of the whole place. It was then he saw the men: two, in green Army jackets with dark patches on the sleeves where insignia had been snipped off. They stood staring at him. Their hands, coffee brown with pale nails, hung at their sides. Their faces, expressionless, could have seen forty summers, or eighty.

He forgot about the picture, turned, and skirted a clump of brush. The breeze hummed in the sage. He passed a wall tent, a derelict wagon, a smoking fire. He glanced back. The men were keeping pace. His scalp crawled, and he lengthened his stride; he realized he had been getting farther away from the agency, and when he angled back that way the Apaches moved to cut him off.

Ridiculous. They couldn't mean any harm—could they? He had done nothing, at least so far as they knew. The agency looked like a clutch of white islands across a wide bay. He made a big loop, striding with his hands in his pockets, resolutely watching the ground. His pulse pounded in his temples. He heard their steps. He was an inch away from breaking into a run, but kept his head, kept on walking, faster now, the rustling of their feet getting closer. He stopped and spun around.

They halted a few yards away. Slowly, from the front of his blouse, one of the men drew a knife. It was a thick-bladed knife with a wooden handle. The man's face was immobile, unreadable; wiry white hairs stood on his upper lip and chin, like porcupine quills in a dog's muzzle. The man spat in the dirt. "What you want?" The whites of his eyes were tinted red. A pale scar pulled the corner of one eye toward his mouth.

"Answer him," the second man said, so softly Fry wondered

if he'd heard it. The second man looked a trifle younger. Tarnished buttons up the fronts of both coats, grease stains on the collars. The second man straightened his arm and shook it, and an iron bar slipped out of the sleeve and into his hand.

"What you want?" The question more insistent, a touch of frenzy to the words.

He wanted to be lifted out of this hole. To rise lightly to one of the mountains ringing the valley, a pine-fresh slope where the sun shone and the air was clean. To be, please Jesus, in his cubicle back in Washington, typing.

What he did was feel for the string in his pocket, close his trembling fingers around it, and pull.

The click was loud as bone-snap.

The scar-faced man lifted his head. "Got a gun." He stared at one, then the other, of Fry's hidden hands.

Fry's heart filled with hope. He tried to make his cracking voice deliver a threat—but more quickly, the Apaches spread out.

"You get one of us," the man with the pipe said, "the other gonna take you."

Fry backed slowly, feeling with his heels.

It made them all jump—the slug howling over their heads an instant before the *boom* blew past. They looked and saw a stocky man in a suit, white-haired, fifty paces, holding a pistol with both hands. The Apaches crouched and dodged off through the brush; they ducked into a crease in the hill and vanished.

McLaughlin came over, the revolver dangling at his side. He hefted the heavy gun. "Borrowed it." He shook his head, twisted his little finger in one ear. "Damn," he said. "Won't be able to hear the dinner bell for a week."

Fry's legs felt liquid, and suddenly he had to sit down in the grass. Hugging his knees to his chest, he caught his breath; it took him a while to find his voice. "Thanks," he said weakly.

"Don't mention it." McLaughlin made as if to holster the pistol, realized he had none. "You have to watch your step." He lowered a hand and helped Fry to his feet. He jerked his head toward the agency, and they set off for it. McLaughlin patted Fry on the shoulder. "Out here," he said, "fires are still burning."

"I thought you said if I treated an Indian like anyone else, I'd get along just fine."

"I didn't think," McLaughlin said, "you'd be green enough to walk into an Apache slum." He stood by the window in the observation room, watching Signet being coupled to the train. "Those Apaches will die with a knife in their hands and a curse in their throats."

Outside, voices shouted and couplers gnashed. A car inspector came back, tapping on the trucks with a hammer, listening among the bell-like pings for a dull sound that would tell of a crack or a broken weld.

"Chiracahuas," McLaughlin said. "The ones that got after you, the ones in the uniforms. Geronimo's old band." He turned his face toward Fry, who still appeared excessively pale. "Thirty years at Fort Sill. The army let them go this spring, trucked 'em to the Mescalero in cattle cars. Bilious old bucks." He ran up the window as the car began to roll.

"Why were they at Fort Sill?" Fry asked.

"In prison."

"What for?"

"Murder. Arson. Rape. Who knows? Who even remembers?"

"Where's Geronimo?"

"Drank himself to death."

Fry nodded. "Yes. It was in the papers a few years back."

McLaughlin took one of the plush armchairs. He said, "I'd like you to take some dictation. Use a fresh book. This will be"—he paused, stroking his mustache with thumb and fore-

75

forefinger, staring out the window—"an ongoing project with us.

"Sitting Bull," he said. "Or, as a witty white man once quipped, 'Slightly Recumbent Gentleman Calf.'" He looked up, his blue eyes whimsical and clear. Fry took a chair, crossed his legs, cracked the fresh steno pad, primed his pen and waited.

McLaughlin turned back to the window. The train was rushing south through the Tularosa Valley. To the east, through soot-dirtied windows, could be seen blue ripples of mountains; to the west, a vast desert of glistening white sand.

"'The Death of the Noted Sioux Indian Chief Sitting Bull, or, How He was Martyrized by the Sensational Press.'" McLaughlin cleared his throat. "We shall start with the first time I laid eyes on the man.

"It was September tenth, eighteen eighty-one. I remember it precisely, because on that date I took over as agent on the Standing Rock Indian Reservation, Dakota Territory."

McLaughlin indicated with his hand that what would follow was not to be recorded. "I don't intend, Mr. Fry, to dictate a polished prose. Far from it. I just want to get my thoughts down. So make this a verbatim transcript. If and when I decide to do something with it, I'll work from your typed notes."

He settled back in the chair and directed his gaze out the window again. "The country was drier," he said, "much drier than at Fort Totten, my first posting. I was not yet forty, still young, still full of vinegar." He set his elbows on his knees and touched the tips of his fingers together. "It was a spare and arid place, yet pleasing to the eye—cottonwoods still green along the river, which is muddy and broad. The Missouri. The Big Muddy. Beyond the river, rounded grass hills, and beyond the hills, a sky so vast it overwhelmed the senses; so blue it stunned the eye."

McLaughlin stopped for a moment, and Fry was made

suddenly conscious of the mile-gobbling clicking of the rails bearing them west.

"My wife, carrying our youngest, led the other children down the plank. Roustabouts worked at unloading the steamer, winching down hogsheads and bales, lowering a milk cow in a sling.

"Fort Yates looked a prosperous place, plenty of stores and spic-and-span houses. The post had a grassy parade ground, an officers' row, enlisted men's barracks, ranked caissons, cannons, and Gatling guns, square after square of corral. Out on the flats stood the tipis, mud-colored and with smoke-smudged tops. They reminded me, as always, of some natural component of the landscape, such as prairie dogs' dens or cliff swallows' nests.

"Sioux Indians. From *Nadowessioux*." He spelled the word for Fry. "It means 'snakes' or 'enemies' in Chippewa. The ones on Standing Rock were of three bands: Yanktonais, Sihasapa, and Hunkpapa.

"He stood with a handful of others seated around him, apart from the rest. The seated Indians were looking not at me, the new agent, as might be expected, but at the standing man—as if he had just finished with some pronouncement or was about to make one. He was of medium height, chunkily built although somewhat peaked looking. His blanket was shabby. He wore moccasins and braids wrapped with fur and yarn.

"Face like a red full moon pocked with meteor hits. Cheek-bones pronounced, almost swollen, mouth a dull sickle with the ends turned down." McLaughlin paused. "What I remember most vividly were his eyes—black, and full of hate.

"I noticed the armed guard around the landing and especially around the band of seated Indians with the standing man in their midst. The soldiers prodded with their rifles, and the Indians rose.

"The gangplank was clear. The steamer, paddle wheel turning in the current, stood ready to cast off. The Indians waited for the standing man, who slowly limped up the plank. They followed him onto the boat.

"I knew then that the man was Sitting Bull."

Outside, the hoarse whistle of the locomotive; the train clattered through a switch point, past a sided freight.

"Sitting Bull was on his way to Fort Randall, to jail. At the time, I was dead set against jailing him." McLaughlin half-turned his head, his brows a thick cloud bank above his eyes. "He had just surrendered out of Canada, where he'd fled after the Custer fight. I said, 'Give him to me. Let me keep him here at the agency.' Tame him, I figured, and the others would all fall into line." He laughed ironically. "Might as well have tried to tame a prairie wolf.

"The next time I saw him was over a year later. A glorious spring day in eighteen eighty-three. Strong light came flooding in through the agency window. It lit the dust that rose from his robe each time he slashed his hand to make a point, or punched his chest with his fist to emphasize *miyah*—the Lakota word, the Sioux word, for 'I.'

"As a matter of course, I always used an interpreter. I could speak a workaday Lakota, but I wished always to be perfectly understood, and to keep a certain distance between myself and the man.

"My interpreter was the half-breed Louis Primeau. 'Sitting Bull says,' Primeau told me, 'that he will not plant anything this season. He will look around, see how it's done, and maybe he'll be ready next year.

"'He says he will be the big chief and draw all the rations and pass them out to the people himself.

"'He has with him a paper with the names of the Indians he wants as subchiefs under him.'

"The members of Sitting Bull's band sat in chairs around the room—a collection of more savage faces I had never seen. One man wore welders' goggles with one of the lenses missing.

Another had on a bloodstained railroader's cap. A third wore a dozen scalps sewn to his shirt. Another had a necklace of dried toads. They stared at me, waiting to see how the agent, the one they called 'White Hair,' would react."

The train rolled past a long, broken bluff, the light from the white-sand desert behind the bluff flashing intermittently on McLaughlin's face.

"Sitting Bull said in his high, singsong voice, 'The Great Father has written a letter to Sitting Bull, saying he must now return to his own country and live among his people. He will be honored as the head man. A fine house will be built for him. He will be given herds of cattle and horses, and many buggies and wagons. He will be allowed to gather his people from all the other agencies, and bring them here to Standing Rock.'"

McLaughlin stood, got a paper cone of water from the cooler, and sat back down.

He sipped from the cup. "I thought I had calmed myself, but when I looked into those black, hateful eyes, my stomach tensed and my gorge rose.

"I spoke to Primeau. 'Tell the'—I almost said 'Chief,' but I would not—'tell Sitting Bull that to be honest with him I must be frank.

"'Say to him that the Great Father never wrote any such letter as he claims, never wrote him any letter at all.'

"At Primeau's words, a sudden angry buzzing, like when you slap your hand on a beehive. My police stood just outside the door. It was impossible to say what weapons these Indians had hidden under their robes.

"I looked him in the eye. 'Tell him that the Great Father thinks the biggest chief is the Indian who learns the white man's ways. The Indian who plants crops and builds his own house. Who learns to live by the sweat of his brow. Who goes to the white man's church. Who sends his children to school.

"'You and your people will receive your fair share of the

goods and supplies that come to this agency for distribution. You will be treated in all respects in the same manner as the other Indians of the agency. You must not expect anything more than others who are equally deserving.'

"The silence was thick. I turned to his followers. 'The Great Father has sent me to take care of you and to labor in your behalf. I hold the same relation to you that a father holds toward his children. And, as the first thing that is required on the part of the children is obedience, so must you willingly obey me and follow my commands.'"

McLaughlin raised his hand and spread his fingers; with the index finger of his other hand, he folded one finger down.

"'You will not leave the vicinity of the agency without my express permission.'"

He folded another finger down. "'The use of alcohol is strictly forbidden.

"'Each head of a family will choose a plot of land and begin to plant crops. Not next year, *this year*. Look around you. The game is almost gone. In a few years the buffalo will be gone and you will no longer see the footprints of the deer.'

"I looked at Sitting Bull. His eyes were downcast but strangely peaceful. He wore buckskin leggings and a stinking tattered shirt, a loop of beads from behind which a crucifix glimmered—the icon could have been no more than a bauble to the man. Beneath the moth-eaten robes would be the angry, disfiguring scars.

"'On this agency the rite you call the Sun Dance or Wiwanyag wachipi is strictly forbidden.'

"That finished it." McLaughlin drank down the rest of the water, crumpled the cup.

And suddenly he was tired, weary to his bones, aching in his soul, wondering. He heard again the question that had gnawed at him for a quarter of a century: at dawn when he came awake, at Mass when the priest nattered on, in his bath, lighting a cigar, hailing a cab, bogged down in niggling negotiation at some remote reservation—the question brought to mind by the story he was telling, and by the strange, piquant picture of the Indian girl fixed in the mirror corner in his stateroom: Did I treat him—and all the rest—did I treat them right?

10

Memories of him, good and bad, came to her as she drove the last faint mile of wheel ruts, found the familiar place (her retreat, for when things got too grim at the school), and set about making camp.

She remembered how, when she was a child, he would put her up on some high place—way up on top of the icebox, in the hayloft's door, on the rusty roof of the shed—and bid her jump: She would raise her arms above her head, shut her eyes, and soar down fearlessly into hands that never let her fall.

When she got the mumps that time it was he who stayed up with her all night, telling her stories, rhyming and singing songs, bathing her forehead, whittling slivers from an ice chunk for her to suck on.

He told her, when she was edging into adolescence, that she would look rather better if she were to keep her lips pressed together when not talking, as they were quite full, and it did not appear seemly for them to be hanging slack. The remark had embarrassed her severely and stuck with her ever since—even now she would find herself unconsciously tightening her lips, tucking them properly in.

She remembered the day he and Mother McLaughlin put her on the train to Carlisle. She had been twelve years old. They had stood on the platform looking up, and he motioned for her to slide the window down, but she couldn't, the thing was jammed in its channel. He brought out from behind his back a big bouquet of roses; where he had gotten them in the depths of a Dakota winter, she had no idea. Handing the flowers to Mother, he reached up and flattened his palms against the glass, pulled down on it, gave it a hard slap, pulled again—still the window wouldn't budge. The train had started creeping, and he had taken away his hands and stepped back, an annoyed look on his face, and they had gotten smaller and smaller, Mother still holding the roses, a spot of red that seemed to glow as the old couple and the dingy station diminished.

Another memory, a darker one: It had come in the night, and today she carried it with her as, the camp now fixed, she walked across the dusty flat.

She stopped, drew down her Levi's, and squatted to relieve herself. Standing, tucking in her shirt and buttoning her pants, she watched the spot of urine go from twinkling to dark to tan as it sank through the dust. Dust unto dust: Hadn't he said it in her dream? Hadn't he said it that night, in real life, her white-haired father?

They were in the small barn in back of the house. The lantern light showed harness, tools, old jars, spooled string, a scythe. There was a horse, hers, the mare Dandelion. The mare lay on its side in the straw. She held the beast's trembling head, patted its dappled nose, and rubbed the bristly fur between its eyes, which were half-shut and glazed with pain, while he knelt at the mare's other end.

She saw quite clearly his gray-white head and broad shoulders as grimly he worked, his lower lip caught between his teeth, eyes gazing into the distance as his hands moved inside the mare. No good, she heard him say. Been three, almost four hours, and an hour for a mare is like a day for a cow. Sweat stood on his forehead; he wiped it away with a sleeve. Frowning, he reached deeper, gave his shoulders a sudden twitch. The mare screamed.

He withdrew his hands, toweled them, and came around to

the front. Then he knelt, patted the mare, scratched behind the one white ear.

You have to decide, he said. He turned and looked at her suddenly, fiercely. It's no good, she can't handle it, it's too big for her. It will be a great big horse. But it has to die, or she does. Both of them can't live.

Why not?

Because it's too big. We have to take it, one way or the other.

Turning back to the mare, he laid his cheek against the long plane of the horse's head; his hand stroked the sweaty hair on the broad, rippling neck. She knew how that hand felt: a father's hand, and a blacksmith's hand, hard, implacable, he would dig out a splinter expertly and coldly, gripping the afflicted hand or foot and holding the limb vise-steady no matter how much the rest of her might twitch. He would. An untreated splinter could lead to infection, it was for her own good. And when something was for her own good, there was no swaying him.

You have to decide, he said again. The foal is worth more than the mare. Colt or filly, it's worth much more. He was a big stallion and a top horse.

She was mute. No way could she decide. She loved her friend Dandelion; she also loved the colt (she had decided it was a colt) growing inside of Dandelion. So she drew back in terror until she fetched up against a bale of hay. He looked at her for a long time. Then he rose and took up the sledge.

The sound was a rock falling from a great height onto sand. Dust unto dust. New life out of old, rising from a welter of blood. He had opened the mare quickly, dragged out the sack, slit it with his barlow, toweled the colt roughly with burlap until it drew breath. Holding it up with one hand, he had beckoned her with the other.

The memory left her. She stopped her aimless walking, closed a fist around a stem of sage, and pulled. Raising the handful of stripped leaves, she drank in the pungent, dizzying scent. Birds talked faintly; heat waves wagged the yellow hills.

How could he have done it? How could he have made up his mind? Was every single decision arrived at by reason, founded on logic, on some calculation of right versus wrong, dollars and cents? How could he have been anything but paralyzed, numb? An unfair question, she knew, but allowed herself to ask it anyway. She wouldn't answer it. Couldn't answer it.

Dust unto dust. He burned the afterbirth in a drum in the backyard. She remembered a long discussion about what should be done with Dandelion, there was talk of giving her to some needy family to butcher, but in the end they roped her and teamed her out of town, into the sage where the coyotes and foxes ate her, the mice whittled her bones. The colt was hers, but it had never seemed to waken to the world, it refused to nurse from the roan mare, and the next night it died.

She sat down cross-legged. The wind tugged at her hair, buffeted her back. It seemed to blow through her, eddying dust near her knees and feet. She leaned back into it, stretched out in the dust as if in a hot bath, luxuriated in it, heedless of the stones digging her shoulders, the sticks scratching her neck. The sky was wide and blue. Tips of sage wobbled at the edges of her vision. The wind sieved dust through the shimmering silvery leaves.

11

They parked the autos beneath thick-trunked cottonwoods in a fluttering, dappled shade. The Rio Grande flowed past, its surface breeze-hammered into countless dimples and dents. Vermilion flycatchers darted after insects, and a kingfisher's cry came rattling down the corridor between the trees.

Fry lagged behind. Though the others had shifted to shirtsleeves, he had doggedly kept to coat and vest. Out of the shade, the heat hit him so hard he almost stumbled. He stopped, blinking. Alleys fed off to either side behind low adobe dwellings with white beehive-shaped ovens in the yards. The houses' small windows were curtained. A brindled mongrel with coyote-pricked ears patrolled along the top of a waist-high wall.

He had resolved not to let the Apache incident daunt him. Indeed, what remained sharpest in his mind was not the terror he had felt, but the picture he might have captured. It would be an incredible shot—not that he could ever publish it, since McLaughlin, if he saw it, would surely recall.

The old woman sitting in the shade of a brush ramada appeared to be doing nothing. She glanced at him and looked away again, as if gray-suited men with flat-crowned Eastern hats came past her house daily. He thumbed the sweat from his eyelids. Steadied, pulled the string.

The Indians were waiting in front of an old adobe church with three bell towers. Slight, dark-skinned, fine-featured people, they were as physically unlike the ponderous, pale Osages of Oklahoma as Greeks were unlike Swedes. The Pueblo men wore ruffled and pleated white linen shirts, and dark broadcloth trousers with scarlet sashes. The women had on bright plaid shawls and doeskin leg wrappings that made their calves look immense.

The heat was quicklime sticking to his shoulders, his neck, the top of his head. His pen channeled the words onto the page. He saw it all as an Indian might, white men coming to the village in noisy machines, speaking fervently about a flag, an event half a continent away when a president cut into the earth at the spot where a monument would be raised to a dying race. As if some stranger laid hands on your shoulders and turned you around to face a hole with sharp-spaded edges, a mound of fresh earth, a marker bearing your name.

"I wish to say a word before we sign. I trust that the statue will be more of a memorial to Mr. Wanamaker than to the Indians."

Fry came quickly to the present. It was the interpreter, speaking on his own. The man's hair lay upon his breast in two hanks; he had an aquiline nose and one eye slightly lower than the other, a demonic cast.

"I feel that I cannot sign this declaration," the man said. "I feel that my people have not been treated right by the United States government's people. They have wronged us and tricked us, and now they want to tax us for lands that the Spaniards said were ours forever. Protect us as did the Spanish government, as did the Mexican government, and we will sign with all our hearts."

Dixon reached out and took the interpreter's hand. "My friend," he said, "the signing of the Declaration of Allegiance does not mean that you have been treated fairly. It means that you are going to do your part. If you do not sign, the government in Washington and Mr. Wanamaker will be offended, and they can do much to right any wrongs that may threaten the Pueblo people. You have hold of my hand; it is an honest hand, and it represents an honest heart, and whatever the other people have done in the past, this is no trick."

The Indian removed his hand from Dixon's. "We have been under the American flag for a long time, and have honored and respected it. We have been treated better than other Indians because we do not have lands that the white people covet. We own our few acres, we grow our crops, we honor the saints. But until our rights are protected, I don't think we should sign."

Dixon's neck was thick and red, and his eyes bulged like hens' eggs. "If you sign this Declaration of Allegiance, what is the government going to say? They are going to say, 'The Pueblos are loyal to the flag, and we are going to help them.' You be the first man to put your name down. This is not a trick." He opened a palm to McLaughlin. "Here is a man you can trust until the stars burn out."

"I do trust him," the Indian said.

"Then sign, and you will simply be putting your name in the records of this great memorial in New York."

"We cannot sign."

"We are here today to help you," Dixon said in an exasperated tone. "I want you honorable men of the Pueblos to be linked to a great monument that will chronicle the story of your noble race and Indian character years and years after you are all gone. Now if you will just put down your names, you leaders of the different pueblos. . . ."

"Why is it so important that we sign? This is just a piece of paper. When has a piece of paper ever meant anything to an American?"

"You speak with a straight tongue and a clear mind," Dixon said. "But this is not a treaty—it is a pledge. It is *your* pledge, and if anyone breaks it, it will be you yourselves, and not some white man."

The interpreter crossed his arms and shook his head. Dr.

Dixon expelled air through his nostrils, raised his hands and let them fall. The interpreter watched with amusement. Then he looked at the Pueblo superintendent, come down from Albuquerque with the expedition. "What do you advise, Mr. Lonergan?"

"Sign."

The interpreter turned to McLaughlin. "Inspector?"

McLaughlin looked bored with the situation. "I would be sorry to leave here without having the Pueblos sign, because it would leave a gap. Every other tribe so far has signed. There is no good reason for you not to sign. The stenographer has noted your comments, and the Commissioner will read them when we return to Washington. I advise you to go ahead and sign the paper."

The interpreter withdrew to confer with the governors of the pueblos. Fry scanned the Declaration of Allegiance, the thick white parchment with its message in elegant calligraphy that began (in somewhat mixed metaphor): "The Indian is fast losing his identity in the face of the great waves of Caucasian civilization that are extending to the four winds of the country. . . ."

The Indians bickered. Dixon brightened suddenly, nodded to himself, turned on his heel. He went among the Pueblo leaders. The bickering continued, but it was of a more expansive sort. Fry could not be sure, but thought he saw something shiny change hands. Immediately after, the Indians came forward. The interpreter stepped to the table where the Declaration of Allegiance lay and took up the pen.

12

In Gallup he visited the next shop on his list. Overnight his plates were developed and printed; the next morning he made his selection in a back alley. He found that he missed doing his own lab work, missed watching the image appear in the developer, watching it come up ghostly and then darken until it looked too dark, then into the water bath, and when the lights came back on, there it would be, a person caught dead to rights on the dripping sheet.

At the post office he checked under General Delivery for any mail in his name. There was none. He paused before pushing the envelope across the counter to the bored clerk, paused long enough that the man's eyes unglazed and looked inquiringly into his.

He was working in a vacuum. No word from Kravitz; all he knew was that the pictures had aroused the ire of the Commissioner of Indian Affairs—but the Commissioner was a naturally irascible man. So he wondered: Were people paying heed to his photographs? Did they simply page on past? Were they amused by the unwary subjects, or offended, or made edgy by the shadows captured by his lens, shadows in which might be glimpsed an unexpected shared humanness among races, among men? He relinquished the envelope, paid postage, walked out. Back at the train it was rush-rush-rush, Dixon instructing the porters, and instructing Giannetti, who would remain on Signet until the Grand Canyon station, last-minute provisioning, packing of bags, and meeting the automobiles, which came roaring down the street in a boil of dust.

The two cars, Reos, were modern-day ships of the desert. A greasy wooden box, which previously had held rifles, was bolted to each running board; one box contained cooking gear and provisions, the other had gasoline cans and water jugs. Three spare tires, a board wired to the back bumper for a table, a rack to hold the grips. The drivers were men in their middle twenties, upon whose heads sat lofty Stetsons encircled by snakeskin bands.

The road led past massive rocks like the bows of scuttled ships, past red hills barnacled with sage. Gallup had been coal yards, railroad shops, saloons, a wire-scarred sky, and when the town disappeared over the horizon, it was as if it had never existed.

The car jerked and clanked, and scalding air poured in under the tonneau. "Hot as hell with the blower on," the driver commented cheerily. He had given his name, Alfred. He wore, in addition to the heroic Stetson, a flannel shirt of a delicate rose color, stovepipe Levi's, and narrow pointed-toe boots of dyed escalloped leather. He peered at the road, or what there was of it, through green-tinted goggles. His gun belt, unbuckled, lay coiled in the center of the seat.

"Excuse me, Alfred," Fry said. "Why the six-shooter?"

The brow creased above the goggles. "Lowlife. Rattlesnakes, redskins, and such."

The weapon was a single-action Colt; Fry had seen enough of them in the movies to know. He touched the white-and-brown horn grip. "What kind of redskins?"

"Navahos. Utes."

"Did you ever use it?"

A broad grin. "Me and Davey, up in the first car, bet we sent a baker's dozen of greasers t' kingdom come."

"Greasers?"

"Mexicans," Booth said knowingly, leaning in from the back seat.

"I remember this one," Alfred said. "Little place called Rosita. They was havin' a dance. Men on one side of the hall, women on the other. We mixed right in and cut the girls away from the men. Ever' time the big bull fiddle give a whoop, why, we'd take another snort of mescal.

"I figgered it was my lucky night; I had got the little worm out of the bottle and had me two pretty senoritas, one on each arm. Then I seen this big greaser. Right away I smelled trouble." Alfred swerved the Reo to miss a large rock, then directed its nose back down the road. "Up he come, not a word. Smiled, and his hand kind of blurred, and when I seen the knife I jerked and shot. Fast. *Too* fast—took him just below the knee, which blowed his one leg out from under him.

"Spun clean around and took a swipe at me, down through my vest, which it was brand new, just bought at the J. C. Penney in Tucson, down through my shirt and undershirt." He shifted gears, the motor roaring, the car laboring up a rise. "Left a little pink scratch across my chest, like a woman will make with her fingernails when you take her on beyond. If you know what I mean." Alfred smiled, moistening his lips.

"When he come round again, I give him another ball. Down he went like an old ragbag, shit himself, and died."

Booth whistled softly. Fry thought, the Old West: ringing on and on, a struck bell.

After a while, Alfred's face blanched. He braked hard, kicked open the door, and fell out. Fry could hear him retching alongside the car. He hauled himself back in and wiped his mouth with a bandanna. "The heat," he said with embarrassment. "Sometimes it's too much for a body to bear."

The sage and mesquite went whirring past. By now they had entered Arizona and the Navaho Reservation, which covered the northeast corner of the state and spilled over into New Mexico and Utah—a vastness, said McLaughlin, greater than New Hampshire, Massachusetts, and Connecticut combined. Fry felt like belting out a song; it was grand to be crossing this wide-open place, free of the train's cramp, of combing soot from his hair and blowing it out of his nose and digging it out of his ears. He had grown oppressed by the clicking of the rails, by the car's constant erratic shuddering; even now, when he walked on level ground he felt as if his legs were being borne in one direction, his torso in another, his head in a third.

To the north, mountains lay like blue, rust-streaked cutouts. A vulture flailed up in front of the car's grille, seeming to expand as its wings cupped the wind. Two ravens sculled past, backs glinting, heavy beaks catching the sun.

They stopped for lunch, and Alfred heated tea water in a blackened billy over a greasewood fire. They ate hard-boiled eggs and meatloaf sandwiches. The sun lowered, and shadows began inching away from rocks. Clouds passed, expanses of land winking into shade, brightening again. Far away in sheltered depressions and copses of pine, Navaho hogans squatted: low mounds of earth and logs, with holes for doors. Miles lay between the rude dwellings.

They came upon a band of sheep milling beside the road. The sheep bleated at the lead car, then trotted off and halted to watch it pass. Alfred stopped. Fifty woolly white faces swiveled as one. A figure stood on a low rise, a Navaho woman, her arms crossed and her back to the road. Her skirt was turquoise, her shawl black, and a crimson scarf covered her head. No trace of her body was visible, not her hands, her face, not even her hair, only the vivid fabric of her garments against the sky.

"Hey, sister!" Alfred yelled.

The wind rippled her skirt.

"Got any turquoise to sell?"

She stood stiff-backed and unmoving.

"What are you, deaf?"

The wind rocked the car, making its springs creak. Alfred ran up the motor and retarded the spark, causing a backfire. The sheep bucked and scattered through the brush. The woman did not turn around. "Surly bitch," Alfred muttered, putting it in gear. "These Navahos want to attract tourists, they'd better start actin' a sight friendlier."

As the car passed, the woman turned slowly, presenting only her back.

The air grew cooler and the colors deepened. The clouds, many and fleecy earlier in the day, had given way to a few massive thunderheads from whose opalescent bellies lightning flashed; no thunder could be heard, for the clouds were too far away. They marched across the land trailing veils of rain.

Booth's elbows and head appeared between Fry and Alfred. He had discovered in the back a gun case containing a .22 rifle. He was holding the gun muzzle up. "I want to shoot a coyote," he announced.

"Coyotes are mighty scarce," Alfred said. He laid his Stetson on the seat, peeled off his goggles. "We'll get you a crack at something, though."

A roadrunner raced across the road, a limp snake in its beak; doves whistled over, toward hidden water. Fry spied a jackrabbit crouching, button eye blinking, mulish ears fingering the air; he said nothing, and Alfred, not noticing, drove past. Booth shifted restlessly in the backseat, checking out one side of the car, then the other. The road skirted a shallow canyon and curved across a flat. Alfred glided the car to a stop and darted a finger past Fry's nose. "Badger! Shoot quick!"

Booth thrust the muzzle out. Fry glimpsed a grizzled back, black paws, a striped face. The gun cracked. The badger whirled, kicking sand. Booth leaped from the car, tromboning the rifle's action.

"Careful," Alfred said, "or he'll cut you deep, long, wide, and consecutive—"

Booth shot again, and again. He advanced, gun ready, and touched the muzzle to the badger's eye. It didn't move. Blood seeped into the sand. Dirt clung to the badger's muzzle and its long tapering claws.

"What're you going to do with it *now*?" Fry said.

Booth shrugged. "Maybe cook it up for your supper."

"Too tough," Alfred said.

"Take it along and give it to the Indians?" Booth suggested.

Alfred shook his head. "Get the car dirty."

Booth nudged the badger with his boot, slumping it into its den.

They drove on in silence. The other car was far ahead, riding under its plume of dust. The desert seemed quieter, pulled in on itself. Fry looked at blood-colored mesas and tawny haystack hills. Distant colors seemed to bloom and fade. He felt alone, a stranger, marooned on the land. "Alfred," he said. "Your name. You never said—is it your last name or your first?"

The road dipped, the car scraping bottom.

"Fellow oughtn't to ask such a question."

Fry's eyes widened. The Code of the West. He stared. Alfred's face was white where the goggles had been, gray with dust everywhere else.

"Oh, for Pete's sake, stop looking at me like that." He yanked the wheel to avoid a pothole. "Alfred Tennyson Smith. If you *must* know. My mother's idea, she's the literary one in the family." He downshifted as the tires slipped in loose sand. "I have a brother," he sighed, "Samuel Coleridge Smith. A sister, Charlotte Brontë. My father's just plain Jack. He's in sales. Champion Brand Mortuary Fluids."

"Where are you from?"

"Ithaca. Came out here five years ago. I had the con, now it's almost gone. The air's done wonders for my lungs. My weight's back up, and I hardly cough at all." He gripped the steering wheel at the top; knobs of bone paled the skin on the outsides of his wrists. "I took this job a year ago. Now my life is a different thing." He looked at Fry. His eyes were hard. "I really have killed a man."

He laid on the gas. Soon they caught up with the first car and drove along behind it in the fading light. A wash came into view, a curving channel of sand with a vein of water that mirrored the sky. A herd of horses grazed. In a field, corn stood in green clumps. Low sandstone buildings, fences, a conical hill. Ganado, Arizona: Hubbell's Trading Post, where they would spend the night.

"Never point at a rainbow." The trader, Lorenzo Hubbell, was a small man with oval bifocals, a soft white beard, and white hair that rested on the back of his neck. "Do not whistle in the dark," he raised a cautioning finger, "or you may summon a ghost."

They sat in the great hall—Dixon, Booth, McLaughlin, Fry. A fire danced above the hearth. The walls were hung with woven baskets, the mounted head of an elk, oil paintings of Indians, pueblos, and glowing desert rock.

Hubbell sat in a rocking chair. "Never watch snakes mate," he said. "It will cause hip problems." He laughed lightly. "I have seen snakes mating on several occasions, and my hips remain as supple as those of a twenty-year-old. Well, almost."

"The Navahos have more superstitions than dogs have fleas," McLaughlin said. "They'll have to get rid of them before they can come properly into the twentieth century."

Hubbell smiled. "Tell me, Major. Do you avoid walking under ladders? Have you ever"—he tapped his knuckles on the arm of his chair—"knocked on wood?"

McLaughlin grunted. He looked into the fire, where the flames were dying down, the logs collapsing into ash.

"Don't burn insects or snakes," Hubbell continued, "as it will cause sickness and sores. And never call yourself by your own name, or your ears will dry up."

"I find the myths and customs of the Indians quite beautiful," Dixon said. "Very naive, very natural. Charming, really."

"The son-in-law," Hubbell said, "and the mother-in-law must never come face to face, else they will go blind."

"Practical too," McLaughlin said.

Hubbell chuckled. "Superstition almost cost me my business many years ago. I was tending store when an old man came in. He bought a can of pears—bilasáanaa bitsee-i hólónígí yadiizín biigi, the Navahos call them, 'apples with tails on them in a can.' The old man paid for his pears, sat down on a bench, and slumped against the wall. One look and I knew he was dead. Let me tell you, I was in a pickle! If the people learned that a man had died in my store, they would never have set foot in it again.

"I got my clerk, and together we sat on the bench, one on each side of the old man. 'Grandfather,' I said in Navaho, 'you look tired.' 'I understand,' I said, although he had not replied. Several customers were watching. 'As you wish,' I said, 'we'll take you outside.' The clerk draped one arm over his shoulder, and I took the other arm, and together we helped the old man out. We took along his pears and left him in the shade of a tree, where, I'm sad to say, he was later found to have died."

Hubbell leaned forward and prodded the fire with a poker. "Do you know, Major, the ethnologists say that my Navahos are johnny-come-latelies. Also your Sioux. The Navahos are of Athapascan stock, same as the Eskimos, and they arrived from the far north as recently as five centuries ago—just as the Sioux, from the east, came late onto the plains. Neither tribe had a strong culture, and both borrowed heavily from the local inhabitants. Both were adaptable, aggressive, warlike. Or, as one learned man put it to me, 'culturally insecure.' Of course, if you ask a Navaho, he says, 'We were always here.'"

"The Sioux say the same," McLaughlin said.

Hubbell turned in his chair. "You knew Sitting Bull better than any other white man. Tell me, were his powers real?"

McLaughlin shook his head. "He—and every other medicine man I've ever met—was a charlatan. Which fact, unfortunately, did not prevent people from believing in him."

"You mean he couldn't turn himself into a fireball and go whizzing about the reservation at night," said Hubbell. "But could he prophesy? Could he heal?"

"I never knew him to heal," McLaughlin said. "He was no prophet, either, just a cunning man who craved attention and fame."

Hubbell placed another log on the fire; it smoked for a time before bursting into flames. "Tell us a story about Sitting Bull. After all, he's the most famous Indian that ever lived."

From outside came faint sounds of laughter, then singing— a low tune that gathered, rose, crested, and fell: Navahos grouped around a fire of their own.

"One day in the spring," McLaughlin said, "I drove out to his camp. He had a couple of cabins along the Grand River, near where he was born. A good site, deep soil and lush grass; I should say some of the best land on the reservation." The Major rocked forward and held his palms to the fire; the glow lit his face. "It was eighty-eight, one of the dry years. The crops needed rain, and we had prayed for it often.

"I met with Sitting Bull to hear his grievances—he never lacked for them—and to discuss what supplies he might need. A crowd of Indians gathered, and I remarked that if the drought held on much longer, the crops would amount to nothing. Sitting Bull replied, 'Yes, the crops need rain, and my people have been importuning me to make it rain. I can make it rain any time I wish, but I fear hail. I cannot control hail, and should I make it rain, heavy hail might follow, which would ruin the grass as well as the crops, and then our horses and cattle would starve.'

"He said this in all apparent candor, and there wasn't an

Indian there, including several Christians, who didn't seem to believe him."

Hubbell nodded. "And did it rain?"

"No. A couple of times, maybe. The crops withered, anyway." McLaughlin rocked for a moment, as if to continue the story, then abruptly he rose. "I'll turn in now. Tomorrow's a full day."

"Yes," Hubbell said. "The glorious Fourth, the Expedition of Citizenship, and I'm sponsoring horse races and a chicken pull. You'll have a good gathering."

"And you shall have our sincerest thanks, Don Lorenzo," Dixon said, "both for your preparations and for your fine hospitality."

"Gentlemen." Hubbell rose, and bowed slightly. "I will ask Hostiin Chee to wake you in the morning."

A coal-oil lamp lit the room, its yellow light reaching out to twin brass beds, plum-colored walls, ceiling beams of peeled piñon logs. The floor was covered with Navaho rugs, against whose gray backgrounds chevrons, stripes, and stepped-edge diamonds stood out in red, black, and white; the dazzling angular patterns made the floor shimmer before McLaughlin's eyes.

Sitting on the bed, he unlaced his shoes. This was not his first visit to Hubbell's. The last time had been—when?—the Moenkopi squabble. It was winter, and before dawn the servant would creep into the room, build a fire, put a pan on the stove. How fine it had been to worm back under the covers, listening to the clumps and clicks of the wakening household; from outside, the stamping and nickering of horses, the chink of harness chains, the rasp of tarpaulins spread across loads, and when he got up, the room was warm and washwater steamed in the pan.

Anyone and everyone found a welcome at Hubbell's.

Teachers headed for lonely day schools, archaeologists, miners prospecting for copper and chalcedony, missionaries searching for souls. Roosevelt had slept here on one of his hunting trips. Artists would stay for weeks, painting in the clear desert light, and when they went away they would leave behind one of their works, although this was not necessary, and Don Lorenzo was offended if ever a guest offered to pay.

He set his collar on the nightstand and took off his shirt and trousers. He stood, stripped down to his wool union suit.

Around the room, at eye level, hung a row of small portraits, heads of Indians sketched in rust-colored chalk. One caught his eye.

The artist had worked from a photograph. This he knew because he had been present when the picture was made. The set of Sitting Bull's face, caught by the lens, had not survived this second translation: The man who stared from the wall was a softer being, one whose eyes did not meet the viewer's and knife their way to the back of his skull.

"I see the dog has a new master."

The soft roll of Lakota syllables had stopped Shell King in his tracks. McLaughlin, at his desk in the agency office, had gone to the door and looked out. He had just met with Shell King, who had agreed with but little urging to send his son to Hampton, to school. The boy was tall for his age, clean-featured, friendly; years earlier McLaughlin had helped him choose a name, Henry, and entered it on the tribal roll.

On the porch, Sitting Bull blocked Shell King's path: Sitting Bull in braids, blanket, moccasins florid with beads; Shell King in clipped hair, dungarees, denim jacket, new boots. The men stared. Neither gave ground. Henry Shellking, who reached nearly to his father's shoulder, did not shrink from the medicine man, either.

"So, Pompeska yatapi, how does it feel to be a white man?"

Shell King made a fist and exploded the fingers outward, toward Sitting Bull's face.

It was an insult of grave proportion. Sitting Bull, however, only flexed his mouth in a smile. "You've switched sides as easily as a woman."

Again the contemptuous backhand finger-flick.

On the sidewalk and in the street, people stopped and began edging in.

"Tell me, Heton cikala." Sitting Bull, shifting his gaze to the son, used the boy's Lakota name: Antelope. "Tell me. Are you proud of your warrior father?"

"Keep him out of it."

"Hen-ree," Sitting Bull sneered. He turned to Shell King. "You've thrown him away. At a time when the tribe needs its young men."

"The tribe will live through young men who know enough not to follow fools like you."

"Hold your tongue."

"You are a fool. You ruined us."

"I did what a chief must do. I fought the invaders."

"You dragged us down."

Sitting Bull raised his voice. "See what Shell King has done. He has given his son to White Hair. Next he will give away all your land and all your children to the whites."

"I say keep the land," Shell King said hotly. "And if we hadn't gone to war on the advice of ones like you, we'd have a lot more of it left today."

Nods and grunts, *hau*, from bystanders.

"If we hadn't followed you we'd still have many guns and horses. We wouldn't be forced to eat the white man's food, which he gives to us like dogs, and terrible it is." Shell King tore off his hat, slapped his thigh with it, and leveled it at Sitting Bull. "You knew we couldn't win. But you kept holding out because you knew that once it was over, your strength with the people would dry up and blow away."

"I still lead."

"Your day is done. We do as we wish, we don't ask you any longer."

Sitting Bull raised his chin. "Wakan Tanka forbids you to insult me this way."

"Wakan Tanka turns a deaf ear to Sitting Bull."

"He hears! Listen, Hunkpapas! Shell King insults you and your god!"

Shell King jammed his hat on his head. He elbowed past Sitting Bull, his son following.

"He hears!" Sitting Bull had spun, and shouted at Shell King's back. "He judges! And he will punish you!"

McLaughlin shivered; the rust red face floated against the wall. He remembered another day, weeks later; he had been helping the issue clerk grease a wagon. The afternoon was close and hot. Swallows dipped in and out of the warehouse, scolding. He had skinned his knuckle on the hub, and sweat stung in the cut. Thunder: far away, then nearer, like something shifting and breaking of its own great weight, a hissing and ticking and a sudden violent *craack,* the deep sound slatting off across the river. He muttered the prayer, almost a reflex now, *Father, let it rain.*

Footsteps slapped across the yard. Jim Shaw dashed in, eyes shining and black. "*U wo!*"

They dropped the tools and ran. Hands greasy, beards dripping sweat, they sprinted up the river road, raindrops glittering in the air. The smell of ozone came up rotten-strong. The clerk, tall and stout, dropped back; McLaughlin ran at the heels of fleet Jim Shaw, not knowing where they were going or why. Fat drops raised puffs of dust. The sky was slate, the broad river leaden, lightning slashed and thunder rumbled. Once, once he had run like this, to catch, to catch a boy for school, Catch him, the father said, and he is yours, and he ran the boy down, three miles till they fell, his arms around the lad, breathless, the smell of crushed sage in the air.

Two horses lay on their sides in the road. Drops pelted furiously, then stopped. He slowed, lungs wracked with pain; heard a woman wailing, gasped at the charred-flesh stench.

Henry Shellking lay with one leg pinned beneath his horse. The beast's shoulder twitched and was still. Henry's hat still sat on his head, and his hands clutched the reins. Great burnt patches covered his neck, side, and leg, and his mouth, gaping, drooled in the dust. People hovered round crying and wailing, so like Indians, he thought, carrying on when something must be done. But nothing could be done.

He pressed his fingers against the boy's neck. No pulse. He closed his eyes and concentrated with all his might: nothing. He quick-crawled to the father. The bolt had blown Shell King from his horse, and he lay on his back, his eyes closed. Smoke rose in wisps from his hair, and a fist slowly unclenched, fingers blooming like petals. A woman shrieked, "He lives, he lives!" and McLaughlin laid his ear on Shell King's chest and heard only a great stillness, like an icebound river. Sunlight fizzled and Merrill asked, "Should I go get the doc?" and McLaughlin said not to bother. His eyes fixed on one of Shell King's boots. It sat there upright, laces dangling, as if taken off before bed. He had lifted his eyes, his throat constricting, and slammed his hands in the dust.

"Major?"

The rust red Sitting Bull stared.

"Major McLaughlin?"

He felt a touch at his elbow and looked into Fry's face. The stenographer stood there in pajamas. The blankets on both beds had been turned down.

"Yes," McLaughlin said. His own voice sounded distant, jarring. He stepped woodenly to the nightstand. He turned the tongue of wick down into the lamp's brass housing, cupped his hand behind the chimney, and blew out the flame.

13

The crowd ringed the trading-post yard, and small boys perched in fruit trees and on the roofs of sheds. Fry sat balanced on a fence rail, Navahos on either side, black hats shading their faces, hair bunched behind their heads in hourglass bobs. Another Navaho squatted in front of the fence, smoothing the sand around a rooster he had just finished burying to its neck. The rooster's white head bobbed and its red comb jiggled; it clacked its beak and blinked an amber eye.

Horses milled at the sun-swimming end of the yard. The riders were bareback, wearing pale loose tunics to midthigh. One of them, a lithe, wiry man sitting a tall black, Fry recognized: Billy Trimble, one of Hubbell's clerks.

At a shout, the horses broke and ran. They pounded across the yard, hoofbeats reaching up through the fence. A rider closed in on the rooster, caught one hand full of mane, leaned down, stretched out and grabbed—missed the target and swept on past. Another bent among the jostling horses, overreached himself, fell. The crowd whooped as he scrambled away from the hooves.

Through the melee, Trimble maneuvered the black horse toward the rooster. He dipped and caught it, the white bird thrashing sand from its wings as it came up. He wheeled for the finish line but the others were on him in an instant, shoving and grabbing. The rooster changed hands again and again. One man beat another with it, to the crowd's great delight; when the beaten man gave ground, the first rider charged the gap. Before he could reach the line, the black swooped in and Trimble snatched the bird. Flattened on his mount, beating its flank with the rooster, he plunged toward the line and crossed it at a gallop. Rising to a crouch on the black's humping back, he raised the broken bird. Its blood shone in the harsh light.

The only light shafted in through a small barred window. Fry sat on a stack of blankets, the plaster cool against his back. Scents of wool and hemp, coffee and leather. At the counter, Trimble waited on a wizened Navaho. The old man dipped tobacco from a tin cup nailed to the counter and rolled a cigarette; Trimble pushed across a box of matches.

Before coming in, Fry had preset the shutter to "bulb." When the old man struck a match and raised it—the flame lighting his wrinkled forehead, throwing his sunken cheeks into deeper relief—he opened the shutter, *thousand one, thousand two, thousand three,* and eased it shut.

The old man opened a gunnysack and took out a silver necklace hung with beads and a half-moon pendant clasping a blue stone. The silver came from melted Mexican pesos and hammered U.S. dimes; the turquoise the old man had found in the desert—*Hola!* There it was, smiling up in beauty from the ground.

At breakfast Hubbell had warned that many Navahos, especially the old ones, would not let themselves be photographed. "If they did, and something happened to the picture, they believe they would die." The trader tugged on a string dangling from a beam above the table, and in the kitchen a bell tinkled, bringing forth a servant with an ornate silver tea service. "I'm not saying they would shoot you," Hubbell said, "but they might break your camera, also your arm." Peering through the lower halves of his eyeglasses, he spooned sugar into his cup. "Once a pelicano came to Ganado with a magic black box. This wizard could put a person's shadow on a piece of pottery that you could see through. He made a portrait of my wife, the one on the mantel there, and he wanted to photograph the Navahos. All refused, except Billy Trimble. Billy was just a boy, but he went out in the yard and faced the camera bravely. The pelicano ducked his head under the cloth, fussed around in there, and made a picture. After developing the plate, he showed it around.

"Next day the ground was black with people. They all wanted to see the piece of pottery with Billy's spirit on it, but none wished to pose. I asked Billy to stand before the camera again. 'Let the others take a look.' A young man was persuaded to place his head under the cloth—he yelped and popped back out. 'Why does Billy stand on his head?'

"He was seeing him in the ground glass, which, of course, inverts the image." Hubbell sipped his tea with a soft slurping sound. "Soon a young woman came by. The men urged her to stand in front of the box, and when I explained that it wouldn't harm her, she took Billy's place. Immediately a long line formed. After each man had his look, he emerged from beneath the cloth with a long face. You see, they expected that when the camera turned the woman upside down, her skirt would fall down over her head."

Sitting in the trading post, remembering the story, Fry grinned. He would have to keep a close watch on this plate, lest an old grandfather in a lonely hogan, surrounded by brittlebrush and coyotes, should sicken and die.

Trimble took the necklace and piled silver dollars in its place. The old man spoke. Trimble produced a sack of flour, took back a dollar, laid down change. The old man spoke again. Cans of condensed milk. Trimble slid the coins into his palm and replaced them in the register. Sacks of Bull Durham and coffee, bright bolts of cotton and velveteen, a dozen sticks of barber pole candy, a harness, a lariat, an awl. Presently the old man pocketed his remaining money, placed his goods in the gunnysack, and hobbled out.

A family came in, hulking father, big-boned mother, children like sprites. Fry tried another shot. The man and woman will turn out, he thought, but the children will be blurs. After the family left, he went to the counter himself. He asked to see a Navaho water bottle, a trim wicker vessel sealed with pine gum and capped with a cork. "How much?"

"Three bucks."

He laid the money down.

"This country makes a man thirsty," he said.

"You have an Eastern throat."

Fry nodded and was pleased to employ a Westernism, one he'd heard McLaughlin use: "So dry out here you have to prime yourself to spit."

Trimble grinned, touched the tobacco tin. When Fry shook his head, Trimble got out a book of papers and rolled one for himself.

"I hear you went to school back east," Fry said.

"Carlisle."

"I grew up just down the road. Harrisburg."

"No kidding?" Trimble waved the match out, eddying the smoke. "They used to take us there. Sundays, we'd sing in a big stone church. At Christmastime we'd shop for presents. The Capitol had a big dome on it, like a thirty-thirty slug. What I remember best was the river."

"The Susquehanna."

"Never seen that much water before or since. With green islands in it, ducks and geese, seagulls even. We walked across it on a bridge, and I looked down and there in the water was fish, big fish, all green and gold, a whole flock of 'em grazin' on the bottom."

"When were you there?"

"Graduated three years ago." He added proudly, "I ran track with Jim Thorpe."

"We used to watch him play football." Fry's grandfather would come in the phaeton and they would drive down the pike to the Indian school, the close-trimmed gridiron set among autumn-gold trees. He remembered Thorpe as tall and barrel-chested, rough-featured and older-looking than the collegians from State, Princeton, William and Mary, Yale. William and Mary: He wondered idly if he'd seen Booth play.

The back of the store gave onto Hubbell's house, and Don Lorenzo came from there now, in a white shirt with sleeve garters. He greeted Fry and told Trimble he would take over at the counter.

Trimble hung his apron on a peg. "Why don't you come to my house?" he said to Fry.

They walked down the road, the lowering sun beating on their backs, past a sign, paint peeling, black letters, TRADITION IS THE ENEMY OF PROGRESS. The last word had been cramped to fit the space. "Who put it up?" Fry asked.

"The Methodists. They got a church in Ganado."

"Do you go there?"

"Congregationalist. Also I go to the sings." He grinned. "I like to cover all the bases."

His small house was painted sky blue, its corners resting on concrete blocks. Rose and yucca grew in the yard, and the black horse grazed out back. Trimble's wife was a tiny, exquisite woman with an almond-eyed, near-Oriental face. "She don't speak English," Trimble said. "This one, though," he grabbed the hands of a small boy, swung him so his shoes grazed the ground, "this one I'm teachin' English to." He hauled the boy up; the child clamped his legs around Trimble's waist and smiled at Fry impishly. "Say hello to the man, Calvin." He whispered in the boy's ear. "Hi Bud," the boy said. "Hi Bud, hi Bud."

"Hi." Fry shook the small hand.

They took chairs outside, tilted them against the wall, and watched the sun going down, a dazzling disk that danced sometimes gold, sometimes blue. Clouds lay along the horizon, purple and thin.

"This country," Fry said. "It's all so new and strange. I've never been west of Pittsburgh before."

Trimble tossed his head away from the sun. "It don't seem likely that all of that is back there. When I went to school it was like I went down, way down, through a crack in the world, and there at the bottom was this green land.

"It was like being in a foreign country. Nice, though. Plenty of girls from lots of tribes, and we did our best to knock every one of 'em up." He grinned, showing small even teeth. "There was some other Navahos but we couldn't talk together, they caught us talkin' Indian they'd wash our mouths out with soap.

"We learned to talk English, read and write and figure out sums, how to fix things made out of tin, except nobody makes things out of tin anymore. They were very big on tin. The old man started the school, Captain Pratt, he was a tinsmith before he went in the army.

"When I finished up, I came back out here and old Double Glasses gave me a job." He rolled another cigarette, dexterously and swiftly with one hand. "The people did a Night Way. That's a ceremony, what we call a sing, it gets you in the tribe. Been gone so long I was the oldest boy there."

"They never washed our mouths out at school," Fry said. "It was always the paddle. Only I was so quiet I never got noticed, let alone paddled."

"If you were that good, bet you never got a girl in trouble."

"God, no." He smiled at his shoes. "I never even, you know, did it."

Trimble shook his head. "Don't let it go too long, you'll get all gummed up inside." He lit his cigarette. "Where do you go from here?"

"California, the coast. East through Idaho, Montana, the Dakotas."

"You stop in Idaho?"

"At Fort Lapwai. The Nez Perce."

"Lapwai. Sounds about right. When you're there, look up a friend of mine. She teaches school in the TB sanitarium. Annie Owns the Fire."

"The name sounds familiar," Fry said.

"She went to Carlisle. Maybe you knew her from there?"

Fry shook his head. "A Nez Perce?"

"Nope. One of McLaughlin's Sioux." Trimble winked. "Tough woman. Watch your step."

"Why, did you get her in trouble?"

"Her? Tight as a bull's ass in fly time."

Fry snickered embarrassedly. "Any message?"

"Just tell her Billy says hi."

"Sure."

Trimble said, "Hey, I meant to ask. D'you like being a stenographer?"

Fry realized he no longer considered himself a stenographer: He was a photog who sometimes did shorthand. But he wouldn't let anything slip; he wouldn't take a chance. "It's okay. I won't be a stenographer forever. I have some plans."

When nothing was forthcoming, Trimble said, "I got plans too. Gonna buy a big flock of sheep. You know I won fifty dollars in that chicken pull? I win money with that black horse all the time.

"Get some land up near Chinle, gonna quit my job and move up there, build a hogan with a dirt floor and the door facing sunrise, and we'll live there, Calvin and Desbah and me. We'll look at the stars at night, smell the rain and the wind." He finished his smoke, snubbed it. "That's what I want. It's not what they taught me to want, but that's how it's gonna be."

Fry looked at the flattening, melting sun, about to kiss the horizon. Maybe Trimble had it right: your own life, to live as you please. Stenographer—photographer. Which was he?

• • •

Trimble led them into the Canyon de Chelly. He was a smooth rider, and Fry enjoyed watching him; now and then he would sweep low to pluck a blade of grass, or heel the black horse and suddenly spurt ahead. With the cook and the wrangler he spoke Navaho, which seemed to Fry a dissonant tongue at once bitten-off and slurred, and sprinkled incongruously with English: "Farmington," "Post Toasties," "Ty Cobb."

If Trimble looked born to the saddle, McLaughlin seemed reared to it; the Major rode legs easy and arms loose, his thickset body passing off the shocks. Dixon and Booth jolted along like feed sacks; Fry had been given a homely nag, an old plodder that provided a stable platform from which to observe.

At first the canyon was little more than a crease in the ground, then cliffs rose on either hand, smooth and rust colored, fencing out the desert. The creek glided past. On its scalloped banks lay sun-bleached branches, toothed leaves, a dragonfly husk, a raven feather. He remembered Trimble's East: a crack in the world, and down in it this green land. In the canyon it was truly that way, the earth verdant between the rock walls, with grass and cottonwoods, plots of corn and melons. Huts of wattled willow—the Navahos' summer homes—were airier and more graceful than the crouching winter hogans.

Rounding a bend, they came upon a camp. Horses and sheep grazed, and a fire whispered. In the shade a woman sat before a frame on which a half-finished rug was stretched. Dixon held up his hand. "Exactly what we want." He and Booth dismounted and began unstrapping their equipment. When Dixon spread the legs of a tripod, the woman got up and hurried away. Dixon, paying no attention, mounted his camera on the tripod's head.

Trimble spoke with a short, dark man whose hair was tied up in a red cloth.

"He don't want you to make a picture," Trimble said.

"Five dollars." Dixon kept working, turning a cogwheel to raise the camera.

Trimble turned back, spoke for a while, laughed. "Ten. And he wants the money first."

The man in the red headband had to speak sharply before the woman would return to her loom. She lowered herself to the ground and folded her legs back along one side, facing the sun-lit vertical strands. Dixon turned a second cogwheel to extend the bellows. He pushed a plate holder into the camera's back. He disappeared beneath the black cloth, fine-tuned the focus, emerged, and set the aperture. The woman sat still as a doe in the brush. Dixon pulled the slide out of the plate holder and grasped the India rubber bulb at the end of the cable.

Fry stood where his own lens would catch both subject and photographer.

A photograph of a photograph: an image stolen of an image bribed: an instant frozen from separate points of view.

At a ruined pueblo called the White House, Trimble, the wrangler, and the cook—in headbands and pale blouselike tunics—were instructed to ride back and forth in front of the ruin, a series of apartment-like rooms stacked up in two stories, while Booth made pictures. McLaughlin explained to Fry that the White House was an Anasazi dwelling; the Anasazi were thought to be the ancestors of the Pueblo and Hopi peoples, who now lived elsewhere, in towns on high forted rocks. The Anasazi themselves had vanished, leaving ruins all across the Southwest. No one knew why they had disappeared—perhaps disease or drought.

The White House was fifty feet up, tucked in under a soaring cliff pocked with half-moon scars like the imprints of giant hammers. Looking up, Fry cringed: In the fast flow of clouds, the rock wall seemed to tumble.

He went in the opposite direction, wading the creek, hiking through thinning brush. On a low cliff, drawings were pecked into the rock: a deer rearing with a spear in its flank, a line of ducks, a squiggly snake, a tall trapezoidal man with a huge erect penis, a dozen handprints—small, almost childlike—made with ocher paint, in which could be seen whorls and creases of fingers and palms. Turning away, he did a double take. Another man-figure, smaller, stood off to one side as if watching, a small circle in the center of his chest.

"Thou shalt study the Book of Nature, God's great open book."

Dixon was holding forth at the camp fire, reciting something he called "The Ten Commandments from the Indian to the White Man."

"Thou shalt breathe through thy nose and not through thy mouth, for the wavy air passages of thy nose and the gluey mucus therein hold, then emit, the disease germs floating in the air."

McLaughlin's mouth twisted. Fat lot of good it would've done the Sioux in the winter of eighty-nine, when influenza, and then the whooping cough, mowed them down without cease.

"Thou shalt not repine nor become demoralized because of self-pity; the echo of 'better days' shall not enter thy lodge door."

Where does he get this tripe? Must make it up. McLaughlin glanced around. Booth sat dozing, Fry listened intently, the Navahos looked amused.

"Thou shalt believe in the dignity of labor; gladly, cheerfully, openly shalt thou put thy hand to any common task."

Try handing a hoe to a Sioux warrior. *Woman's work.* How they had sneered at him, White Hair, who counseled the drudgery of farming, who could be seen sweating in the agency garden, scattering manure, scratching with a hoe.

"Pomp and ostentation shalt thou in all ways eschew. . . ."

Hell, Indians *breathe* pomp and ostentation. And what is this expedition, if not pompous, ostentatious?

"Lastly, thou shalt love and reverence and obey the powers above. Every energy of thy life shall in earnestness and self-extinction be devoted to the Great Spirit. Then all of life shall be a sacrament, and death a glad translation."

Dixon looked up. "My name is Dixon—a very old name of British heritage. I am proud of my name, yet somehow it pales before the sublime expressiveness of Indian names."

Trimble nodded. "Like my aunt, Mary Whiskers."

The cook had a husky voice. "Archie Manygoats."

"And Sam Hides the Sausage," the wrangler said. "Don't forget old Sam. Hopi. Tell me this, how come the Hopis have all the fun?"

The foolery, McLaughlin noticed, seemed lost on Dixon.

"Most intriguing of all are the naming practices of the Plains tribes," Dixon went on. "A man may have a dozen names, or no name at all. If he performs a valiant act and wishes to commemorate it, he gives himself a new name."

That had all died out years in the past. Now Red Bird's daughter becomes Amelia Redbird. Leon Striped Elk, Ralph Drops-at-a-Distance, Gertrude Looking Eagle, Annie Owns the Fire. Although Dixon did have the particulars about right. Sitting Bull, before he became that, was Slow and Jumping Badger and Sacred Standshot.

"Suppose a warrior makes a dash on a camp and carries off a woman. He then calls himself 'Eagle' or 'Hawk.'"

Nope, gets clapped in the penitentiary for kidnapping, unless the woman is white, in which case the posse brings a rope. McLaughlin was reminded of his own names. White Hair, The Iron Worker, and, nice touch of irony, Man-Who-Bothers-His-Friends-for-More-Land.

"Rain-in-the-Face, the great Sioux warrior, was so named because he persisted in leading an attack in the teeth of a raging storm."

That was perhaps the least inventive way Rain-in-the-Face explained his name. Rain was a braggart and a malcontent who went around telling all who would listen how he had cut the heart out of Captain Tom Custer, the general's brother, on the Little Bighorn.

"The noble names: Bear Claw and Red Cloud and Crazy Horse, Plenty Coups, Runs the Enemy, Sitting Bull."

Sitting Bull. How many times must I hear that damnable name? "Seeda Boo" was how the old reprobate said it in English. In Lakota, Tatanka Iyotanka. The buffalo bull, *Tatanka,* was wise, powerful, life-giving. *Iyotanka* was hard to translate—not quite "sitting," more like "situated," "located," or "in residence." The wise and powerful one who has taken up residence among us.

Dixon chuckled. "Young-Man-Afraid-of-His-Horses. Poor chap was branded with this name when he tried to save his horses during an attack, abandoning his family to the enemy."

"Hogwash." Heads swiveled toward McLaughlin, who immediately wished he hadn't spoken. He said, less cuttingly, "Tasunka Kokipapi. The correct translation is Young-Man-*They*-Are-Afraid-of-His-Horses. He was such a fierce fighter that the mere sight of his horses would make his enemies quail."

Dixon's face was stiff. "I bow to your greater knowledge of the Sioux tongue."

A silence descended, which McLaughlin filled with a story from the time before the buffalo had vanished, before Sitting Bull arrived at Standing Rock, and the Ghost Dance smothered the reservation with turmoil and grief.

"In eighty-two," he began, "the buffalo were thick on Hidden Wood Creek. Running Antelope came seeking permission to take the people on a hunt. 'As soon as the crops are planted,' I said, 'you may go. . . .'"

•   •   •

A country of grass, broken by draws and hillocks and occasional outcroppings of stone, it rolled westward to the horizon, which ever receded in sameness as they rode. The people had gone on ahead; it was easy to follow the horse dung and travois ruts, the paper and cans.

The sky was clear and the sun shone brightly. The spring rains had been munificent and flowers garlanded the plain: purple coneflowers, red clover, tomato-colored mallow, purple-and-yellow mariposa lilies. Horned larks flew high in the air trailing song. He rode the fine gray gelding that Crow King had given him. Crow King had handed him the hackamore with his eldest daughter astride the horse. "Take her for the school, Father," he had said.

They crossed Cedar Creek. On flat stretches the prairie dogs stood on their doorsteps and whistled shrilly, the piercing cries spreading through the colony from mound to mound. They rode past muddy wallows strewn with matted black fur; here and there the remains of a buffalo, leathery hide and gnawed bones, staring skull heavy with horn. At each of these winter kills the policeman, John Eagle Man, would dismount and, with a certain degree of embarrassment in the agent's presence, turn the rotting face east, toward the rising sun.

The camp lay near the Black Hills–Bismarck Trail. The lodges were empty save for a few old women. Beyond, the people had gathered, two thousand of them seated in a large crescent whose horns opened to the west. Around the inside of the crescent sat the prominent men in all their savage finery: Running Antelope, Long Soldier, Red Horse, Gall. The last time he had seen Gall, the massive warrior had been wearing a nail apron and wielding a hammer, shingling the physician's roof.

Behind Running Antelope a fire smoldered, and in front of him, around a painted stone perhaps a foot in height, sat eight young men, the scouts, all good hunters and youths of high standing in the tribe. With a charred wooden spoon Running Antelope dug a coal from the fire and placed it on the tobacco. He touched the pipe to the earth, raised it to the sky, placed it between his lips, and drew in smoke with a stuttering hiss. The pipe was passed to the first scout, who placed his hand, holding the bowl, on the painted stone and drew in one puff of smoke; thus the pipe went around. When the last scout had taken his puff, the onlookers sprang to their feet, shouting and bringing up horses.

He turned to Eagle Man.

"The scouts will be taken ahead, Father, and then the escort will turn and race back to the circle." Eagle Man indicated a line of three freshly cut bushes, set up about ten yards apart. "The leader must knock the bushes down. If he fails, we may as well go home—no good will come of the hunt. If he knocks down one, we'll have a fair hunt. Two, and we will make a good bit of meat. All three, and we'll kill as many as we need."

The gray wanted to go with them, a howling mob of three hundred, and he let it. The Indians dashed about on their ponies, joking with the scouts, touching them with bits of fur, wands of sage, sticks to which feathers had been attached. He kept the gray reined in and, as the idea jelled, looked sharp about him.

They went a mile, another, the Indians still capering their mounts, he walking the gray: It had come many miles already, but still seemed fresh. For an instant he saw it all as a skylark might, the horses long like schooling fish, the riders in buckskins emboldened by feathers and beads, the one white man in a bowler hat and vest. He saw deer peeking from the draws, coyotes skulking, and beyond the hills, beyond the curve of the earth, the placid black herd.

Hiyiyiyiyi! They wheeled and the race was on. Quickly the field stretched out. Close to the gray's neck he rode, feeling bold, feeling lucky, feeling foolhardy, swept up in the fever of it. His eyes slitted against the flying dirt, and strands of mane lashed his face.

He drew near to the leaders and rode behind them. A stony ridge rose ahead—he had spotted it on the way out, and he cut right to keep to level terrain. He passed several riders. They turned their heads and looked, astonished.

The Indian ponies slowed for a marshy patch and again he swung wide, again he gained ground. The air rushed down his throat, from which, he realized, a beastly scream issued. He spotted the crescent. One last horse to beat, a paint, and slowly the gray drew abreast of it, thank God for good government grain, and pulled ahead, and the crescent grew and became people as he went pounding past the bright blurred faces. The gray made the turn and headed toward the bushes, wanted to flare but he dragged down on the bit, kicked and manhandled the beast down the shuddering green line. He reined, twisted in the saddle. All three bushes were spinning. A howl rose, and they were helping him off his horse, touching him with their talismans, proclaiming his medicine good and extolling the hunt to come.

He let it be known that he wanted a live calf. On the first day of the hunt he killed five of the great cattle himself, stopping finally to aid a man who had lost three fingers to a bursting gun. The hunters paid no attention to the wounded man but pressed on with the slaughter, the black vastness grunting and bawling, squealing and shifting as the riders cleaved through it.

"I had a good stiff ride back to camp that evening." Looking up, he saw the firelit faces. "We had killed two thousand. Before the hunt was over we would kill three thousand more, a good thing, because the crops failed and the beef issue never came through that year.

"When I woke in the morning, the camp had gone on ahead. Around my tent, tied to stakes, were twenty-two calves.

"That was the last buffalo hunt on Standing Rock."

• • •

In the morning Fry opened his eyes to a dim blue light. The sounds that had wakened him came again: a chorus of yelps that swelled into howls, discrete points of sound that flared and faded, flared again. He sat up. A dark form appeared on the canyon rim, then another, and a third; the coyotes trotted along the edge before drawing back and disappearing.

The others still lay in their blankets. Movement at the stream caught his eye. Trimble squatted, dipped water, rubbed his face. Skinny, hatless, cowlicked obsidian hair. He straightened, turned toward the east, and spread his arms.

Fry joined him at the stream. The sky was paling, the stars were flecks of ash. An owl flew over on silent wings, and a jay scolded it from cover. Higher up, a raven soared. It caught the sun and flamed, then, dropping, became a cinder again.

The stream smelled fresh and clean. The breeze awakened and came up the canyon, and together they turned, as if to greet someone entering a room. Trimble held out his hands, palms up. "The wind gives us life," he said. "It blew life into First Man and First Woman—I always figured they were born in a place like this." He touched his fingers to his lips. "The wind coming out of your mouth keeps you alive. When it stops, you die. There, on your fingers. See it? The wind."

Fry looked. On each fingertip the lines showed clearly, whorling about a tiny central point, dark loops and pale ridges. The wind rose, bending the grass, making the cotton-woods sing. Far off, the coyotes howled again.

"De-jiss-je," Trimble said. "Let's build a fire."

14

When she woke, the empty foothill country was filling with light. She lay with one hip touching the wheel, against which she had sat, watching the fire, until finally she fell asleep in the night. Now the fire was dead. The day world was coming alive. She checked the sky, vast, unobstructed, and brightening fast. No boxes out here. She spread the blankets where the sun would dry them and rose stiffly, kneaded her thighs under the stiff denim, circled her shoulders and neck, heard the bones softly pop. She reached for the rifle in the wagon bed.

The boys, Sibley in particular, had taught her to shoot. The rifle was a Winchester 1886 Takedown, caliber .45/70. At a hundred paces, despite the wallop and the ear-splitting boom, the holes made by her three shots could be covered with a hand. The rifle had come into the family when she was six years old. The previous owner, an Indian youth whose name was not known, had driven brass upholstery tacks into the buttstock in a design suggesting an eagle or a hawk. She worked the lever, chambering a cartridge, then let the hammer down to half-cock.

Grass stems caught the first light in tiny waving shafts of gold. Halos stood above the bushes of sage. She threaded her way between the dew-soaked clumps, setting down her moccasins carefully, feeling for twigs and avoiding them, shunning the loose chattery stones. She moved down the drainage, into the breeze. The stream course was summer-dry but full of green grass. In the grass the insects were waking with all their small ticking talk. High overhead a hawk screamed; she looked but could not spot it.

A doe grazed, shaking off flies with her short, black-tipped tail. Her fawn butted in to nurse, forelegs bending, rump held high, tail going like a pinwheel. It was a big fawn, nearly half-grown, but the doe remained tolerant, standing placidly while it suckled, finally disengaging herself and moving a short ways off.

Annie drew back and made a wide circle into the freshening wind.

She could not, as old Foam could, smell a buck before seeing it. Like curdled cream, he said; like the white man's barnyard. Try as she might, she could not sift this essence from the myriad other wild smells. But her eyes were keen. Standing in a shallow crease that fed into the grassy draw, moving only her eyes, she picked out the straight horizontal line so at odds in a country of curves. The head raised above the back then, showing velvety knobs.

His jaw worked side to side. His eyes were dark and round. The scoops of his ears turned this way and that, rested on her, went on and touched another quadrant, reversed themselves to listen around behind. She kept still. He lowered his head to feed.

She waited, until her heart had settled and her arms felt steady and strong. He looked up again, a young buck, not too big, a yearling. When again he dropped his head she cocked the rifle and pointed it. He raised his head, and she shot him through the neck. The sound went rumbling through the hills. The buck took two splay-footed bounds, slumped, and fell on his side. His blood washed the sage. She hauled his hind legs around uphill, stuck him above the brisket, and let him bleed out.

She thought of Sib, her stepbrother, who had taught her to shoot, and of Foam, who had taught her to kill. Sib was dark and quiet, shy, stammered painfully, was twelve years older. He was much given to tinkering with mechanical things: He liked to mend farm machinery and fix kitchen gadgets, and he even reloaded the brass cartridge cases that they spent at target practice. Old Foam liked black pepper stirred in his coffee, and would often smuggle her a nice cut of cold boiled pup, which, to his chagrin, she always refused, out of deference to Father McLaughlin. Foam wore an eagle feather tied in his long gray hair, a seashell choker, a mirror on a thong. He laughed with great, rude amusement whenever she stubbed her toe or fell. He took her with him hunting prairie chickens and rabbits, slaying them with a bow and blunt-headed arrows. After she was granted use of the rifle, together they hunted for deer in the creek bottoms, and the big high-racked bucks would get him so rattled he would empty the magazine without touching a hair.

She was the better shot. Foam showed her how to walk in silence and how to use the wind, where the deer would lie in the days of the full moon, at dusk and at midday, during the rut, in summer and winter, in the hours before a storm.

"The animals are better than we are," he said. "They see and hear and smell so much better than we do, and they don't have any evil inside of them. They don't hate each other. If they kill, it's only for food. When we kill them"—his eyes left his work of gutting, his bloody hands paused inside the steaming cavity—"when we eat them, we get some of their goodness."

She thanked the little buck for his life, as she had seen Foam do—held onto one neat jet hoof and gave slow and silent thanks.

That night she ate backstrap fried in a skillet; the rest of the meat she would jerk tomorrow, over the fire on a wooden frame, and it would last until she returned to the school. She finished her meal as the quarter moon was sinking. She let the fire dwindle. Coyotes yapped. Far off, an owl hooted. She leaned back against the wagon wheel, sitting on one blanket, the other wrapped around her. It took a long time for the light to leak from the sky, the darkness to settle. The stars came out and spangled the black expanse. She found the coyote and the bear and the turtle Foam had shown her up there, also Pa yamini pa, the monster with three heads. Then she picked out the Big Dipper, the two stars that formed the end of its gourd pointing up at the Pole Star, which started the handle of the Little Dipper. She found the constellation that looked like a crunched *W*, and the one shaped like a cross hovering straight overhead: the things Father McLaughlin liked to single out in the night sky.

The land glowed in the starlight. She heard the horses ripping out grass and grinding it. Stars everywhere, coming down to the horizon, a sudden scratch of fire as a meteor abraded to nothingness. She let her head rest in the pocket between two spokes. The stars began to swim, to run together, all the little flecks of brilliance swirling and melting like a rage of windblown snow. She lowered her face and wept.

15

They held the ceremony in Polacca town, at the foot of the mesa below the old stone village of Walpi. Walpi seemed to have extruded itself out of the rock, its doors and windows no more than natural cracks. Polacca, Arizona, was a few poor adobes, a church, a school, a laundry, and a row of bright-painted government houses lately built by the Indian Bureau in hopes of luring the Hopis down from their lofty rock.

Fry found shade beneath an eave and kept to it. Tugged on his water bottle between speeches. He stood a bit removed from the action and had to strain after words and fudge on some of the quotes, but figured no one would know, much less care:

"The President of the United States . . . dug the first shovel-ful of earth. Chief Wooden Leg of the Northern Cheyenne continued digging with the thighbone of a buffalo. . . ."

By now Fry could do it in his sleep. The muted words wafted by.

Children gamboled, naked as new spring leaves. McLaughlin was down to shirtsleeves and a straw boater, while he, Fry, stayed with coat and vest—what a natural he must seem, or maybe just prim; nor was he unaware of the possibility of keeling over in the heat, and when they went to loosen his clothing and revive him they would find it, and the jig would be up.

Dixon was in full cry: "You Hopis live in a high place; you live where the wind blows hard and the sun is hot." Hot, by

Jesus, yes. Fry felt besieged by the heat, which roared down out of the sky, bellowed from the walls, danced above stick ladders and chimney pots. In the heat waves the Hopis seemed to shimmer, ghostly in their pale cotton wraps, a dark spidery people doused with dust.

"I want you Indians to feel today, as you dedicate yourselves to this great, this God-loved banner, that you will fight to defend it until the last thread of this flag has faded away, until the last drop of Hopi blood is shed."

Hollow words. A flag stood for nothing out here. Concepts of "nation" and "citizenship" and "government" were unreal. Real was the glaring sky, the shafts of sun so solid they hurt, the wind that picked up grit and sand, flung them like mockery in the face.

A Hopi man, small and with a bowl-shaped head of hair, climbed onto a crate. "I am very glad that I have been presented with this flag by the government. A while back I didn't know the pathway of the white man, and was opposed to it, but now I am taking it up. I have found that the way of the government is bright and good. I want to own some stock. I want a Model T. I want to ride in an aeroplane."

Is he really saying this? Fry looked at his pen, marching mechanically. The symbols recorded the words on the pad. Spoken honestly, or in irony? Did it matter which?

There was the usual swirl when the ceremony ended. The Hopis, shyer even than the Navahos, would turn away or shield their faces with their hands or blankets when Booth and his Kodak hove into view. Booth advanced anyway, grinning as the people covered up or ran. Fry got a picture of him stampeding the Hopis. Also a shot of four demure maidens with their hair done up in queer black orbs that blossomed one from each side of the head; an old man dangling an acorn-brown child; and a flushed, heat-embattled face— McLaughlin's—set against the sun.

• • •

The team was in no hurry. Buttes like overturned pie plates shimmered in the starlight, and a distant mountain spread a low black smudge.

He sat on the hard seat next to McLaughlin, who had let the reins fall slack over the kickboard. The harness creaked steadily and the wheel rims grated over rocks. Fry was in a sulk. Dixon and Booth had stayed behind and would spend the next day photographing the Hopis, whom the Santa Fe Railroad touted for its tourists as "the real aboriginal stock of America, in all their picturesque life and customs." When Fry had asked to stay too, McLaughlin had said grumpily, "Let them loot their damned pictures, we've got work back at Keams." So they had left for the Keams Canyon Agency, just when a long line of men with mud-smeared legs and grotesque bright masks had come filing out of an adobe to the steady pulse of a drum.

"Would've liked to have stayed for that dance," Fry muttered.

The Major looked at him. "Well," he said. "Yes. Sorry about that."

"I've never seen a real Indian dance."

McLaughlin waved a hand. "I have. All too many. Broken up my share of them too."

"Yes?"

"When I took over on Standing Rock, first thing I did was to outlaw the dances. Kept my Indians out of circles. We had a meeting, they sat in rows, in chairs. The circle, Fry, is a baneful pagan symbol. The Sioux perform all of their rites in a circle, including the Sun Dance." McLaughlin spat over the side. "What they do at a Sun Dance is a pity. Gash their chests and drive sticks down behind the muscles; the sticks are tethered to ropes dangling from a pole. Some of the more creative dancers dice 'em in through the cheeks under the eyes, or beneath the muscles of the back.

"The dancers trudge around the pole, staring at the sun,

chirping on little whistles. They lean back on the ropes until they tear free. Hours, days—the longer he suffers, the more blood he sheds, the braver and more spiritual the dancer has proven himself." He sniffed. "Show me an Indian who's been through a Sun Dance, I'll show you an Indian in no shape to haul freight or mend fence or band hay. The Ghost Dance? We'll get to that later."

The wagon crept up a hill, paused, descended. "The average Sioux male was an underfed, improvident child," McLaughlin said. "He lived for warfare and strife." He gave a scoffing laugh. "A warrior could count coup—perform a valiant act that would earn him great fame—by giving his enemy a little swat with a stick. Even, criminy sakes, if the enemy was already dead. They squandered days in council bragging about the pony stolen, the scalp lifted, the buffalo killed."

From out on the desert there arose a thin cry, a high tremulous note that sustained itself for a moment—then abruptly was cut off. The horses pointed their ears at the sound. "Rabbit," McLaughlin said. "Owl or a coyote got him." He picked up the reins and gave them a desultory shake; the team, which had not deviated from its moderate, comfortable pace, kept walking.

"It must have been hard," Fry said, "to turn them into farmers. In one generation to go from mounted hunters to tillers of the soil."

"Hard? More like impossible."

"They had to take allotments, choose one little parcel of land, when before they had ridden over oceans of it?"

"It had to be done."

"Couldn't they just have been left alone on their reservation?"

"They were starving. The buffalo were gone. The land was needed for homesteading. Plus, it was felt that the influx of white settlers would be beneficial. Schools would be built, towns develop, centers of trade and culture spring up. . . ."

His voice trailed off. "We followed the Allotment Act of Eighteen Eighty-seven. The head of a family could select a hundred and sixty acres for himself and forty acres for each minor child. Should the land be suitable only for grazing, the acreage was doubled. A family might end up with hundreds of acres." He paused. "And there it would lie. You can't live by dancing. You can't live by sitting there looking at the land, can't turn your family out to graze.

"Well," he said, "I wish it had worked out. But the wind sucked the moisture out of the soil and burned the crops to nothing. Or it blew in clouds of grasshoppers to pick the fields clean. In the bottoms, where the best soil lies, there was a constant danger of frost. Every two, three years we'd get the good spring rains, the crops would push up, everything would look jim-dandy. Then along would come a hailstorm to thrash the wheat in the fields, or a drought to shrivel it. Now they say we were shortsighted, that with larger allotments the Indians might have prospered raising cattle. But we feared raising cattle. It would have nurtured the old nomadic ways.

"Look at the Dakotas today. Wind's blowing the soil away. Homesteaders packing up and leaving in droves—good farmers, Germans, Norwegians, Swedes, foreclosures everywhere. And still people are pouring in, taking up claims." McLaughlin was quiet for a time. When he spoke again, his voice was thin. "A brutal land," he said. "Sometimes I dread going back."

The rambling log hotel, El Tovar, stood on the absolute rim of *it*. It was the holiest American shrine. It was reached by a railway that terminated in five sidings. It sat there in sublime silence, beyond the station with its sedate ranks of Pullmans, its black-on-white Santa Fe cross, beyond the Indian welcoming committee (Navaho youths listlessly shaking rattles and thumping tom-toms, wearing imitation Sioux warbonnets made of turkey feathers in Moline, Illinois), beyond the Hopi House (built to look like a Hopi village, and stocked with authentic Indian goods marked up several thousand percent), beyond the parked autos and carriages and omnibuses, the strolling, camera-toting tourists: yawning, immense, dropping down in great pastel shelves to a twisting brown band, the Colorado River, which had carved out this canyon that was, truly, nothing short of grand.

At the post office—like El Tovar, constructed of peeled pine logs—Fry checked under general delivery. He was given a promisingly thick manila envelope postmarked Washington, D.C. He carried the envelope to the hotel. In the dining room he found a seat by the window. He ordered a steak dinner, an extravagance, as his per diem would cover only the meal on Signet. The waitress, in a snug black uniform with a white apron, set his plate down with genteel precision. His palms were damp, but not just because of her. As he ate, he looked out the window. Imminent slopes were freckled with pine. The canyon was crowded with mountains whose peaks stopped just below the level of the rim. The top halves of the mountains glowed pumpkin orange, while the lower slopes lay in maroon shade. Shadows streamed from side-lit buttes like trails of departing souls.

He finished his meal and ordered an iced tea. He sipped the drink, chewed the ice. He stared at the envelope, his pulse running. Finally he opened it.

Inside was a check for $120. The *Dispatch* had run eight of his photographs in each of three consecutive Sunday editions, paying him five dollars per picture. Fry's salary was $17.50 a week. Kravitz had enclosed a letter: "Dear Ansel: It is just as I predicted, your pictures are standing this town on its ear. People have sent in dozens of letters; some say the photos are trash but others rave about them. Art critics have submitted essays attacking or defending candid photography. People line up at the building to buy papers every Sunday. I await, with great anticipation, your next shipment."

Along with the letter and check were the newspapers. Fry chose one and started from the front. In an advertisement, a handsome baseball player smiled at the sweating glass of Coca-Cola in his hand: "Drink the Drink the Nation Drinks." An article on the United States Navy showed photographs of dreadnoughts steaming forward, alert admirals, officers at mess. A portrait of a jowly industrialist, a millionaire in rubber bands. The German emperor's recent boar hunt, the stiff-backed Kaiser bent at the waist, reviewing a company of bristly, defunct hogs.

Arriving at the center spread, he looked through the round portals and saw . . . people. *Real* people. Squinting scarecrow of a man and his stout wife, between them a girl with a goiter, her fingers just brushing the disfiguring lump. Railroad worker, his jaw jutting, ejecting a quid of tobacco. *Oh my God*— Dixon, his eyes shut and his hands raised, Indians kissing the flag, while in the background two Cheyenne men looked on with undisguised scorn. Giannetti protecting the Edison from Indian attack, Booth ogling an Indian woman's shapely behind. Oh no, oh no, oh no—a boy in a dress, on his leg a ball and chain.

His heart rose and toppled. Why had he sent these? He'd half-forgotten having done it, out there on the desert. *Why?* So stupid. He was lost. Or was he? Hurriedly he tucked the envelope under his arm, paid for his dinner, and left. The sun had gone down, and the canyon was filling with gloom. He walked the raked gravel path along the rim. Halting, he stared into the canyon. He was looking, he knew, at a minor portion of an abyss that twisted in fifty miles from the north, elbowed here at Grand View Point—identified by an incised wooden sign—and snaked off two hundred miles to the west. Into its maw you could dump every battleship and rubber band and baseball player and bottle of Coca-Cola in the world, every Indian monument, every Kicking Kickapoo and sad dirt farmer's daughter and jittery candid photographer (there was only one, so far as he knew)—and the Grand Canyon would not so much as belch.

His meal sat heavily in his stomach, and a tightness plagued his chest. He touched the camera lurking beneath his vest. Trust in it, he thought. The Major will figure it out! Trust in yourself, in the truth. You're gonna die for sure! Keep on pulling the string. They'll never catch you. Never.

"Scandal! Disgrace! It makes the ceremony look like a fraud!" Dixon's eyes started out of their sockets, his hands fisted, then became claws. "I am made to look like . . ."

McLaughlin said, "A snake-oil salesman."

Dixon glowered, the skin over his temples pulsing. "*Candid* photography. It's contemptible, it's warped, it spreads ill will." He slammed his palm on the paper, and the sugar bowl jumped. He pointed: "The day the Kickapoos, those cads, walked out on us. And these Cheyennes, the smug ingrates . . ."

McLaughlin's chair was backed against the dining-room wall. His white hair shone in the light from a Pintsch lamp. "Doctor Dixon, the Commissioner is every bit as interested as you are in halting the activities of this photographer. The Bureau has made inquiries at the Washington *Dispatch*. In fact, the Secretary of the Interior contacted the editor himself." The Major clenched a stub of cigar between his teeth. "They refuse to give a name. Odious 'freedom of the press.' Also, they're selling one hell of a bunch of newspapers." The cigar had gone out, but the Major appeared not to have noticed. He turned to Fry. "The Commissioner first brought this matter to our attention when?"

Fry checked the logbook. "June twentieth."

"So he's been at it at least a month." McLaughlin patted

himself for matches, located a small box. He lit the cigar stub, keeping Dixon waiting, fuming. The Major waved the match out, held it until it cooled, and placed it on the table edge. "I've questioned every agency superintendent since that date. This picture"—he held up the newspaper and pointed at the boy in the dress—"was taken at the Darlington school. I know, because I saw that child. I questioned the superintendent, and not a hint, not a rumor of any photography, clandestine or otherwise. Yet obviously that shutterbug snuck in there."

Dixon gripped his chin and gloomed at the newspaper. Booth sat straddling a chair backward. "After that picture of me," he said quietly, "I would break every finger on each of his hands, in such a manner that he would never wish to operate a camera again."

"Benjamin!" Dixon's face was liverish. "If you had kept yourself under control you would not have embarrassed this expedition in the first place."

Booth looked at the floor and scowled.

"Mr. Giannetti," Dixon said, "your theory about this photographer's camera."

Giannetti nodded. "There's a spy camera, a glass-plate job, makes a round negative like this. It has a good shutter and lens, which would account for the sharpness and the generally high quality of the images. Used mainly for police work, detectives, undercover surveillance, things like that. Very small and compact. You wear it under your coat."

"Note that, Mr. Fry," McLaughlin said.

Fry sat like lead.

"Mr. Fry?"

"Yessir. Got it."

McLaughlin clenched his teeth on the cigar, angling it upward. He looked at Dixon. "Suppose we find this 'candid photographer.' What right have we to make him quit?"

Dixon blinked. His mouth fell open and clicked shut. "Couldn't he be prohibited from entering the reservations?"

"On what grounds?"

Dixon said, "I'm not sure."

McLaughlin immersed the cigar butt in his coffee dregs, *hiss*. "Let's keep our eyes open," he said. "Watch the crowds at every ceremony. We may see a familiar face." He shrugged. "Though even if we do, I can't say there's any way to stop him."

At that point Booth smiled grimly and raised his head.

16

They went down into the canyon on muleback. Fry's was a noxious blear-eyed creature who looked ready to turn and bite at any moment. Yet Fry rode easy. After all of that talking, fingering about for a candid photographer, nobody had looked at him once, let alone twice.

Poor bland Ansel: the clerk, the insignificance with a pen in his hand. He grinned to himself. He was free. Free to absorb the sights of banded cliff, cotton-ball cloud; the smells of bitter alkali and sweet sage; the sound of the desert, which was no sound at all, a profound silence that swelled until it seemed to fill him to brimming.

Free to make his pictures, though by God he'd be more careful from here on in.

They descended the steep trail, strung out in a line. Dixon, in front, was doing his best to play the role of "leader of the expedition." He rode ramrod-straight, pioneering the way (the trail was beaten, obvious), now and then raising a hand to stop them and point out some new sight. Surely there would be a letter to Rodman Wanamaker about this difficult leg of the trip; Fry began composing it in his head: ". . . a perilous and trying descent, at every turn I expected to plummet to the bottom of the precipice with the mule on top of me. Vermilion walls rose sheer on either hand, a thousand feet"—make it two thousand—hell, five thousand feet—"while below us, eagles rocked on currents of wind. Blowing sand assailed us, spiny cactus blocked our path, heat caused the water in our canteens to boil. Thus we approached the Havasupai, carrying the saving banner of citizenship, the blessed, glorious flag."

Next, Booth. Big block-headed Booth, the mule taking a pounding from his weight, stirrups adjusted too short so that his thick legs splayed to the sides. Break my fingers? You'll have to catch me first. I take every precaution. My trunk is always locked, I go over every square inch of the bathroom after changing plates, and you have no reason to suspect me, none at all, though you make it plain you do not like me. Just that morning, for instance, Booth had languidly reached out and closed his hand around Fry's elbow. "Small Fry, you remind me of a cat. You always look so damned guilty." Booth had laughed and added, "Makes me want to chunk a rock at you."

After Booth came McLaughlin, in line in front of Fry. The compact broad back moved with stops and starts, shudders and jounces, as the mule picked its way down the trail.

If anybody puts it all together, it will be this man. This tough, shrewd, sober man. And what would it have been like, to be Sitting Bull and to square off against him in his prime? This bulldog of a man, tenacious, untiring, with the weight of authority, of arms and Army, behind him; an honest man, Fry was sure of it, but so certain of himself, so blind to other possibilities and points of view.

He brought to mind again the photograph in the file back at Bureau headquarters: McLaughlin with his Indian policemen, "Survivors, Sitting Bull Fight." A shoot-out, yes, but what had happened? What led up to it? Well, it looked as if he would find out. Fry had been annoyed at first when the Major saddled him with the extra dictation. But what a chance to learn what really happened, from a man in the thick of it! Now he looked forward to their sessions. They had filled one pad and most of a second.

They continued down the steep trail, Fry battling with the saddle horn, enduring the heat and glare. In an hour the trail leveled out. A stream of water bubbled from the ground; the mules all rushed to it and drank. They rode along beside the pale blue stream, bordered along its course with thick beds of watercress below overarching willows. The stream sank back into the ground, and stark desert returned. The stream re-emerged, bringing the verdure with it. Then desert again, then greenery, the stream wider now, deeper and bluer, with them for the rest of the ride.

The canyon opened to an oval park fenced in by red cliffs. On the valley floor, fields of alfalfa glowed like green enamel. Before the agency were gathered brown-faced women in calico, with headdresses of brilliant handkerchiefs sewn together; they chattered excitedly as the riders drew up. The Havasupai men were shy and silent, their short black hair in unkempt thatches.

Early the next morning they held the ceremony, raising the flag on a two-by-four scabbed to a building wall, since the agency had no pole. Dixon knelt below the limp flag, piled up some dirt with his hands, put a stick in the top: the monument in New York. The interpreter was a fat young woman with a puzzled face; doubtless her English was poor, for the Havasupai never seemed to catch a glimmer of where New York was, or what a monument might be. A sad and scrofulous lot, many of them toothless, with pale, trachoma-scarred eyes and the swollen ulcerous joints of secondary tuberculosis.

A young boy, whose twisted torso looked like a shirt badly hung on a hanger, attached himself to Fry. Wherever Fry went, the boy followed; whatever Fry did, the boy mimicked it. When Fry took a drink, the boy raised an imaginary canteen. When Fry wrote on his pad, the boy wrote on an imaginary pad.

"Beat it," Fry hissed.

"Bea' it," the boy hissed.

"Scram."

"Scram."

Fry glowered, made a shooing gesture with his hand. The boy did the same.

After the ceremony, down the canyon from the agency, they visited a village. Dixon took portraits, for which the Havasupai willingly posed. Fry stood under a tree and ate a yellow plum; the boy, still shadowing him, acted out the eating of a plum. Fry threw the pit away and licked his fingers. The boy threw the fanciful pit away and licked his fingers.

Between the leaning stick-and-mud huts, the very ground stank. Piles of human excrement lay about. When it's cold, Fry wondered, where do they go? Inside, on the floor? He peered through a window opening. Flies zoomed through the hut, crawled the plank table, clustered on the walls.

How could a child grow up here? How could it escape disease, infection, early death? Become anything but an imbecile like this one trailing me around?

He bent toward the boy. The child had puffy cheeks and a slack mouth. Fry stared, trying to read something, anything, in the black eyes. And here the eyes did not duplicate his. They were not just dull, they were dead. No light, no spark of humor or curiosity or resentment. They were holes full of nothingness, holes in canyon walls.

The Vanishing Race. Four little, three little, two little Indians, one little Indian boy. Locked away on a reservation, out of sight and out of mind. Put him on the penny, now the nickel, maybe someday he'll make the dime. Dixon there with his camera, securing portraits of "types," the Bureau with its relentless push toward assimilation, Wanamaker's memorial with its gleaming bronze Indian on top, a statue to be seen from a distance, marveled at—ultimately forgotten. James McLaughlin: Where did he fit in?

Dogged by the boy, he reconnoitered until he got a good angle—huts and people, trash, a dog nosing in a pile of excrement—and got the picture (blamed if the ninny didn't mimic the whole thing, the pause, the hand twitching in the pocket, even the click), though the image didn't feel good, didn't feel like it had any life. Well, he couldn't send it, anyway: no one else visiting this cramped arm of the canyon except the expedition. But maybe someday. Because people needed to see other people living like this, as surely as they needed to see themselves, caught in unposed, unvarnished life.

In the afternoon heat, McLaughlin and Fry sat in the shade of a big cottonwood. At a nod from the Major, Fry opened his pad and uncapped his pen.

"The calico dresses," McLaughlin said, "what the women were wearing today? Straight out of the eighties. Reminded me of reservation days. Bundles would come from the Eastern cities, from church groups, charity packages of clothes.

"We'd put them out in the yard and the squaws would paw through them, squabble over the dresses, strip down right there in the middle of town and put 'em on. They'd wear that old calico until the next charity package arrived—never a washing, though we showed them how, gave them buckets and washboards and soap—and then go through the whole unseemly process again.

"But not Sitting Bull's wives. He wouldn't let them demean themselves like that."

The Major poured himself a glass of water and drank half of it. He and Fry sat on folding wooden chairs. The pitcher rested on a stool.

"At first he lived near the agency, which was convenient for me, because I could keep an eye on him. Then he moved on down to Grand River, where he was said to have been born.

"He lived on Standing Rock for seven years. Seven years of gradual improvement for the Sioux people, although he fought it whenever and however he could.

"Much of that time he was away from the reservation. He

went to Washington to meet the President. He traveled to Canada and the Eastern cities with Cody's Wild West." McLaughlin drank off the rest of his glass and filled it again from the pitcher. They all drank constantly in the unremitting heat; the thermometer on the agency porch stood at 110.

"It was a different age," McLaughlin said. "The railroads had just been extended across the continent, in obvious testimony to the white man's dominance. The country was growing by leaps and bounds, everything was booming, and any obstacle to progress, especially if it had to do with Indians, brought down the scrutiny of the whole land." He raised his face, surveying the twisted branches with their thousands of pale green leaves, none of which moved. "Reporters were always snooping around the agency, waiting for something to happen. There we were in the howling wilderness of Dakota Territory—yet it hardly felt that way. Something would happen, a rancher killed by Indians, chiefs jostling for power, a blizzard, a tornado, even a big jackrabbit hunt—and they'd know about it the next day in St. Paul, Chicago, New York." He spoke with a wondering tone. "The things that happened. Once an Englishman came to town, one of a hunting party. An Indian girl walked into his tent, wrapped her arms around him, kissed him, and kept kissing him, and wouldn't quit. Well, he came up for air and married her on the spot. And she back to England with him.

"Sitting Bull was much in demand. They had him up to Bismarck to lay the cornerstone for the new capitol. He stood on a wagon tongue and hawked his autograph, which he'd learned to write in Canada, at a dollar-fifty a crack." McLaughlin sniffed. "Everybody wanted the signature of 'The Generalissimo of the Sioux.' Even the brass hats, I saw them chuckling at it, great men seeking a savage's autograph, but then it was only for a grandchild, a favorite nephew or niece.

"They handed up stationery with the Northern Pacific seal on it. Villard, Governor Ordway, General Grant.

"This was before Sitting Bull went with Cody." McLaughlin gave a trifling nod. "I had my shot at him. Took him to St. Paul. First I showed him a bank. Banker was a wheezy little man, pale and pudgy. 'Major McLaughlin and Mr. Sitting Bull, step this way, please.' The door opened on hinges big as your fist. In the vault the banker showed him sacks of gold. Sitting Bull? He yawned.

"'Thousands of dollars in cash,' I said, 'and more in securities and bonds.' Louis Primeau took great pains to explain, but I don't think Sitting Bull quite grasped the concept.

"I gave my little speech, told him that when the Sioux accepted their allotments in severalty they would receive a generous amount of money from the government, which they could use to buy seed, stock, tools, and the like.

"The banker stood there staring at Sitting Bull's bowed legs, his quilled moccasins, his greasy Pendleton robe and black stovepipe hat. If I had told him, I imagine he'd have jumped out of his socks: The eagle feather in the band of that hat, its tip had been dipped in the blood of a Ree chief.

"Outside, people stood crowding round the hack—I had hired it to force a passage. Shouts went up, and not a few curses; I kept my eyes peeled for a gun. This was only eight years after Custer.

"The driver whipped up and went. A fine mist hung in the air. I pointed out a Catholic church, a hardware store, a lumberyard, a power station. Sitting Bull smoked his pipe and looked around. He turned to Primeau and spoke.

"'He finds this a strange way for people to live,' Primeau said. 'Even the hornet doesn't build so crowded a nest.' Sitting Bull went on, his cadence slow and thoughtful. 'The Hunkpapas will never live this way—the Little Yanktons, maybe, for they are easily led. But the Hunkpapas—never. Not in your lifetime, Father, and not in the lifetime of your son, or your son's son.'"

The Major fell silent. The sun's glare filled the canyon. A

leaf fell in the upper branches of the cottonwood, came ticking down, and landed at McLaughlin's feet. Someone could be heard coughing inside the superintendent's house. Fry looked at McLaughlin, the thick white brows, the chiseled nose with slightly flaring nostrils, the austere lips. The Major was staring at the sun-baked canyon walls, and his lips grew thinner as they drew back along the side of his jaw.

"Perhaps I didn't impress him on that trip. But I did later.

"It was in the agency office. Simplicity itself. We'd just had a new telephone put in. I asked the operator to ring up Mrs. Parkin, a mixed blood living at Cannonball River, twenty-five miles up the Missouri. I called Bull over, handed him the earphone, and motioned for him to speak into the mouthpiece.

"'Hallo! Hallo!' he bellowed. 'You betcha! You betcha!' That about exhausted his store of English. He had spoken in the white man's tongue because he figured it was all the machine would understand. Then, as planned, the voice came cutting through the hum and crackle; a woman's voice, coming straight from hell."

He looked Fry full in the face. Fry saw a triumphant smile, the eyes bright, the chin uplifted, the lips pulled back from the teeth: the smile of a man so certain of his rightness that it made Fry draw back involuntarily.

"The voice answered in Lakota," McLaughlin said. "In Sioux." He leaned back in his chair. His head settled against the ropy bark of the cottonwood. "He was hardly heard from for months on end. He began to farm a little, to raise chickens and cattle, to live in a house. He requested a school for his children. Of course I had it built."

17

The stories had been clipped from a San Francisco daily by one of her Carlisle classmates and mailed to her in Idaho two summers before.

Now, she sat waiting out the heat of the day, resting in the shade, small brown birds sitting mum around her in the thicket as a sparrow hawk hover-fluttered overhead, the fierce little falcon lifting at the movement of her hand, flashing away as she smoothed the clipping against her leg and read:

STARVING INDIAN PROVES ENIGMA

Sheriff Provides Food
but Finds Prisoner Unable
to Speak Any Known Language

[*Special Dispatch to The Call*]

OROVILLE, Aug. 29.—An Indian clad only in a rough canvas shirt that reached to his knees was taken into custody yesterday near Oroville by Sheriff Webber.

The Indian evidently had been driven by hunger to the town's slaughterhouse, as he was almost starving, and at the sheriff's office ate ravenously of the food set before him. Not a word of English can he speak.

Where the Indian came from is a mystery. The most plausible explanation seems to be that he is the sole surviving member of a little group of uncivilized Deer Creek Indians, who were driven from their hiding place in Tehama County two years ago.

In the sheriff's office he was surrounded by a curious throng. He made a pathetic figure crouched upon the floor. He is about sixty years of age. His feet are almost as wide as they are long, showing plainly that he never has worn either moccasins or shoes. In his ears are rings made of buckskin thongs. Over his shoulder he carried a rough canvas bag containing a few manzanita berries and some sinews of deer meat.

She got out the second clipping.

WILD INDIAN IDENTIFIED AS OF DEER CREEK
State University Professor
Pronounces Him
"Least Civilized Man"

OROVILLE, Sept. 1.—A two years' search came to an end in the county jail tonight, when Prof. P. T. Waterman, instructor in anthropology at the state university, came face to face with what, after an extended conversation, he termed to be a member of the Deer Creek or Mill Creek Indians.

The identification was so complete that there can be no question about it. At the close of the session Waterman was jubilant. If this man is, as indications point, the last of his race, Waterman says that with him would pass away all knowledge of his language, for he is the only man on earth who understands the tongue in which his tribe conversed.

Waterman went to the cell in which the Indian has been confined and talked to him in five different Indian languages without receiving a response. He then turned to the language of the northern Yana Indians, on the theory that the Indian was probably a southern Yana, or as the tribe is better known, a Mill Creek or Deer Creek Indian. Despite the fact that the dialect of the northern Yanas bears about the same relationship to that of the southern Yanas that Italian would bear to Spanish, he was soon able to make himself understood.

"The southern Yanas," said Waterman, "were a warlike people, and two years ago when I attempted to get an Indian to lead me into Deer Creek, where their village was, I found that they were still held in the greatest fear, although half a century had passed since any Indians had seen them and their tribe practically had been depleted.

"Not only from this man can we learn something of their language, but he is absolutely untouched by the modern world, and from him we can learn of the customs of the Indians and their civilization such as it was."

Two years ago a surveying party drove a small band of Indians from their last hiding place. As far as could be ascertained, the remnant of the once proud tribe at that time consisted of four bucks and one squaw. It is believed that the Indian captured here is the last of this band.

"I judge this person to be the least civilized man in America," the professor said.

It was the picture, more than the story, that moved her. The Least Civilized Man wore only a scrap of tattered canvas. His bare skin, visible in a dark shining vee from the breastbone up, showed sharp high ribs and a collarbone like the emaciated torso of a tubercular child. He stood barefoot, slightly stooped, facing the camera dead-on. His face looked Oriental. The corners of his eyes turned up. The corners of his mouth turned down. The nose was long, the cheekbones high and fine. She fell now into a kind of heat-stunned trance, staring at the face, her own flesh-and-blood eyes fixed on the paper ones. Haunted eyes, attractive eyes, doomed points of light; once she had focused a magnifying glass on them, and they'd fallen away in a grid of gray and black dots.

She had felt a wild communion with those eyes. In a dream once, the Least Civilized Man had chased her, his cape flapping, across the plain. He was so frail and weak, she'd had to slow down and let him catch her. He threw her down, and covered her there under the harsh sun. He planted within her the seed of his child, his wild Indian child, and her body felt liquid and awash, the plain rocking them all like sea swell. She surprised herself by not feeling ashamed. Then as she sought out his eyes, the sun lanced through him, and the man grew flat and flimsy, became the transparent stuff of shadows, until finally he faded away to nothingness in her arms. She had wrenched herself awake to find her back arched, her body streaming.

Now she raised her face and blinked at the dry yellow hills. Beyond the hills lay heat-shimmering mountains. The country of the Least Civilized Man lay farther west, a golden paradise where streams gushed and tumbled, where deep canyons were choked with scrub and chaparral. His people had all been eliminated (hanged, shot, infected, displaced) by the new ones. So in the end he had been reduced to following faint runways of trails like the most timid mouse. Now, the newspapers said, they kept him in a museum. It was better than death, she supposed, but it was still a bitter end.

She looked eastward toward old Foam. Sometimes when she was with him, she had seen the air moving: looked at the ether above an anthole and, for a moment, watched brilliant motes swerve. At night she had seen pale glowing lights floating quickly this way and that—Foam said these were the spirits of the dead. He had a song, an old Ghost Dance song, which even now she could hear on the wind.

The wind stirs the willows, the wind stirs the grass. Fog! Fog! Lightning! Whirlwind! The rocks are ringing, they are ringing in the mountains. The sun's beams are running out, the sun's yellow rays are all running out. But we shall live again. We shall live again.

She breathed deeply, folded the clippings, and put them away. The sun had lost some of its fire. She had not seen a human face for days. She thought of Foam ("that old blanket Indian," Father grumblingly called him), who for some reason had taken a liking to the shy skinny Hunkpapa girl being raised (because one parent was dead and the other was drink-

ing herself swiftly into oblivion) in the agent's house. She saw
Foam, sloe-eyed and slope-shouldered, old as the plains, in
his ramshackle cabin, trash all around, tipi and sweat lodge
out back, bits of red yarn tied to sticks and stems, fence posts
and lodge poles, the yarn animated by the wind; she saw
scuttling chickens, grazing horses, the placid cow, the gang of
dogs. She wondered if Foam was still in this world or had gone
on to the next.

Then she saw Father McLaughlin, who, in the course of her
life, had been of greater influence than Foam. It had not
seemed a strange life, growing up in Fort Yates, in the
McLaughlin household. But in retrospect perhaps it was.
Raised as a white, then thrown in with the Indians at
Carlisle—she thought in English, they did not; for her the
reservation was simply home, not a place of exile and pain;
Catholicism was her only remembered religion, it fit her as
comfortably, if as casually, as an old shoe—then graduated
into the wider world, there to be seen and treated as an
Indian. In Lewiston, everywhere she went—to the shops, the
theater, the library, the park—she saw the heads swivel. Was
her slip showing? Had she absentmindedly put her blouse on
backward? Honey, you're a digger. And that's halfway to a
nigger.

Like when she had rented this wagon and team. The livery
man followed her down the runway between the stalls, showing, by the casual way he spat near her feet and picked his
teeth, that in no way did he deem her a lady; she thought he
might actually unbutton his trousers and urinate in her presence. After all, she was an Indian. No matter that she could
parse a sentence and he could not. That she knew European
history and he was unaware of the friction between Germany
and France in the Alsace-Lorraine. That she read D. H. Law-
rence and he (if he could read at all), the "Katzenjammer
Kids." He showed her nags, she pointed out swollen cannon
bones and spavined hocks, which gained her a grudging mea-

sure of respect. When he demanded a deposit twice as large as he should have, she paid readily but insisted on a receipt and demanded it be notarized. Then told him, climbing into the seat, arranging her skirt, taking the whip from the socket, "I always get a receipt." He pulled at his lip with thumb and finger, looking at her quizzically, almost genially. No, she shouldn't have said it, it demeaned her more than it did him, it destroyed any small progress she might have made, but she was brittle with rage, her heart was poor. "White men." She spoke haughtily. She waved the whip so that the tip whispered. His eyes narrowed and he stepped back. She snapped it at his feet, *crack!*, so that he jumped. "White men," she said again. "Steal the wheels off a moving wagon if you let 'em."

Now she shrugged, turned the motion into a stretch, and stood up straight on her long slim legs. She looked around at the landscape. She could read it like a book. She could hear, she could smell, she could see. She could hunt. She took out a piece of jerky and tore off a corner with her teeth, which were white and sound and perfectly straight—superior, she reflected, to the teeth of almost every white person she met.

She looked at the land, which was a remnant of the territory once held by the Nez Perce, but in the midday glare she could not see the luminous shadows that would be Nez Perce souls; anyway, it had been a long time since she'd glimpsed any such shades.

Well, she could get the Antelope Creek School; if need be, she would use the McLaughlin name. Foam's cabin lay along Antelope Creek, which flowed into the Grand. No Least Civilized Man back in Dakota; but the shadows would be there still, in the wind-tossed grass of the bottomland, lingering above the spilled blood and the bones.

18

The car was a marvel to get back to, with its food and comforts, its solidity, its opulence. (He would have to write Kravitz about it. Or send a picture. Kravitz had, he suspected, socialist leanings.) Fry returned to his soft berth in the observation room, where oak-bladed fans paddled softly in the ceiling. He ventured down the long carpeted passageway with windows on the left and staterooms on the right; through the dining room with its clawfoot table and cherry sideboard where the stewards set the silver covered dishes; past the stewards' room, pantry, kitchen, all crammed together; into the anteroom with its storage locker containing dozens of new American flags, flags for the tribes, still stiff with the manufacturer's sizing; then through the door and into the vestibule, which screeched like a demented owl, letting onto the rest of the train.

Signet was always the last in line so it could be coupled on and detached again easily: Signet, then a coach or two, a car with sleeping and smoking compartments, dining car, baggage car, tender. Then the locomotive itself, huge and black with a long cylindrical boiler standing high above the wheels, driven by eccentric rods that pushed back and forth, blurringly translating the urgent pressure of steam.

It filled him with—how else to describe it, except glee? He walked around brimming, gleeful to be racing across the land, ever heading toward that next exotic destination, the train gobbling up the miles, carrying him, Ansel Fry, candid photographer, deeper into the West.

He'd been up in the dining car for a birch beer and was coming back down the passageway, watching his reflection in each of the night-black rectangles (skin browned from the desert, looking lean and hardened, ready to take on anything) when the Major's door swung inward. McLaughlin stopped short, blinking surprise. "I was coming to get you."

"Sir?"

"Bring your pad."

He realized it was only the second time he'd been in McLaughlin's room. It was stuffy in there, yellowish with gaslight. And the clipped-out photograph of the girl—the candid photograph of the pretty, preoccupied Cherokee woman—still sat in the upper right-hand corner of the mirror on the wardrobe door. Fry stopped and studied it: drank in the sight of her leaning forward, shoulders yearning and full of life, attention riveted on something outside the photograph's frame (he couldn't recall what it might have been), one hand barely touching her waist, the other hand raised. . . . "Major McLaughlin," he said, "why is this here?" He tore his glance from the picture and faced the older man. "Why have you cut this photograph out and kept it?"

Annoyance flickered across McLaughlin's face. He gave his head a short shake as if to dismiss the subject. "A picture," he murmured, "nothing special. . . . Reminds me of someone."

"Who?"

McLaughlin waved briefly, turned away. "Sit down." He indicated the chair by the window. Fry sat, and the Major lowered himself onto the bed.

McLaughlin handed him a newspaper. "Another one."

More candids, more people like the Cherokee girl. People different from the set faces staring out of gilt frames or printed in magazines and books. People alive, not egos composed for posterity. He wanted to thrust the paper into the

Major's hands and say, Look at them, living, just being, for God's sake, themselves. They are you, they are me!

"We've got to stop him." McLaughlin grimaced slightly. "I say *him,* but I suppose it could be a woman taking these. Cribbs is fit to be tied. He's getting blistered by the SAI."

"The SAI?"

"Society of American Indians. Bunch of do-gooders in Washington. They've got some clout." McLaughlin fixed his pince-nez on his nose and motioned to have the paper back. He pointed. "This one, this one, this. Indians in uncomplimentary situations or surroundings."

Why can't he understand? It's too much to hope for, too much to expect. "If it's somebody out to get the Bureau," Fry said, "then why all of the other pictures—the trainmen, people in towns, whites, Negroes, ordinary folks doing everyday things?"

McLaughlin bit his lower lip; his eyes were narrowed and his look was inward, as if trying to build a picture of some half-familiar face seen once too often in the crowd. "He's close to us. Think about it. That one edition. Pictures of Dixon, Giannetti, Booth."

Fry felt a knot in his stomach, tightening, growing hot. He made his voice smooth as glass. "Suppose this *candid photographer*"—he said the words with a faint, deliberate distaste—"happened onto one of our early ceremonies in Oklahoma. Here's this big exciting event, it draws a crowd, it distracts people, they're paying attention to flags and speeches and bands. He takes some pictures. He sells them, and they cause a fuss."

Fry took a breath, the air coming easier. "He decides to follow us around. It'd be easy, our itinerary's in all the papers. Whenever this person wants to take some more pictures, he shows up where we'll be."

McLaughlin nodded absently, shook the paper so the pages rattled. "But these touchy ones, the ones that make us look bad." He smacked the paper with the fingertips of one hand. "Must be some kind of do-gooder."

"Pictures like that sell newspapers."

"Indeed they do." McLaughlin put his pince-nez away. "A minor mystery. I wish we could clear it up and get Cribbs off my back." He looked at Fry. "You're sweating like a racehorse."

"It's hot in here."

"Hot as the hinges of hell. Let's go out on deck."

From the observation room they dragged two chairs onto the narrow platform. In the darkness the train clattered steadily along, fruity snatches of coal smoke coming back, light from the coaches flashing yellow against cactus along the track. The air, although hot, rushed agreeably through the awning struts. McLaughlin turned on the overhead light; Fry nodded that it would be enough.

"Did you enjoy the canyon?" McLaughlin said.

"Loved it. Walked all along the rim and saw it at dawn and at dusk. Bet I sent a dozen cards."

McLaughlin said, "I think, if I ever have an incurable disease and only a short while to live, I'll go there. Dying on the edge of that abyss"—he stopped, groping for words—"wouldn't be like dying at all. Just changing over from one realm into the next." He frowned a bit, as if embarrassed at such talk. "Where's your home?"

"Harrisburg."

"I've been through it. River town, scenic. A good place?"

"A good place to be from."

McLaughlin settled into the chair, the slipstream ruffling his hair. "I was on Standing Rock for fourteen years. I'm seventy-one, so that's—what?—a fifth of my life. A fifth. Yet it seems like the only place I ever lived."

"Do you miss it?"

"Some of it. The space, the sky, the great openness. Certain things, no." He gave a short guffaw. "Heard about the Dakota farmer who was driving in to town when one of his oxen died of sunstroke? Before he could skin him out, the wind turned around to the north and froze the other ox in his tracks."

Fry grinned.

"In the towns—I'm serious, now—in winter they string ropes along the sidewalk so you can haul yourself along. Cold"—he made a fist, knocked it against his forehead—"like a wrecking ball. In other seasons hailstones the size of hens' eggs. Mud and flood." He said bitterly, "The land of opportunity. There was a sign in the land office in Fort Yates— 'Where the Manless Land invites the Landless Man who knows how to farm, to come and possess it and become independent for life.' What that land did best was to break men, white and red."

There was a roar as another train approached from the opposite direction, a deafening shriek as it hurtled past, palpable blows of air and soot, for Fry the retained image of a man leaning back in a barber's chair getting a shave: a dice train, eastbound, the Deluxe. When it had passed, McLaughlin was ready.

"The Sioux," McLaughlin said. "In point of fact, not one people but a conglomeration of tribes. Three main branches, the Dakota, Nakota, and Lakota, a linguistic split. The Dakota are in Minnesota. The eastern plains of North and South Dakota are the home of the Nakota. Farther west live the Lakota, the prairie dwellers, the roughest of the bunch."

He fished a cigar out of his vest pocket. He laid it on the metal rail and, securing it there with his hand, used a penknife to cut it neatly in half; he put one half back in his pocket, placed the other half in his mouth, and, cupping his hands, lit it with a kitchen match.

"When the first white man set foot on this continent," he said, "he was predestined to come into the inheritance of the Indian. There's no use quarreling with natural law. The strong always outcompete the weak. It has been so throughout history. Thus it was foreordained that the Indian should be conquered by the white man, and so it has come to pass."

McLaughlin paused and surveyed the dim desert rushing past, and again Fry was made wary by the set of his jaw, the absolute certainty of his tone. The Major's was a mind in which there was only black and white, not a single shade of gray. And what freedom that must give you, Fry thought: the freedom of never having to doubt.

"Dakota Territory, eighteen sixty-eight," McLaughlin said. "In the three years preceding, the combined bands of Lakota Sioux have flexed their muscles and driven the whites from the new Bozeman Trail. Now the settlers are clamoring for the army to come and pacify the Sioux once and for all. But the army is still weak after the Civil War. The better alternative is to buy the Indians off.

"The Treaty of Eighteen Sixty-eight grants clear and absolute title to a Great Sioux Reservation, stretching west from the Missouri River, across Dakota Territory to the Wyoming border, a place where no whites can venture except government employees on essential Indian business. Also an Unceded Territory to the west, including large chunks of Montana and Wyoming, where the Sioux can go hunt. A permanent reservation, a place for the tribe forever. The Indians get cash, clothing, food for four years, schools and teachers, and any Indian who takes up farming receives implements, seed, a team of oxen, and a cow. All they have to do is quit picking on the other tribes and fighting with the whites.

"Most of the Lakota bands sign—the Brulé, the Minneconjou, the Oglala. One major Hunkpapa leader signs, Man-Who-Goes-in-the-Middle, also known as Gall. The other key Hunkpapas—Four Horns, Black Moon, Sitting Bull—stay away and never sign." McLaughlin removed the cigar from his mouth and rotated it between thumb and fingertips, inspecting it. Evidently it was satisfactory, for he stuck it back between his teeth.

"Eighteen sixty-eight. I was your age, maybe a few years older. Smithy in Wabasha, Minnesota. When winter came that year our finances necessitated that I leave Louise with a baby in her arms, and go sell watches, tools, household utensils, and jewelry, town to town and door to door in Kansas, Iowa, Missouri."

Fry surprised himself by interrupting—something he never did when taking dictation. "The Great Sioux Reservation. How many acres?"

"Acres, hell. Not including the Unceded Territory, ninety thousand square *miles*. For twenty-five thousand Indians.

"In eighteen seventy-four Custer led troops on a reconnaissance of the Black Hills. The Black Hills are holy mountains to the Sioux, and within the bounds of the Great Reservation. Custer went there illegally—'a place where no whites can venture except for government employees on essential Indian business.'

"I suppose it *was* essential, however, that the government find something there that would make it too valuable for Indians to own. What Custer found was gold.

"The Army tried to keep the fortune hunters out, and the ones the Sioux found they butchered." McLaughlin leaned back in his chair and rested his feet on a crosspiece in the railing. "Don't bother taking this down. I have an article in a drawer somewhere, one of the fire-breathing editorials, believe I can recall it word for word: 'This abominable compact with the marauding bands that make war on the whites in the summer and live on government bounty all winter is now pleaded as a barrier to the development of the richest, most fertile section in America.'" He gave a fat chuckle. "It gets better. 'What shall be done with these Indian dogs in our manger? They are too lazy and too much like mere animals to cultivate the soil, mine the coal, bore the petroleum wells, or wash the gold. Having all these things, they prefer to live as paupers, fighting and torturing, hunting and gorging, dancing all night to the beating of old tin kettles.'"

He cleared his throat. "The Sioux are offered six million dollars for the Black Hills. At the council, angry mounted Lakotas, whooping and waving rifles, charge the commissioners' tent. The baldheaded white men"—McLaughlin's eyes twinkled—"make doors and windows where there aren't any. Back in Washington, resentment is expressed at the high and mighty attitude of the Sioux, fomented, it is decided, by bands of nontreaty Indians roaming in the Unceded Territory. That fall, in defiance of the Treaty of Eighteen Sixty-eight, the Army decrees that all Sioux in the Unceded Territory must return to their agencies on the reservation proper, or suffer the consequences.

"You don't budge an Indian out of a snug tipi with winter coming. So the Army went looking. The next spring, up on Rosebud Creek, General Crook hooked up with Crazy Horse and a thousand Indians. Nobody won that round.

"A week later on the Little Bighorn, Custer dashed his brains out against an immense force of Sioux and Northern Cheyenne.

"Sometime before, so the story is told, Sitting Bull sponsored a Sun Dance. He asked his blood brother Little Assiniboine to cut a hundred pieces of flesh from his arms. Little Assiniboine complied, using a knife and an awl. Thus prepared, Sitting Bull took his place in the sun, piping on his eagle-bone whistle, shuffling in the slow circle of men around the ash tree. Around and around he went, the blood dripping off his fingertips, until he collapsed and saw a vision: soldiers on horseback coming down like grasshoppers, with their heads low and their hats falling off."

McLaughlin plucked the cigar stub out of his mouth and threw it over the railing. It hit between the rails in a shower of sparks.

"On or about the day when Sitting Bull had his vision, I was installed as agent for the Upper Santee Sioux, Fort Totten Reservation, eastern Dakota Territory."

You and Sitting Bull, Fry thought, coming closer together.

"In time, the Sioux were defeated or at least subdued through starvation. The buffalo were gone, which destroyed their food supply as well as the seat of their religion. The various bands returned to their home territories, gathering around the agencies that had been set up there.

"Sitting Bull never signed the treaty selling the Black Hills. Some other Sioux, people the whites said were chiefs, sold the Hills. And soon the rest of the Great Reservation was being coveted." McLaughlin reached in his pocket for the other half of the cigar; struck a match along his trouser seam.

"There were two commissions and two treaties," he said. "One in eighteen eighty-eight, which was rejected, and rightly so, and one the following year, accepted by the Sioux.

"Eighteen eighty-eight. By then I had moved from Fort Totten to Standing Rock. With the possible exception of Pine Ridge, Standing Rock was the toughest assignment an agent could get.

"Around Fort Yates were gathered seventeen hundred Lakota of the Hunkpapa band, Sitting Bull's band. Also an equal number of Yanktonais who had been moved there from east of the Missouri and who were not Lakota at all, but were of the Nakota.

"We were the first agency the commission treated with. If the Indians at Standing Rock could be persuaded to sign, the other agencies would follow. The bill would have split the Great Reservation into six smaller and separate tracts, with the land in between opened up for homesteading. The selling price was fifty cents an acre. Highway robbery. Off the reservation settlers were giving a dollar an acre, more.

"Before the council I got John Grass and coached him. His words one afternoon, of all the thousands, still stick in my mind. 'It seems you want us to give the whole land away,' he told the commission. 'Look at our children in the schools. If you are saving anything for your children, so are we trying to save something for ours. I want to know which people will go out of existence first: the whites or the Indians? If you know that one is going to live as long as the other, you ought to listen to what we are saying.'"

McLaughlin puffed on the cigar, whose end glowed redly. "A week into council I was ordered to speak. I stood on the platform before my Indians, many of them wearing the cheap issue blankets branded with acid, USID, United States Indian Department—'Uncle Sam's Idle Devils,' the settlers said. And because I had no choice but to do my duty, I urged the Indians to sign the new treaty, wipe out the prejudices of the past, take up their allotments and farm the land. But first, under provision of the Treaty of Eighteen Sixty-eight, the consent of three quarters of the adult male Indians had to be obtained.

"The clerks passed out the papers, two to each voter, one blue and one red. The blue paper had a picture showing the commissioners shaking hands with smiling Indians, a schoolhouse with children ready to go inside, the prairie graced with shocks of wheat. An Indian accepting the treaty was to make his mark on this blue paper.

"The red paper showed the same commissioners being turned down by scowling Indians, children fleeing the school, the prairie barren and bleak. An Indian opposing the treaty was to sign this.

"The bill hadn't a ghost of a chance. My advice to John Grass, plus Sitting Bull's presence, threw it into a shambles. None would sign the papers. They just threw them on the ground and the wind blew them away.

"The next year, brand new commissioners, a brand new offer, and it was fair, dollar and a quarter an acre. Again Standing Rock was made prominent, this time as the final and deciding agency visited.

"And I did it," he said. "I turned them around. It was for their own good. The money could be held in trust, and when they had accepted their allotments it could go toward stock and seed and modern equipment, we could set them on their feet, on the road toward independence." He finished his smoke and chucked it also over the rail.

"Did they want to sell?" Fry said.

"Didn't matter."

"If they didn't want to sell, was it right to make them?"

McLaughlin frowned, turned in his chair. "If they didn't sell they'd have still lost the land. Congress was ready to take it." The level gray eyes put Fry in his place. After a while McLaughlin relaxed. "I kept expecting him to show up, but he never came. On the last day, General Crook was at the podium, and I heard hoofbeats racing in. I said to myself, Where have you been? Out in the brush making hocus-pocus? Mumbling in a sweat lodge to prairie chickens or badgers or deer?

"My police intercepted the ponies. Ten followers, a dozen, no more.

"From the change in volume I knew Crook had seen them. He said, 'I understand there have been threats made against Indians who sign this bill. Don't be afraid, because these people will not be allowed to interfere with you.'

"Sitting Bull clamped his legs on his horse's sides and rose up and called out over the heads of the crowd, 'No one told us of this council, and we only now got here.'

"Incredible as it may seem, Sitting Bull apparently had not heard about the new commission. They knew of it in Boston, New York, Washington, in every parlor in the land, and yet word hadn't gotten down to Grand River, forty miles south of Fort Yates."

McLaughlin hesitated. "I blame myself for that. I should have seen to it that he knew. If I could have convinced him that it was utterly necessary to sell the land . . ." He shrugged, and his voice resumed its normal vigorous tone. "General Crook turned to me and said, 'Did Sitting Bull know we were holding a council?'

"'Yes sir,' I said. 'Everyone knew it.' Because it had never occurred to me that it was possible he hadn't heard. I raised my hand from the tabletop so that none but John Grass should see. He came forward quickly and put his X on the ballot. Mad Bear followed him. Then feet were churning and hooves stamping, a man yelled, a woman began to wail. I caught up the tribal roll as bodies were jostled into mine. 'Be still!' I shouted. 'Your leaders have signed this! What they have done does not bind you. Every man must do as he pleases!'

"Big Head signed, and Bear's Face. The pandemonium was general. I raised my hand again, a fist, and my policemen moved to restore order. They closed ranks around Sitting Bull and shunted him to one side.

"He rode. The vaunted Sitting Bull showed his heels and rode."

19

He finished his prayers for the souls of Imelda, Thomas, and William McLaughlin. The chapel was lit by thick white candles whose flames, unwavering, appeared unreal. Saint Francis reposed in a wooden bier, his face slick from touching, rich violet robes glittering with tin: tin legs and eyes, tin arms and heads, kneeling figures, crosses, madonnas.

Imelda: a madonna herself, a dark beauty, perfect blend of his fiery determined Scotch-Irish and Louise's self-possessed persevering Sioux. Dead these long years, these bitter years, dead in childbirth and the baby with her. William: cut down from sturdy manly health in less than a week. A blue norther, and he'd gone out in it to tend stock, and taken a chill, and now was under the sod. Tom, only this spring, drunk again, how many times had he lectured him? A fall from his horse, a broken neck, another useless death. The boys, raised on a reservation, had grown up wild as weeds. Poor Tom, dead in a ditch like a common drunk, and a father, an old father, called home to bury yet another son. In the quiet of the chapel, sequestered from the desert glare, he closed his eyes, crossed himself, and prayed again: Lord, grant peace to their souls.

Outside, he trudged across the atrium and continued through a gate. Climbing the dusty hill east of the mission, he had to stop and rest, breathing hard, a pink tinge to his vision. Finally he gained the hilltop and sat on a bench at a small shrine, looking out over the Santa Cruz Valley, which stretched away to dry, low-lying mountains, the Santa Ritas to the east, the Sierritas to south and west.

The mission lay before him, cruciform church with twin buttressed towers, pendentives and groins, bubble-like nave, all shining an immaculate eggshell white. A worker limed a wall. Two nuns walked past the dormitory wing. A man in gray crossed the atrium, left via the arched gate, and made his way across the sandy yard. In a minute he reached the Papago village, low rectangular baked-mud huts.

McLaughlin shielded his eyes. Something about the man. Yes. It was Fry. The stenographer lingered at a corral across from a woman bent at some work; he appeared to study her for a moment before moving on. His path intersected that of a Papago couple, the man in overalls, the woman pushing a wheelbarrow; again the gray figure paused, hands in his pockets, seemingly absorbed, as if pondering which way to go.

An odd one. Competent at his work, perhaps too often daydreaming or wandering off somewhere on his own. Eastern boy, raised on the dime dreadfuls. No real way of understanding how it had been. McLaughlin raised a hand to his mouth, stroked it down over his mustache. He leaned back, idly thanking Saint Xavier, whose mission it was, for the skim of clouds that had spread to blunt the sun. Closing his eyes, he dozed.

He was in the carryall behind the roan mare whose white-tipped ears made a gun sight against the sky. A moonless, starless night. Soft feminine hills, billows of sage. The mare shied as a ferret humped across the road, and he flicked the reins, spoke soothingly, brought her back to a trot. It would not do to dawdle. He checked over his shoulder: Along the horizon, lightning exploded silently.

He'd spent the day with Talking Crane. Earlier, he had learned that one of Talking Crane's wives had died. In a measure it was good news, because now the man, having only one spouse, could be accepted into the church. The dead woman, called simply Ant, was an unreconstructed savage; likely her corpse stood scaffolded somewhere on the plain.

He urged the horse on. The sweep of the western sky flickered ominously. A squall line, a big storm by the looks of it, to bring the needed rain.

He had found Talking Crane sitting on the bed, smoking. A big man, a noted warrior in his time, now flaccid and bent, with a red nose lumpy as a sack of shot. The younger wife, Plum Woman, nursed a swaddled baby; in the infidel manner she had hacked at her hair and cut flesh from the backs of her hands, mourning the departed one.

He shared the bread and cold sliced beef Louise had sent, as well as greetings from Talking Crane's children: He had saved two, in school at Fort Yates. And as he ate he watched the baby, whose black eyes followed his every move. It was through the children, not the confused, embattled adults, that the race would live.

Under clouds like rumpled bed linen he and Talking Crane chopped weeds in the garden. He always carried a hoe and shovel in the buggy; one never knew when they might prove instructive. The garden was dying from drought. The tops of the corn plants were black and withered, the tomato vines looked like baler twine. Still, they laid out a plot for potatoes, and McLaughlin urged the seeding of more alfalfa to feed a second cow. Talking Crane agreed to the improvements in the polite, infuriatingly noncommittal Lakota way.

Driving off, he had turned to look back. The house stood sad and alone, scarcely more than an outcrop on the plain. Its door listed, and from the crooked metal chimney a streamer of smoke lined parallel to the ground. Talking Crane was one of his greatest successes.

The first rumble reached his ears, like prayers in a cavernous temple. Lightning crinkled between sky and earth. He fidgeted on the seat—lightning could set the grass on fire, explode the prairie into flames. The belly of one cloud flickered, another to its right was lit, another and another until the whole sky flashed with pink and amber light. A cool current came welling through the darkness. He stopped in a grove, unhitched and hobbled the mare. He had just finished tying down the curtains when the first drops hit.

It had been a year since Shell King and Henry had been struck down. He scoffed at what some said, that Sitting Bull had sent the lightning that killed them. He climbed back onto the seat, drew the rosary from his pocket, and pulled the slicker tight. In any case Sitting Bull was half a continent away, performing with the Wild West. Reports trickled back: Cody's top attraction, everybody's favorite to revile or acclaim; he was fast friends with Annie Oakley; he was making money hand over fist. A blinding flash, an ear-splitting *bang,* and rain lashed the curtains and blew in the open front.

The face came looming, plucked eyebrows, jutting cheekbones, lank hair. The baleful, probing stare. Always a glint in those eyes, like a wolf in a pen: At any time you expected him to throw back his head and howl.

And to think the whites lionized him. Him! The single biggest impediment to Indian progress—to all progress, that of James McLaughlin included. There was no denying it, Sitting Bull stood between him and the recognition a good agent deserved.

He started at a close strike, whose flash froze the horse in a plunge. Rain sheeted, and hail rattled on the roof. Power? What power had he? The power to paralyze, demoralize. Not the power to bend God's elements to his own ends. A bolt crashed onto the rise to his left; he heard a faint ticking, smelled a hint of sulfur. *Our Father who art in heaven.* There was a loud bang above his head. *Hallowed be thy name. Thy kingdom come, thy will be done on earth, as it is in heaven.* A branch fell like a dying bird. The rain roared down, the grove lit endlessly with only an occasional dimming; the thunder so constant and deafening it seemed eerily silent. . . . *as we forgive those who trespass against us.* The ground appeared to boil, the singletree vanishing from the tip up.

Flood. Even as he realized it, he felt the carryall lurch. He tensed to jump but the back end was already sluing around. The seat tipped, he heard a loud *crack,* he was falling and the water wrapped his slicker tight and shoved him over, face-down. It filled his nose and ears. He rolled free, gasping. The carriage circled slowly, like a wounded beast. Falling backward, flailing his arms, he fought to pull away, the water shoving and shaking him, guiding his foot between the spokes. He went under again and felt the leg bending. Blessedly there was no pain. He saw Louise's face and was filled with sadness. *And lead us not into temptation.* Darkness engulfed him, a dull, steady roar. *But deliver us from evil.* Time passed, a long, uneventful stretch of it, and he heard another, fainter *crack,* was rolled over again, and came up choking for breath. Pummeled along, tearing at a clump of sage, he hauled himself to high ground. The rosary was twined with sage leaves in his hand. Lightning seared the sky; he sensed it could not touch him now. Then thunder—chord after exultant chord. He fell back, laughing, and drank the sweet rain.

The blood pounded in his temples as he rose from the bench and descended the hill to the Mission San Xavier del Bac. The church stood white against the desert. He could hear the comforting drone of children engaged in recitation. He went through the gate and stopped at the facade, a rich terra-cotta against the white walls. Above the thick mesquite door (at one time protection against Apache attack) was the portal arch, framed by reliefs of flowers and vines. A window crowned with a scallop shell, perhaps a symbol of pilgrimage, or baptism. Pilasters led his eyes to the Franciscan coat of arms. Shallow alcoves held figures, nearly effaced by rain, of female saints.

"Hello, Major."

He glanced over. "Hello, Fry."

Fry raised his face. "Look up there, on top of that scroll."

McLaughlin found it: a small sculpted animal. "A cat."

"Yes. Now look on the other side in the same place."

A mouse.

"I was talking to one of the Indians," Fry said. "He says that when the cat catches the mouse, the world will come to an end."

The expedition stopped at three reservations in a week: the Mohave Indians in Parker, Arizona, July 18; the San Carlos and White Mountain Apaches in San Carlos, Arizona, July 21; the Yuma Indians in Yuma, Arizona, July 23. At each stop there was the clanging of the train's bell, black smoke rising, people looking up, people climbing down, people cheering, derbies and boaters, round-domed Stetsons, black flat-brimmed reservation hats. Speeches, faces coppery and pale, and always flags. Flags stretched between dark hands, flags kissed. Flags charging up poles and getting stuck and jerking back down and getting untangled and hitching up again. Big ones, little ones, receding into windy blue.

Fry felt divorced from the ceremonies; increasingly they struck him as stilted and insincere. His pen marched on, setting down words and phrases that now and then stole back to whisper a grim report: red man, white man, inevitable tread of destiny, children of nature, bold but wasting race.

He could count on burning up a six-exposure plate at each ceremony. And there were other chances—on the reservations, in the desert towns, when the train stood for an hour at the station, at the Harvey Houses where the coach passengers ate. They gave their orders to the conductor, who wired on ahead, and the food would be steaming when the train pulled in, travelers and tourists and drummers and soldiers all piling out of the cars, hustling in and sitting, pitching into roast beef dinners, meatloaf platters, fried chicken, shoveling down the food, waiting for the gong that said the train was poised to go.

He had polished his technique. The oblique approach, the barest pause (head turned as if his attention were elsewhere), the subtle click, turning and moving away again, on the prowl.

Nervous? Yes, and sometimes downright scared. Like when he shot three bindle stiffs crouched over a coffee fire near the tracks. They saw him and came up the bank like mean dogs, and he knew again the stomach-churning fear. But all they wanted was spare change, and he jingled a silver trickle into each cupped palm, and when they stood there, heads bent, poking at it, counting their take, he shot them again.

He grew confident. Confident, but not cocky. Get cocky, you'll leave your kit in the bathroom or a photo on your desk, a round photograph like a staring eye—and everything will blow sky-high.

20

Bullbats were booming in the rosy dawn, and she stopped her loading to watch. The dark birds fluttered up, higher and higher in the sky, on pointed, raked-back wings; they would level off, hold themselves in place for a moment, and then dive, pulling out at ground level, making their weird buzzing sound, soft and raucous at the same time.

She harnessed the team and climbed up. She meant to be under way before the heat came on; it would take most of the day to get back. She wrapped the reins around one gloved hand, took up the whip, popped it above the right horse's haunch. "Giddap." You're as lazy as I am, she thought. She drove until she came to the twin ruts of Gilpin Road. She let herself through four Morman gates, received a long, hard stare at the ranch house she passed, turned onto the main route leading back to the school. She was not sure if it was Sunday or Monday; she had meant to keep track and had made pencil marks on the wagon bed, but she might have missed a day here or there. If it was Monday, she was late.

When she pulled into the compound, all was quiet, which gave no real hint as to which day of the week it was. Breakfast at seven (cooked cereal, sugar, whole milk), classes in the morning, dinner at noon (easily digested foods like macaroni and cheese, bread pudding, a little unspiced meat), a rest period from one to two, more classes, a recess during which suitable games were played, supper at six of more bland, filling food (and they'd better eat it all, or the matrons would see to it that they did), study time until eight, then bed. It was quiet every day at Lapwai.

A teacher was leaving the green-painted school—Mary Kelce, a Shinnecock from New York, tart of tongue, stuck on herself; she stopped and gave Annie a sidelong stare. Mr. Gable was taking out the trash; dependable old soul, he gave her his usual cheerful wave. Two nurses walked across the porch of the ward, in peaked caps, white dresses, and clopping white shoes.

She stopped next to the office and got down, brushed off her Levi's, and slung her hat onto the bed. She ran a hand through her hair, windblown and full of dust and sticks. Taking a deep breath, she marched up the stairs. The tear-off calendar on the wall said Tuesday.

"Is Mr. Siebert in?"

The secretary gave her a watery smile. "Why, yes he is. If you'll just wait, please." She went away and came back. "He's busy at the moment, but he'll see you in a while."

She waited. Half an hour passed. It was strange to sit in a chair, inside a room. The globes of the hanging lamps looked like dead pigmentless flowers. She heard the power plant rumbling across the compound. She wondered, idly, what she looked like. In all that time, she had forgotten the features of her face. Then her thoughts turned to faceless things, souls.

So many questions. How does it vacate the body? Supposing that the mouth, in death, claps shut: Does the soul slip through the nose, splitting in twain, merging again past the nostrils, rising like a cloud? Or does it pass through the blasted chest unimpeded? Old Foam was sure where souls went: to Father McLaughlin's Milky Way, which was Foam's Wanaghi Tachanku, the Trail of the Dead. That great mass of glowing, twinkling suns split into two branches, one branch spreading gloriously across the heavens, the other branch turning after a short distance and fading away to a faint cloud. At the point in the trail where the branches split, Foam said, the Arbiter stood holding a feathered wand. The Arbiter inspected each soul for blemishes, which revealed impurities and sins. If a soul had but few blemishes, the Arbiter pointed his wand toward the long trail, at whose end the traveler found a lush paradise, a happy hunting ground. If the soul had too many blemishes, the Arbiter pointed at the short trail, which ended at a cliff. The ill-fated soul fell over it and went tumbling for all time.

The secretary, whose name, oddly enough, she could not now recall, smiled at her again. "We were so worried about you, dear." She shook her head. "Imagine! A woman all alone in that wilderness."

What had they expected? For her to vanish? Her soul to whisper out of her body, haunt the earth like a shadow, float up to God in heaven or sojourn among the stars? She stood and strode toward the office, past the secretary, who frowned and said, "Well I never . . . ," opened the frosted glass door, clicked it shut.

His head did not budge, although his eyes, behind the round lenses, moved up, studied her for a moment, then returned to his writing. His pate was as dark and shiny as the bottom of an apple-butter jar. His pen scratched as he wrote.

"Miss *Owns* the Fire," he said finally. "Please be seated."

She remained standing.

"We had *just* about given up on you." He raised his face: small glittery eyes, a high forehead, an undershot chin. He was some brand of Eastern Indian, she wasn't sure which, with a strange way of emphasizing his speech. "You're two *days* overdue. That fact, however, has had no special influence on my decision."

"I'm going home."

"Mr. Gable and some of the *other* men wanted to form a search party, but I said no, she's a *capable* young woman, if not a very responsible one, quite able to take care of herself."

"I'm going home."

"I know." He pulled another page in front of him, signed it, and set it on a stack. "You just said." He replaced his pen in its holder. "It's in the best interest of the school for you to go. I don't know what you plan to do. Nor do I care. If you find some way of remaining in the Indian Service, my *evaluation*"—he slid a sheet across the desk—"will make it unlikely that you should ever rise to a position of real responsibility again."

He took off his glasses. Without them his eyes were large, soft, and brown. "Yesterday, when you should have been here, Ike Catches passed away. The nurses say he asked for you."

She nodded.

"Ellen Ramirez has gone into the ward. She's very weak and despondent. She has a deep and abiding *conviction* that you've been eaten by a bear."

"I want to see them all."

"You may stay, Miss Owns the Fire, until your replacement arrives. There's a new graduate out of Carlisle. I've sent for him already." He put his glasses back on, picked up his pen. His eyes, reduced again to tiny glitters, focused on hers. "You will assume your normal teaching load. And no more of that *Indian* nonsense. The old ways are primitive and fortunately are dying out. It behooves us all to let them pass away quietly."

Ellen Ramirez had acute tuberculosis—"galloping consumption"—and all who visited her or any other patient in the ward donned a hospital gown and mask. There were ten beds in the room, but Ellen was the only patient. She was a long-faced, stick-armed girl of twelve from Laguna Pueblo, New Mexico.

"Miss Owns the Fire," she whispered. Her eyes were bright and feverish. Her words sounded like insects trying to eat their way out of a punky log.

"Ellen, I came back. I didn't get eaten by any old bear."

Ellen's lips made a faint smile. She tried to sit up but fell back on the bed, coughing violently. When the spell passed, sweat stood along her hairline and in the hollow at the base of her neck.

"I'll stay," Annie said. She took the girl's hand.

She slept sitting up in the chair, waking every time the child was wracked by coughing. With great effort, Ellen elbowed herself up to deposit her bloody sputum in the papier-mâché spittoon Annie held out for her, which later would be burned. The coughing weakened her further. Her body contracted into a fetal *N*, her limbs rigid and trembling. She gripped Annie's hand. Ellen's stare traveled through Annie's sorrowing black eyes, through the green-painted walls, through the night, through hills and mountains and mesas, to a place Annie knew not where. Toward morning, she felt Ellen let go.

21

In Los Angeles Fry had his plates developed and printed, and mailed a new batch of photographs to Kravitz. To Miss Etta Deemer, RFD, Anadarko, Okla., he sent a postal card, a view of the Steel Pier with the Pacific sparkling in the background. Inspired, he took a streetcar to the Steel Pier, rented a bathing suit with straps over his shoulders, changed in a little white house, and waded through the surf. He swam out beyond the breakers, where he lay on his back and floated, looking up at the sun. The ocean rocked him in its gentle blood-swell. It gurgled and whispered in his ears. He swam back in and lay on his towel in the sand, and no one talked to him, no one knew his name. He decided he would never tell anyone about his camera, he would never get caught, would always be one step ahead, his pictures would become famous, they would change the way people looked at themselves and at the world.

And maybe they were doing just that, if he could believe Kravitz's latest letter. The photographs were exciting indignation: indignation at living conditions on the reservations, indignation that anyone would photograph another person unawares. Other photographers, Kravitz wrote, were trying to get the same effect, though no one else had come close, no one else was so good, so natural, so invisible at his craft. Aboard Signet, the candids had become yesterday's news; Dixon and Booth grumbled a bit whenever their clipping service forwarded the *Dispatch*, but, since Fry had refrained from sending any more pictures that showed expedition members, they soon lost interest in the quirky photographs. Even Cribbs's letters had lost some of their bite.

The situation looked good. Then two things happened on the coast to remind Fry how vulnerable he really was.

The first occurred in San Francisco. The expedition had returned from Round Valley Reservation early one mid-August day. Morning fog was shredding itself over the bay, and the hills bustled with wagons and men, bristled with scaffolds and forms, bricks and girders rising, the city re-building itself after the earthquake and fire of '06.

The next day at breakfast Dixon announced: "There is in this city a curiosity that we must see."

They caught a trolley, which rang its gong and whined on the upgrade, spraying brilliant blue sparks where its rigid steel umbilicus kissed the wire overhead. The conductor stomped on a bell in the floor beside him to make people get out of the way. When the car arrived at Parnassus Heights, dust and sand clouded with a *phoosh* from its brakes. The affiliated colleges were three brick buildings: dentistry and pharmacy, the hospital, the museum of anthropology. At the museum a guard pointed out an office. Inside, a tall, loose-limbed bearded man stood on top of a desk, reading from a book; high on the shelf above him, a gap in the tomes.

"Professor Kroeber?" Dixon said.

The man looked down, startled, replaced the book, stepped like a stork from desk to chair to floor, and clasped Dixon's hand in both of his. "Doctor Dixon, pleased to meet you."

"May I introduce my companions? This is Major James McLaughlin, Inspector, Bureau of Indian Affairs."

"Professor," McLaughlin said, shaking hands. "Our office has been in touch, relative to your 'wild Indian.'"

"Yes," Kroeber said coldly. "And you can't have him. We found him first, he's ours and he'll stay that way."

Turning on his heel, the professor led them down a corridor. He shot back over his shoulder: "Do you all know Ishi's story?"

"The Major and I," Dixon replied, hurrying to keep up, "but the younger men do not."

Kroeber entered a gallery where urns and pots stood in tall glass cabinets, two dugout canoes sat on the floor, and a totem pole leered from the corner. He stopped before a display case. "Ishi's arrow-making kit." Tiny arrow points, a chunk of deer antler, deerskin rag, shards of flint and glass: blue glass, as from a bottle.

"Milk of magnesia?" Fry said.

Kroeber stared at him. "Mister . . . ?"

"Fry."

"Aha! The ethnologist Lucien Fry from Princeton?" Fry admitted he was not. "Well, you are an observant man, none-theless." Kroeber indicated the blue-glass shards. "All those years he was hiding, Ishi got the glass for his arrow points from trash heaps and dumps." He pointed out a salmon harpoon, a deer-head decoy, a quiver. "The quiver is an otter skin. Note the four holes in the head. Two are the eyes, the other two are where the harpoon went in"—the professor made a snicking sound, jabbed one finger between thumb and forefinger of his other hand—"and came out.

"Two years ago this month," he said, "a man, or rather a vestige of a man—starving, filthy, naked except for a canvas scrap about his shoulders—was discovered at dawn, crouch-ing in the corral of a slaughterhouse near Oroville, a hundred miles north of here. Thank God the butchers didn't shoot him. They telephoned the sheriff, who approached with guns at the ready. He found what he deduced to be a wild man. The man did not resist arrest.

"He had committed no crime, but the sheriff thought the jail would be the best place for him, which it turned out to be when the press and the curious descended.

"'The Wild Man of Oroville,' 'The Least Civilized Man in

America,' transported suddenly from the Stone Age into the twentieth century. When we heard the news, we realized he must be a Yahi, a Mill Creek Indian, as the settlers called them." Kroeber pushed a finger through his beard. "The native Indian population of California was one hundred thousand in eighteen fifty-three. Three years later, with the Gold Rush, forty-eight thousand remained. Thirty thousand in eighteen sixty-four, perhaps twenty thousand left today. And the last, the very last wild one, here with us."

He set off again, trailing words. "In a canyon, in the foothills below Mount Lassen, Ishi and a handful of others survived. Their band was small, never more than a dozen, and no one knew they existed. A good three decades since the tribe had been assumed wiped out. They fished for salmon, hunted rabbits and deer, and gathered acorns and wild plants. They hid. And as the years passed, one after another, they died." Kroeber stopped. "Finally, only Ishi was left. He was the last of his people. When it became too much to bear, he left his canyon and headed south.

"He was dazed when they found him. He didn't belong in jail, being neither dangerous nor insane. So we adopted him. Charming fellow, really. He lives at the museum, gainfully employed"—Kroeber nodded perfunctorily to McLaughlin—"as a janitor. His salary is twenty-five dollars a month, of which he saves more than half. He also gives demonstrations to visiting groups."

He turned and clapped his hands. "Ishi!"

The Indian was sweeping out a cloakroom. He emerged slowly, nudging a push broom, a man of middle stature, moon-faced, clad in tan work clothes. He looked to be about forty years old. Plump. A wide, full mouth and timorous black eyes. A womanish face, thought Fry. Ishi's skin was a light reddish bronze, and his hands were small but strong-looking, with straight, tapering fingers.

Booth was the closest. He grabbed Ishi's hand and pumped

it. "Ishi, old sport," he boomed, "pleased t' meetcha." When Booth released his hand, the Indian stood with a panicky expression on his face, his arm frozen in midair. Then Kroeber introduced the others, Ishi shaking hands timidly, and softly saying "Howdado" to each.

Kroeber beamed at his charge. "One evening, Ishi and Dr. Pope, of the hospital faculty, went to Buffalo Bill's Wild West. After the show one of the Indians came up, a tall Sioux in war paint and a feather bonnet. He studied Ishi in silence. Then he asked, in perfect English, 'What tribe of Indian is this?' 'Yahi,' Pope replied, 'from northern California.' The Sioux picked up a strand of Ishi's hair and rolled it between his fingers. He peered into Ishi's face. 'This is a very high grade of Indian,' he said."

Kroeber led them outside onto grounds shaded by eucalyptus trees. The professor stepped back as Ishi bent over his fire tools. The drill was wood, the length of an arrow shaft and thick at one end; this end Ishi fitted into a socket in a shingle-size flake of wood. Holding the drill upright, its shaft between his palms, he began rubbing his hands back and forth, the drill twirling one way, then the other. When his hands had worked their way down the shaft, he suddenly let go and darted them to the top—the drill standing unsupported for a split-second—and commenced rubbing again. Soon smoke curled from the socket. The drill blurred, the smoke thickened. A tiny flame blossomed in a tuft of thistledown. Laying the drill aside, Ishi placed a wad of dry grass on the tinder and blew gently. Fire was made. His audience applauded. People passing in the park looked up.

Ishi grinned. "Evelyboddy hoppy?" He straightened and walked directly to Fry and looked into his eyes. Their gazes met on the level. He smelled of phenol and honey and dust. "'*Ishi*' means 'man' in the Yahis' language," Kroeber was saying. "Not his real name, of course; like most Indians he would never reveal his true name, fearing a loss of identity."

Ishi stood, staring. His forehead crinkled, and Fry instantly remembered Kravitz's face on the porch of the rooming house, the day Kravitz found him out. Seconds passed, and still Ishi stood regarding Fry, staring first at his eyes, then lower, at his chin, his shoulders, his chest, lower still, finally fixing on the center of his torso, on the shielding vest—as Fry came near to turning and running. The Indian, with his primitive man's sharp hearing, had he heard the shutter click?

Ishi reached out. Yes, Fry thought, he is going to touch the camera. Suddenly he felt quite calm. He raised his own hand, his fingers intercepting Ishi's. The two hands paused, touching lightly. Kroeber was still lecturing. "He will answer to 'Ishi' but he will not say it aloud." Fry sought to interweave his fingers with Ishi's, and Ishi allowed it. Fry felt a quickening sensation throughout his body, as if Ishi bore in his system some special humor, which he was now passing on through the conduit of their hands.

Ishi, with his black eyes, probed Fry's blue ones. What is it like for him, Fry wondered. What does he feel, stranded in this humming city—alone?

"It is as if he has now *become* Ishi," Kroeber said, "become, simply, 'man.'"

"Is evelyboddy hoppy?" Ishi said.

The second incident occurred two weeks later and had nothing to do with photography.

The air was cool and wet and gray. Tall firs and hemlocks shaded the grounds where the Indians had gathered, young Eastern-educated men in suits and cravats and stickpins, old big-bellies with gray mustaches and broad flat faces. Siletz, Clackamas, Rogue River, Umpqua, and Yamhill tribes. The elders did a feather dance, whirling, bending, chanting. After the ceremony, Fry and McLaughlin took a walk.

The road tunneled through a forest where rank scents of bark and woodsmoke hung in the damp air. Ravens rattled from the green spires, squirrels chittered; somewhere a band saw whined.

Hooves pounded on the road behind them, and McLaughlin, without looking back, sprang instantly off the berm. "Fry!" he shouted. As Fry leaped, he felt something hard and massive brush lightly against the heel of one shoe. Sprawling, he caught a corner-of-one-eye glimpse of the horse and rider racing on past.

"Bastard!" McLaughlin shook his fist at the vanishing horseman. He bent and picked up Fry's hat. Fry crouched on hands and knees, gasping for breath: The camera, driven into his solar plexus, had knocked the wind out of him. He choked some air into his lungs, fought his way to one knee. McLaughlin, still sputtering curses, moved to brush the pine duff from Fry's coat, but Fry got quickly to his feet and turned away. He ran his hands over pant legs, sleeves, lapels, chest, feeling the camera—intact, he hoped—beneath his vest.

"You all right?"

"Think so."

"You're out of breath. Hold still for a minute. There. You've cut your chin."

Fry took the handkerchief the Major offered and dabbed at the cut. He turned back to McLaughlin. "Why was he . . . scorching like that?"

The worry was slowly draining out of McLaughlin's face. "If he was Sioux, I'd say his heart was poor."

"I saw him at the ceremony. Quiet, nondescript old man."

McLaughlin climbed back onto the road and peered down it. "I think he's gone. Let's get back."

They walked quickly for a ways, slower as the fear left them.

"You never can tell," McLaughlin said. "You never can tell. I remember once on the reservation. It was March. A chinook had come up, thawing the snow and opening the creeks. The river was still frozen, and the muddy meltwater ran on top. Around the buildings the drifts had rotted and shrunk back.

"A magpie landed on a branch. I hadn't seen a magpie in months; I turned my head to watch it, and as I did I saw an Indian standing behind me in the street.

"He had a blanket wrapped around him, his face hidden behind a fold of the robe. A boy. But who? There were so many, and their names changed so often, that even if I'd recognized him I would have been hard-pressed to call his name.

"The wind had been shifting all morning, coming around to the north again, and a chill was in the air. I turned up my collar and blew on my hands. And still the boy stood staring."

McLaughlin blinked rapidly. He shuddered slightly and knit his shoulders together as if cold. "I saw it, then: the muzzle, sticking down below the robe. I turned and slogged ahead toward the porch. I think I only half-believed I was in trouble, because when I saw the new clerk, Kemp, who was not working out to my satisfaction, lounging on the porch, I told myself I'd have a word with the oaf.

"I kept walking. My boots grew heavy with mud. Kemp looked past me, and his eyes bugged out and his jaw dropped.

"I turned sideways to make a smaller target. The muzzle wobbled absurdly. With an aim like that he was as apt to smash Kemp in the forehead, or break a window, or take the heel off my boot. The boy ached to pull the trigger but wasn't man enough. The muzzle slumped, crept up again, steadied. Good new repeater. The bore looked big as my thumb. Hunkpapa boy, I recognized him vaguely, from the old Sitting Bull band.

"I heard the Lakota words, then. She spoke them steadily, neither scolding nor pleading, as a younger sister might address an older brother. Behind me Kemp snuck through the door. The magpie took off from its perch. The street was empty, except for the boy and the girl, who kept talking. Her words were reasoned and distinct. I knew the words, but it was as if my brain had frozen, and the words flowed over it like meltwater over ice.

"She kept on, speaking evenly, steadily, respectfully, until finally the boy dropped the gun in the mud and stumbled away.

"She stood there in the alley." McLaughlin stopped; half-raised, then dropped, his square-fingered hand. "I lifted her up and buried her face in my neck." He looked at Fry through wide eyes. "Couldn't have been more than five or six. Little slip of a girl. My daughter. She'd saved me, you see. I held her, and rocked her, and could feel her heart beating. I held her tightly, and she shivered in the wind."

One shoulder moved in a slow shrug. "Never learned the boy's name. Never tried to find out. His heart was poor. All the props knocked out. No more buffalo, no horse-raiding, no Sun Dance or war with the Crows. No way for a young man to test his mettle or a grown man to keep his name."

They were back within sight of the school; children played on a swing set in a pale light that trickled down around the evergreens' shadows. "After they had signed," McLaughlin said, "after the Great Reservation was broken up, after the crops failed God knows how many years in a row, after the government reneged and cut rations again—after the Ghost Dance came and went—the hearts of many were poor."

"Your daughter," Fry said. "Her name?"

"Annie Owns the Fire."

It hit him like a horse ridden flat-out down a pine-duff road. *The name on McLaughlin's card in the file drawer back in Washington. The woman Trimble asked me to greet.* He thought of the photograph, his photograph, stuck behind the mirror frame in McLaughlin's room.

"Where does she live?"

"Idaho," McLaughlin said. "She teaches at Lapwai in the TB sanitarium. We'll be there soon."

22

Someone clapped down a step stool, and McLaughlin took her arm and helped her board. She wore a maroon suit with a silver brooch at the collar, a black coat, and a black straw skimmer of a type known as a Merry Widow. The porter took her luggage, which consisted of a hatbox, two wicker suitcases, and a battered leather-faced rectangular case that looked as if it might contain a musical instrument.

Booth and Fry stood on the platform watching.

"You say McLaughlin raised her," Booth said. "A fine piece of ass."

Fry colored.

"I'll be in her bloomers, time we hit Bismarck." Booth fingered an earlobe, his upper lip drawn back. "Small Fry, your average Indian maiden fucks like a mink."

Annie Owns the Fire was of medium height, broad-shouldered, straight of carriage, and with a womanly figure. Her waist did not appear to be girdled but was nevertheless slim—not a "bowling-ball squaw" as Booth called them. She had a rather large nose and a strong chin, symmetrical lips that stood out darkly against the surrounding skin, hair so black it seemed to have some of the magpie's purple in it. Fry had shaken her hand, which was dry, curiously rough, and firm of grip.

After introducing himself, he said, "Billy Trimble asked me to say hello to you"—the words came spilling out, he swallowed and awkwardly added—"from him."

Her face lit. "Billy! You've seen him?"

"He's married and has a little boy. He clerks in a store on the Navaho reservation."

"Back on the res, eh?" She half-smiled. "He used to say he was going to travel. Alaska, China, Japan. But you say he's all right?"

"Right as rain."

She nodded. "And you're the stenographer."

"Yes. I . . ." He cleared his throat. "I take down the speeches."

She smiled again. "Of course. Isn't that a stenographer's job? I learned shorthand myself."

"Pitman?"

"Gregg. Though I suspect I've forgotten it by now."

Then Booth had come shouldering in, tipping his hat, enveloping her hand in his. Booth had held the handclasp for about five seconds too long while tendering his introduction; she had stood, waiting patiently, until he let go. Then she had turned, caught up the hem of her dress, and allowed McLaughlin to guide her up the steps.

The locomotive clanged its bell; steam leaked from nozzles and pipes, and brownish-tinged smoke plumed from the stack. The conductor called "Bo-o-o-ard!" and doors slammed and people hurried, footfalls ringing on the platform. Booth and Fry climbed up.

There was a certain degree of agitation in the car. Giannetti poked his head into the passageway, ducked it back. The steward, shoving a Carpet Cat, stopped and stared, then remembered himself and backed, nodding prolifically, against the wall. She was shown the spare stateroom, the one the Bureau rented and the one Fry had long coveted but which had been kept vacant for visiting dignitaries, superintendents, district supervisors, and the like; she went in without a word and without closing the door. The others trooped behind McLaughlin down the hall. Dixon stood in the dining room, half-glasses draped over his nose, his portraits fanned on the damask tablecloth.

McLaughlin was gruffer, more formal than need be. "My daughter, Miss Owns the Fire, has been posted to a new school in South Dakota. Please inform the Pullman Company. The Bureau will absorb any additional expense. It is deemed that the interim trip will prove educational for her."

Dixon blinked and folded his glasses. She came in then, hat and overcoat left behind, face somewhat hawkish in profile, her movements controlled and graceful, suggesting a fineness of form beneath her skirt. Those mounds under her shirtwaist—are they starched frills on the cover of a corset, Fry wondered, or breasts? Well, he might ask Booth someday. Although—and the thought brightened him considerably— what was it Trimble said? Tighter than a bull's ass in fly time.

"Miss Owns the Fire." Dixon beamed and shook her hand. "You're a schoolteacher?"

"That's right."

"Education, my dear Miss Owns the Fire. I've said it before and I'll say it again. I have, I hope, given it proper due in the speeches delivered on the expedition thus far. Education is the star that will guide the Indian into the future."

"I couldn't agree with you more."

"And you're a Carlisle graduate?"

"Yes." Sober pause. "'Fitted for efficient service,' I believe is how they put it in the school paper."

"Welcome aboard the Rodman Wanamaker Expedition of Citizenship to the North American Indian."

"My pleasure, I'm sure." She glanced down at the photographs on the table.

"Go ahead, my dear, take a look."

Fry saw that Dixon had been building up quite a collection. Navahos, Hopis, Havasupai mother and child, Hupa boy and girl, Cherokees, Choctaws, Chickasaws, great mixed batch from the Northwest, a frog-eyed Comanche name of Bayard

Looking Glass, Fry remembered him, shiny-faced and obese, with a black silk neckerchief and string-wrapped braids. The controlled studio lighting, nose tips a bit dewy, ears out of focus there at the back, blemishes and smallpox scars smoothed away with Giannetti's Gray Value Four, the eyes chipped-obsidian sharp.

"Did you take them?" She looked at Dixon as if seeing him for the first time.

"After each ceremony I try to obtain photographs of representative individuals from each tribe. The images will be on display in the museum to be built in association with the Indian memorial."

"They're very fine."

Yes, Fry thought, very fine indeed—for portraits. These people had pride and identity intact. Yet there was about them that inevitable stiffness. His own photographs, crude by comparison, were fluid, seemingly on the verge of change, less a record of a person's features or clothing or an event than a sliver of time. A viewer fifty years hence might look at Dixon's work and say, "Superb Indian photographs," or "Magnificent types." Fry hoped that the same viewer would look at his candids and realize that the people of 1913— Indians, whites, rich, poor, townsmen, countryfolk—had been just that: living, breathing people, not masks from some dim, distant past.

Annie took the chair next to Dixon and began chatting with him; McLaughlin grudgingly sat too.

Would she like his pictures? Watching her from a seat in the corner, Fry suddenly thought it important.

That night he lay in his berth as the train shook and clattered and howled.

Indians.

No longer did they seem charged with mystery and romance. Some were dignified and peaceful, others were angry and violent, wry, grim, stupid, intelligent, sullen, talkative, cautious, self-destructive. . . . Being people, fate had set them onto paths and wrenched them off again. Like the rest of us they must strive, waver, want, love, die. It seemed wrong to call them a vanishing race: He had seen their thousands, babies and children, young men and women—here a vision of Annie Owns the Fire came to him, her strong cheekbones and straight white teeth, faintly almond-shaped eyes with irises so dark he couldn't tell where they left off and the pupils began; eyes that were frank and forthright, that had seemed to admit his, yet hadn't quite, an outer door opening to reveal an inner one.

He tossed off the blanket, dropped down, and unlocked his trunk. He got out a sheaf of photographs, the next ones he would send. He flicked on the reading light recessed in the ceiling above his bed. Back in his berth, propped up by a pillow, he began turning through the pictures. Gradually he grew disheartened. These people, these strangers: What could he really know of them? A crooked smile: happiness? defiance? irony? fear?

He stared at the dark, ripple-edged sheets whose round images he had supposed to be mirrors on life. Maybe the mirrors were crazed. He dredged up a conversation he'd had with McLaughlin, weeks back. The Major had asked him, point-blank and out of the blue, "What do you think of the candid photographs?"

For a moment he had been speechless. Then he had said, impulsively, probably incautiously, "I like them." The Major squinted doubtfully. "They're real," Fry went on. "They're life."

"But are they?" McLaughlin countered. "Why did he pick that one instant to trip the shutter? Why then, and not ten seconds—ten minutes—ten hours later?"

Yes, certainly he chose the moment to freeze the frame. So

maybe each picture did end up being his own interpretation of the world, a minuscule blink at an infinite, never-to-be-grasped whole. People said that a picture was worth a thousand words. But sometimes a thousand pictures were required for a single word. Could a picture convey grief or joy, love or despair? Could anything less human, less ephemeral, than a dance, a song, a cry?

Her face came back then, tantalizingly strong. He thought of her sleeping thirty feet and two compartments away. He looked at the photograph in his hands, a real humdinger. Two women in San Francisco, backed by one of those fine ornate hillside houses that somehow had survived the quake and fire. He was shocked at how close he must have been. The woman in the foreground was tying a scarf around her neck, eyes half-shut in concentration, the brocade on her sleeve blurred it was so near the lens, while the woman behind her, hair pulled back under a wide-brimmed, flower-bedecked hat, looked impatient, head cocked and lips flattened, maybe thinking, Hurry up, you silly goose, we'll be late.

His photograph, his candid photograph, one of those singular images that had become such a part of his life. He hoped the picture would survive. He hoped someone would see it, and seeing it, know himself a bit better, and knowing himself, know life better. Grab for it. Love it. Cry for it. Burn with it. He said her name softly: "Annie Owns the Fire." Somehow, he thought she would understand.

She was new life injected into Signet. She was the stewards' darling. They loved to shine her shoes (to their dismay she had but one fancy pair), wait on her, joke with her, cook her favorite meals, smell her scent as they made up her bed. From the start she was on a first-name basis with Benny, Ansel, Sam. Not too talkative, a good listener; like a child she seemed to weigh every statement, every question, every wisecrack and pun, seemed to take it all in, consider it, and respond—or not—with candor.

If Fry and the others were glad to have her on board, McLaughlin's feelings were mixed. She was coming home, he thought, in disgrace. And she tugged at his memory a bit too insistently, making him recall things he was only slowly working around to. Like the dim winter day in the aftermath, when he and Louise had gone to the cabin, into the head-cracking stench, the stove dead and the coffeepot frozen, door cracked so that any mongrel could have trotted inside and found her there on the baby board, dragged her down and eaten an arm, a leg, a face, as had already happened that winter to a child in another camp. Hardly even fussing she was—too weak, just as Louise had suspected; the mother, Fidelity, nowhere to be found.

He shoved all of that away.

Leaning close to the window, he cupped his hands around his face, stared out into darkness at a mountain lake like mercury in the moonlight, behind swift-marching black trees. Just as quickly, lake and trees vanished and he saw a vast, sunlit plain. Even smelled it. Like fresh-toasted bread. Grass waving, grass whispering, grass running like fur under the hand of the wind. When he had been new on Standing Rock, the Bureau had sent a circular stating that if each farmer, in the course of breaking the sod, were to plant ten trees, enough rainfall soon would be generated to make the country dependably lush: "Rain follows the plow. Toiling with his hands, man can persuade the heavens to yield their treasures of dew and rain. The polished raindrop never fails to fall in answer to the power of labor and the imploring prayer." And he had believed it and preached it, although the logic, he now knew, had been every bit as warped as that of the dance.

Wanaghi wachipi, the Dance of Souls Departed, the Ghost Dance. It had shaken him to his core, tested his wisdom and competence, his determination and strength, as they had never been tested before. It had finished Sitting Bull, swept away Owns the Fire, destroyed Fidelity, and given him Annie.

He leaned back from the window and was present in the observation room again. Fry sat at his desk facing his pad, held upright in a metal stand; the typewriter clicked drily.

"Fry."

"Yes, sir?"

"Leave off with that typing. Get your notebook and pull up a chair."

"They took it up against my specific orders. Took it up because they were hungry, sick, desperate, and full of guilt after selling the land."

He sat utterly relaxed, leaning back into the overstuffed settee. He had allowed himself the luxury of a glass of Irish whiskey, poured from the flask kept in a drawer in his stateroom. Two jiggers, tempered with water from the cooler; ambivalently, feeling it a waste, he had also poured a jigger for Fry, and sure enough, the boy's mouth puckered at the strong smoky taste, and after the first tentative sip he'd set the glass on the end table and hadn't touched it since.

McLaughlin tipped his own glass and let the whiskey trickle down his throat.

"They danced," he said, "because a cataleptic Paiute from Nevada said they should dance. Man claimed to be the Messiah, the Indian Christ. At one point this Judas, whose name was variously given as Wovoka, which means cutter, and Big Rumbling Belly, and Jack, I think it was Jack, Wilson—at one point this dimwit actually mustered the gall to have a white man draw up and forward to the President a proposal that if he could receive a regular salary, he would keep the people of Nevada well informed of the latest news from heaven and, whenever necessary, furnish a little rain.

"They danced because the Messiah told them to, and because the crops for two years running had failed from lack of rain. They danced because Indians always dance. The young men and women—back from Hampton and Carlisle, trained to teach and farm, to be seamstresses and carpenters and clerks, to eat like white people, pray like white people, sleep in beds and make them in the morning—they danced, and not only that, they used their English to send letters back and forth, spreading the contagion from tribe to tribe.

"They danced, in the end, because their hearts were poor."

Now the train stopped. A trainman went back, red lantern swinging. Up front, the screech and thump of a boom, a hoarse rumbling as the tender took on coal.

"In a way, Sitting Bull started it himself. This was several years earlier, when he went on tour in the East, the time my wife went along as interpreter." McLaughlin swirled the amber liquid in the glass; the fumes tickled his nose and made his eyes water. "He would work the crowds every day. He told the people that in their wars with the whites the Indians were only defending themselves and their land. He said that far from being cruel and wild, as they were always depicted, Indians were actually kindly and humane. Some were; he was not, though he would take up little babes from their mothers' arms and bounce them on his knee, fooling everyone.

"He told the whites how horrified he was at the crucifixion of Jesus. He said—with perfect sincerity, and probably with perfect truth—that if Jesus had come to the red people instead of to the whites, he would not have been mistreated, but rather loved and revered.

"So there it was, the first time ever, this notion of an Indian Christ."

Two whistle blasts, a jerk, and the cars were in motion again. The trainman trotted past, lantern jouncing, feet crunching the gravel; the crunching stopped as he swung himself up, and a door grated shut. The engine gained power, the deep, slow coughing changing over to a smooth staccato roar.

"The leaves had just begun to turn when Kicking Bear came up from Cheyenne River. We were not aware that he was on Standing Rock until he had come and gone; had we known, we would have jailed him.

"That summer, Kicking Bear said, he had taken the Iron Horse to Nevada, where he had met with the Indian Christ. The Christ had lifted Kicking Bear into the clouds and shown him the land spread out. Herds of buffalo and antelope and elk and deer, the old camping grounds of the Sioux reaching on and on forever, not a town or road or farm or train or windmill or mine or mule or white man anywhere. The Christ said, 'The time of deliverance is at hand. All the dead Indians are now coming back, and as they return they are driving before them great herds of buffalo and elegant wild horses free for the taking.

"'The more you dance,' he said, 'the more you sing, the sooner the dead will return. And just before they come back, the Great Spirit will lift you up and cover the earth with dirt, thirty feet of it, smothering the whites beneath.'

"Although this sounds absurd and unbelievable to a rational man, the Indians believed it." He paused.

He turned to Fry and looked at him in a way that made Fry realize McLaughlin was also telling him the story, informing him, not just using him as a recorder. Fry felt a surge of affection for the man, who had based his whole life on honesty and his own particular vision of reality. He was not a personable man. Nor was Fry. And yet they had grown close. Fry felt, for an instant, a prick of guilt at the way he was using McLaughlin, standing in his shadow to make photographs McLaughlin found distasteful—even though they were honest photographs, and maybe someday he could tell the Major, somehow convey to this upright, unbending man that they were both struggling toward the same end: a revelation of truth.

"'Dance,' the Indian Christ said. You know, Fry, it was ironic, because as Wovoka proposed it, the Ghost Dance would have been a harmless enough thing. Dance, but in the meantime tend to your farms, keep the peace, send your children to school—wait for the millennium to come to pass. But the Sioux had never been good at waiting. And Kicking Bear added some attractive embellishments to the story.

"The dancing, he said, would bring wind and fire to annihilate the whites. Some of the whites, the best of them, would be turned into tiny fishes in the streams. Kicking Bear showed Sitting Bull's people how to do the dance, taught them the songs and helped them make the sacred garments, the shirts and dresses that were bulletproof. He told them the whites had lost the secret of making gunpowder. The powder the whites had would no longer burn. But the powder the red people had would burn and kill."

Burn and kill: Suddenly it rocked McLaughlin, he was afraid of going too far, too fast. Fact, event; cause, effect; rational decision, inevitable outcome. He lifted the glass and slugged down the remaining whiskey. It burned his throat and arrived, glowing, in his belly.

Fry sat, his pen waiting.

McLaughlin relaxed again, sinking back into the glow. He sensed he would finally sleep well tonight. He glanced at Fry's glass. "You going to drink that or not?"

Fry nodded. He raised the glass and emptied it at a draught, shivered involuntarily, and blinked back tears.

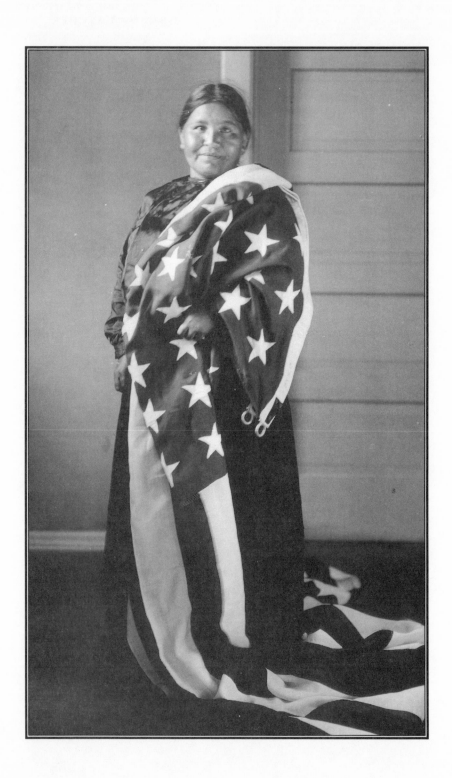

23

She sat on the porch with Mrs. Hay, the superintendent's wife, who was gaunt and twisted as a locust post, and was not well, but this was one shindig she said she wouldn't miss, a chance to put on Sunday best and get out of "if you'll pardon my French, Miss Owns the Fire, that *damned* sickbed." Annie had helped her dress, and fixed her hair, the pompadour of dry static-filled gray drawn up high over a pad, tortoiseshell combs to hold the arrangement in place, on top a dusty black hat trimmed with ostrich feathers.

The school band played a Sousa march. When they broke into a faintly recognizable rendition of "Carry Me Back to Old Virginny," Mrs. Hay dabbed at her eyes with an oft-mended lace handkerchief. "How beautiful," she said. "Arthur and I hail from the Old Dominion, do you know."

The agency lay next to the town of Browning, Montana. At the station the Blackfoot Indian police had met the train and checked the disembarking passengers to see that no liquor was brought onto the reservation. The police were tall, solid men with haughty ways. They wore black hats and dark blue uniforms with silver stars on their breasts, the familiar five-pointed stars with little globs softening the tips. When Annie was a girl and drew a star in school, she had always made it like that: five arms, each with the little glob at the tip. Then the teacher explained that stars were not really shaped like police badges but were, according to the scientists, round like the sun, only more remote.

She saw to it that Mrs. Hay had enough comforters on her lap. It was a bright but cool day. Dixon occupied the dais on the stand in the center of the square.

His fine, fervent words mesmerized her, as did his hands, pale soft doves that described decorous circles, clasped together in harmony, fluttered up again in quest of that reachable goal, then settled thumbs tucking under his arms. "I pray you, my brother Indians, be loyal to this flag. Stand by these stars and stripes. Men have given their lives to keep this glorious banner from trailing in the dust. I want you, through loving this flag, through serving it, to realize the goal of becoming citizens of the United States."

With him stood Father McLaughlin. She had not seen him for two years, since the time he had come to Lapwai on inspection—she had known without him saying it that he had arranged the trip to see her. She had always called him Father. So had the other Indians on Standing Rock, but for her it was different, he truly had been her father; in fact, she could not even remember her real father, except perhaps faintly, more a feeling than a memory, of a dark presence like a cloud on the horizon of her life, and then one day she woke up and the cloud was gone. Her mother she remembered well enough. She remembered the day that Fidelity had come to the McLaughlins' house, in a rickety wagon drawn by a paint mare, and tossed the reins carelessly over the fence. The McLaughlins had seen her in the parlor with the doors shut, and Annie had been given sweets by Imelda (who had not yet gotten married to Frank and had not gotten pregnant and thrashed in awful agony in the four-poster bed—Annie had been given sweets that day as well—until, long hours after, the house dark and quiet, the doctor had clumped down the stairs and shaken his head).

On that earlier day there must have been a screech owl in the parlor with Fidelity, calling in a spooky tremolo like they did in the river cottonwoods, and when Fidelity came out and

Annie hid behind Imelda's skirts, Fidelity screamed and twirled about and grabbed at a picture on the wall and, in falling, dragged it shattering down. The doctor was summoned, and came with his black bag but never opened it, sniffing over Fidelity, who had been put to bed on the couch, and saying in a voice that all could hear, "Nothing wrong with her that a week off the bottle wouldn't cure."

Now the thick, stern, white-haired man stood front and center on the speakers' stand. His voice, as he addressed the assembly, sounded old; brusque as usual, no real style or polish to him at all. Always his hair had been white, but now, finally, she saw him as an old man. Imelda, then William, then in the cold gray March of this year, Tom. Father cabled her please not to come, the trip was too long, she had her teaching responsibilities, Mother was taking it as well as could be expected, and she, numb at Lapwai—where she'd already had more than her fill of vacant classroom seats, undersized coffins, dry-eyed mystified children standing in ranks—guessed she had seen enough funerals to last her a lifetime, and this one for a stepbrother seven hundred miles away hadn't had enough pull. Though now she wished she had gone—not for Tom, or for Mother, but for Father, as it came to her that she loved him truly, despite their having parted ways.

The flag climbed the pole and unfurled stiffly in the wind. Then came the part she liked least, when Dixon reached into the cloth sack and threw the handful of nickels into the air. The children loved it, though, rolling in the dirt, laughing and shrieking, wrestling over the shiny coins. It stuck in her craw to see them grubbing like that. If she were honest about it, the whole ceremony stuck in her craw. As, she could tell, it did in Father's.

She got up and stood behind Mrs. Hay, whom she had not met until yesterday. She rested her hands on the woman's shoulders and, with the fronts of her thighs, gently rocked the chair.

"Thank you, Annie." Mrs. Hay reached back a twisted, wrinkled, age-dappled hand and patted Annie's strong, dark, long-fingered one. "Annie, you're a dear."

"So you met my friend Billy," she said.

"I sure did."

"Billy Trimble was the quietest, shyest boy."

"Really?"

"Oh, quiet as a mouse."

Fry frowned with his eyes while smiling with his mouth. "Way he told it, he was a real rip-roarer."

"Well," she said, "in a way I guess he was." She gave a light, inward-directed laugh. "Do you know how Billy went home?"

"He didn't say."

They were walking down the boardwalk along the main street of Browning. A real Western town with hitching rails and general stores; wagon tracks striped the broad dirt street, which divided the facing lines of buildings and gave them the look of rival gunfighters. The stores' white fronts soared into the sky, the cornices of their tall facades surmounted by faded flags whipping in the wind.

"One day," Annie said, "Billy decided to stop talking." She stopped, turned, and looked at Fry, and remained silent just long enough for him to grow uneasy. "He clammed up." Again a long silence, though now he knew what she was up to, and grinned, and earned from her a smile. "Took to his bed and lay there like a wooden Indian," she said. "No matter what they did, he wouldn't move, wouldn't say another word."

The wind, bustling down the street, brushed at the fine hairs that had escaped from under her hat. Her nose, Fry noticed, was quite long, but well formed, above dark full lips that drew back now, revealing her straight white teeth.

"I didn't see it, of course; another boy told me," she said. "Billy paid. Oh yes, he paid."

"What did they do with him?"

"Started out by slapping. 'We'll slap some sense into him,' the assistant principal said, a Mr. Madison, a fireplug of a man. The slaps turned into punches. Little punches at first, then harder ones. And still Billy wouldn't say a thing. They knew he could talk, he knew they knew it, they knew he was defying them. So he had to pay. Punches to the belly. Hard punches. Punches to the back. Punches that wouldn't bruise the skin." Her face was hard. "Mr. Madison held Billy's head in the commode and flushed it. He did this for quite some time. I was told they had to pull Mr. Madison off Billy, Mr. Madison became so exercised."

Fry sucked in a breath. That small, lithe Navaho; that bright, open man.

"Several people worked on Billy. But Billy wouldn't speak. He wouldn't eat, he wouldn't drink, he fouled himself. His urine showed blood. That discouraged them from beating him."

Fry felt sick, as if from a blow to the solar plexus, as if the camera had been driven into his gut again.

She resumed walking toward the depot. "His last year. If he'd stuck it out another month, he would have graduated. Only it was like he didn't want to graduate, he wanted to throw it all back in their faces." Frowning, she crossed her arms at her breast. "We thought about joining in. Can you imagine it? A whole school of Indians who wouldn't say a word. But we weren't as brave as Billy.

"Shy Billy. Little Billy. Not just a thorn in their side, a big jagged rock. So, thank God, they called it a 'catatonic attack' and put him on a train, strapped him to a litter in the baggage room and shipped him back to Arizona. Probably the Navahos did a sing for him. It wouldn't surprise me, he's a hero to them. Wouldn't surprise me one bit."

Fry said, "I believe he has the qualifications."

"There aren't many Indian heroes," Annie said. "At least we're not taught about them.

"We have our dead heroes, our Crazy Horses and Sitting Bulls, and our live heroes, like Chief Joseph, who put up a good fight but finally came to his senses and settled on the reservation. And people you don't hear about, like Billy." She smiled at him, and it seemed not fully a sardonic smile, despite what she had just said. "We have our heroes, and now we'll have Mr. Wanamaker's memorial." She left him then and went up the steps of the car.

Back through the town he went, brought low by the story. No doubt it was true. At least they hadn't killed him, or his spirit, either; but, good God—he swallowed hard and shook his head, as if to banish a bad dream. And came upon the aftermath of the ceremony, which had spilled over into the town, and the scene was as crisp and skewed as the next dream in a feverish sleep.

Surrounded by a chanting, clapping crowd, an Indian, his body crouched and undulating, gripped a rattlesnake in his hands. The snake's black-red tongue flicked lightning-fast. The Indian brought the head to within an inch of his lips, the crowd whooping and shouting, then opened his mouth and slowly moved the thick pale diamond inside. *Click.*

To beating drums, a dozen men shuffled in a line, belled anklets and bracelets jangling, coach-whip braids shaking, feathered shirts and leggings shimmering. One dancer wore a tall hat like a dunce cap, his cloak pieced together from scraps of an old American flag. The dancers dipped their shoulders, shot their heads back and forth, took manic little hops and spread their arms like wings; they looked like prairie chickens. *Click.*

"Just two-steppin' to beat hell."

He whirled about to face a tall spindle of a man, showing his eyeteeth in a grin. His suit, an ancient black cutaway, smelled mousy and stale; his tie, of some slick fabric, was flecked with egg. "Clinton Keck, at your service." The boomy voice belied the limp hand. "You look to be the kind of man appreciates the fine art of photography," Keck said. "Step this way, please." He drew Fry across the street to a wagon, a black box with C. KECK, PHOTOGRAPHER, on the side.

"Postal cards?" Fry said.

"Postcards, postcards, only the backward say 'postal' anymore." Keck got out a sample book, dozens of cards held in place by black mounting corners. He pointed. "This here's my best." The legend read, "Two Minutes Before Disaster, the Cyclone that Swept Humbleville Off the Map": houses, gobbets of clouds, a gray funnel descending. "Six people killed," Keck added heartily.

He got out an invoice. "Name?"

"Ansel Fry."

Keck flashed his eyeteeth again. "Well, I'll be. Jim Fry's boy, and damned if you ain't the spittin' image of him."

Fry shook his head. "Edwin Fry is my father. He lives in Pennsylvania."

"Oh. Well, anyway." Keck wrote with a stubby tooth-marked pencil. *"Ansel Fry."*

On the far side of the wagon, facing each other, were a large box camera and a chair; behind the chair stood a hinged wooden screen painted with Doric columns and vines. "Dollar for the sitting, cards are ten cents apiece or three for a quarter, you can pick 'em up this evening right here. Were we at my studio in Cut Bank, I could offer the appropriate accoutrements—a ten-gallon hat, perhaps the Holy Bible, a gun, trophies of the chase. But we're not in my studio so you set right here." Keck wiped off the seat, put his hands on Fry's shoulders, pressed down. "Photography is a matter of lighting." He waved his hand significantly at the sun. "The play of light on a surface gives the illusion of life, the necessary third dimension. The photographer lives on shadows, on shades of gray."

"Wait," Fry said. "Can we do it out there?"

Keck shrugged and lifted the tripod, its legs clacking together. They went out in the street. Fry turned his back to the broad plain scattered with tipis like sails. Indians gathered around Keck as he performed his ministrations under the cloth. Fry put his hand in his pocket and gripped the string. Keck emerged, withdrew the slide, clawed for the bulb. The Indians drew back, muttering. They looked from the box to Fry and back at the box. Keck peered around the side and waved to get Fry's attention. "Please look fixedly at the lens and call up a pleasant expression on your face."

The clicks were simultaneous.

"Come November, and still they were at it. On the whole of the reservation perhaps four hundred of them, which was far fewer than on the other reservations, a credit to our control. And most of the dancers, to no surprise, in Sitting Bull's camp."

They were seated on a bench at the Blackfoot Agency. It was a marshy place, and the air felt damp and chill. Dwarf willows showed a hint of yellow in their leaves. Board sidewalks led from building to building, and people were out strolling, doing chores, picking up after the previous day's ceremony.

"And didn't the papers scream." McLaughlin turned a bemused face toward the scribbling Fry. "War on the way! General uprising! Though had there been one, it would have been bloody and brief. The army had forts all through the territory, and the settlers outnumbered the Indians twenty to one.

"Near the reservation, Germans had homesteaded in number. *Die Indianer kommt! Die Indianer kommt!* In Mandan they dug trenches and threw up breastworks, and the women vomited with fear."

Two old men, in bib overalls with red handkerchiefs blooming from their back pockets, worked at taking down the speakers' stand. They pottered about, looking up at the sturdy structure, and now and then one would pry a board partway out with the claw of his hammer, knock the board back into place, then hook the claw behind the protruding nailhead and give it sharp wrench—the nail would squawk out.

"The leaves had all come down," McLaughlin said. "Mistletoe hung in the cottonwoods like clumps of snarled hair. Ducks rafted by on the river every morning, and vees of geese passed over heading south. Yet the weather stayed warm.

"Beside me, Primeau rolled a cigarette, pouring from pouch to paper, his stained fingers working. 'Nothing to worry about, Louie,' I said. He replied with a grunt, a sound he produced as authentically as any full-blood could.

"The streams being low, we forded easily. The road split three ways. We took the right fork, which split again, sending us south, past the police shelter and across another creek. A coyote flushed from the brush; he had a hungry look to him, a wobble in his run.

"We were in the camp almost before anyone noticed. The first thing that struck me was that there were no drums, no thumping of skin-topped buckets. A tall pole stuck up from the earth, and they had decorated it with red cloth streamers and, as they often did to give their ceremonies an air of legitimacy, a small American flag. The people danced around the pole in a circle, men, women, and children, a hundred or more, holding hands and singing, 'Father I come, Mother I come, Brother I come, Father give us back our arrows.'

"They had striped their faces with red and yellow paint. Their garments were decorated with suns and moons and stars, the shoulders and sleeves trimmed with the eagle feathers that would lift them high in the air when the tidal wave of soil came rolling. 'The wind stirs the willows, the wind stirs the grass. Fog! Fog! Lightning! Whirlwind!'"

McLaughlin sat with his elbows on his knees, one thick-fingered hand rubbing against the other. His eyes were on the two old Indians dismantling the speakers' stand.

"Here were people I knew, people I saw every day, at the agency, in town, in church, and here they were, joined in this horrible dance.

"Man, woman, man, child, around the circle they went, fingers linked, faces dripping, eyes rolling up in their heads. Their feet churned up dust, and the wind blew it off. A man collapsed and still the circle spun, the dancers hopping and stumbling over his prostrate form. A woman broke free, pawing at the air, her face purple. She went down in a heap.

"She lay there for some time before two men took her under the arms and dragged her to a tipi. The flaps opened, and inside"—McLaughlin spat vehemently between his legs— "Sitting Bull. His long hair was loose. He looked thinner than a few weeks previous, but the look he gave me showed that his wits were not dulled or his hatred lessened by the rigors of his life. By his side, dressed in skins and baubles, stood Bull Ghost, Sitting Bull's mouthpiece in the séances.

"The woman, still in a swoon, was laid at Sitting Bull's feet. Bull Ghost announced in a loud voice that she was in a trance and communicating with the ghosts. The wheel of dancers came to a halt, and those who were able made their way to the tent.

"Sitting Bull waited for quiet. Then he raised his hands above his head and let a palmful of dust trickle from each. He put his ear to the woman's lips. He had all the tricks of the fake spiritualist. Knowing his people intimately, he could name the dead relatives of the woman who had fainted. He spoke softly to Bull Ghost, who shouted to the onlookers: 'Different Owl has talked with the spirit world!' A great moan went up. 'Throws Himself Down is coming! White Mouse is coming, leading a sorrel horse! Sword and Afraid-of-Him and Bear's Head are coming, driving the buffalo before them!' The dancers replied with shouts.

"It would do no good talking to them in that state. I drove on through the camp, passing in front of Sitting Bull's tipi, his eyes following mine. They were evil, calculating, and filled with hate. I glared at him, thinking: You feed on their misery and despair.

"We stayed at Bull Head's, three miles up the creek. Darkness came early, despite the summery air. Lieutenant Bull Head was one of my policemen, a Ceska Maza, a Metal Breast. We slept on his kitchen floor, and in the morning returned to Sitting Bull's camp. The place was quiet; figures stood clustered about the long row of wickiups in which the Ghost Dancers were taking their baths. The dancers had pitched their tents around Sitting Bull's cabin. At my knock, the elder wife, Seen by Her Nation, opened the door.

"A lamp smoked. A blackened, crusted pot—fixture on every Sioux stove—gave off steam. 'He is out taking his sweat bath. Should we get him?' I said no. Glancing around the room, I saw the other wife, Four Times, sister to the first; three young children; and his half-grown boy, Crow Foot, a dull and nasty lad. I tipped my hat and went out.

"The air was pleasant, and a light dew lay on the grass. I went around the corner of the cabin and almost ran into him. 'Hau,' I said.

"'Hau, Mee-jure.'

"He was naked except for a breechclout and moccasins. He had rubbed his body with sage and was covered with the smell. We shook hands, and I drew him over to the wagon and gave him a blanket, which he wrapped around his shoulders.

"His followers swarmed around us." McLaughlin paused, still watching the two old men working; they now teetered on the platform edge, prying at a board.

Fry tried to picture it. The Ghost Dancers rushing up, the bitter, heartsick tatters of the tribe, only half-believing in this fantastic new religion that offered them back their old life, while here stood the agent, a sober, demanding man, symbol of their defeat, ready to bring them down once again, to reality.

"To Sitting Bull I said, 'I will tell you things you already know.' Primeau's voice started in, wavery with fear, but steadfastly trailing mine. 'You know I speak the truth. We may not always agree, but you know I never lie.

"'I have done many things for you and your people. I told the army to let you go from Fort Randall. I got you plenty of horses and cows. I let you go with Cody.' I went on, reviewing in the Indian manner all the favors I had done.

"'And after all of this, you repay me by disobeying my orders and leading your people astray with this Ghost Dance, this absurd story of an Indian Christ.'

"Sitting Bull replied, 'It is not absurd. It is the truth. Christ has come back to the Indians. He came already to the whites and you nailed him to a tree—even the Black Robes admit it. The dancing is a good thing, and I believe in it.'

"'No,' I told him, 'one look in your eyes tells me you do not believe.'

"The Indians sneered. 'Lies,' Bull Ghost remarked. 'White Hair's pockets are full of lies.'

"Sitting Bull raised his hand. 'Sometimes the father's advice is good, but not today. Being a white man, he does not understand the dance.' He flashed his teeth and said, 'We will go together, you and I, to beyond the yellow faces west of the Utes, where this dance began. Together we will find the Messiah. If we do not find him and all the dead Indians coming this way, I will return to my people and tell them it's a lie. If we do find the Messiah and the ghosts, you will let the dance go on.'

"There it was: a chance. It was conceivable the Bureau would let us go. Two, three days out, dig up this Paiute phony, let them burn a little tobacco, search the skies for buffalo and horses and dead Indians, then cart him back, and if he still spouts this nonsense, throw him in the guardhouse.

"But something stopped me—the childish absurdity of it all. 'No,' I said. 'It would be as futile as trying to catch up with the wind that blew last year. Better for you to come to the agency where we can talk about this some more.'

"'*Hiya, hiya!*'—No!—many voices shouted angrily. And from the back of the crowd came the old rallying cry, '*Hopo, hopo!*'—Let's go!

"He quelled it by lifting a hand. 'I will discuss this with my people, and if they agree, I will come to the agency soon.'

"That was enough for Primeau, who practically vaulted onto the seat. I nodded to Sitting Bull and stepped on up. Taking the reins, I gave him a long last look.

"His black eyes returned a stare so cold I knew he had no regard for me at all. If it suited his purpose, he would have ordered us killed then and there." McLaughlin settled his hands on his knees, pushed, stood; he was still watching the old men, who had fumbled a few boards down off the speakers' stand and were now resting, mopping their faces with their handkerchiefs.

What happened then?, Fry wanted to say. You stared at him. You looked into the hated and hating black eyes. And the next time you saw them—?

But McLaughlin had started down the walk toward the old men, stepping out in his even, purposeful stride (once he had pointed out to Fry the extreme natural evenness of his gait, saying, a bit proudly, that shoe soles lasted twice as long for him as for the average man). Upon reaching the speakers' stand, McLaughlin peeled off his coat and gestured at the

structure; one of the old Indians climbed up and began prying at the boards in earnest, while the Major, sweating freely,
helped lever them off.

He looked at Fry and waved for him to come help.

On Signet the next morning, returning from breakfast, the
train skimming across the empty land, Annie passed by
McLaughlin's stateroom. The door was open, and she glanced
inside. The Major was not present. Seeing the photograph in
the corner of the mirror, she went in for a look, expecting it to
be Mother.

The oddest feeling fluttered up: a picture of her, a sixteen-
year-old Annie. But no, it was some other young girl. She
slipped the picture out from behind the bracket, the newsprint curling in her hand. The image was round. Must be the
candid photographer they're always talking about.

The girl in the picture was watching something intently: a
ball game? a dance? She smiled. A boy. Of course, a boy. What
else would put such life into a young girl's frame?

He came in the door then, looking tired and pale.

"Hello, Father."

"Annie." He was still in his dressing gown.

"We missed you at breakfast," she said.

"I'd a hard time getting to sleep last night." He stifled a
yawn. "I'll get the cook to make me something later."

She held out the photograph. "Who took it?"

He shrugged. "Someone, some sneak going around to the
reservations."

"A candid photograph."

"Candid, secret." He hung his bath towel over the bar on
the inside of the door. "It's obvious the people have no idea
he's there. The pictures show things the Bureau would rather
the public not see."

"Such as . . . ?"

"Poverty. Alcoholism." He put out his hand, and she gave him the cutout. "Isn't it wrong," he said, "to take a picture of someone who doesn't know you're there?"

"That picture doesn't seem wrong to me."

"Perhaps not." His brow drew down. "I clipped it because it reminded me of you." He put it back in the mirror, stood looking at it for a moment. "Daughter—"

She felt herself tense.

"Siebert showed me his evaluation." He turned to face her. Managed a smile. "Jumpy as he could be. I suppose he figured I'd hold it against him." He shook his head. "It's a terrible evaluation, but from what I can understand, totally deserved. He told me about your speaking Sioux to the pupils and that shameful incident between you and the matron." McLaughlin's face had become stern. "I told him I'd back him completely."

"He was right," Annie said. "I didn't do the job they hired me for."

"And now?"

She shook her head.

Meaning she was sorry? She would change, make amends? "You had your problems there," he said. "I wasn't aware. Maybe we should talk."

"You have his paper. It tells what happened." She turned and left the room.

24

D ixon was a celebrity on the Crow Reservation. He had
spent a month there in 1909, bringing together dozens
of aging chiefs from various Plains tribes for a mammoth
jamboree. The event, bankrolled by Rodman Wanamaker,
had been billed as The Last Great Indian Council. It was a
time of feasting, telling tales, and recalling days of yore. Just
over the hill lay the Custer Battlefield National Monument. At
the Last Great Indian Council the chiefs had determined,
after considerable discussion, the answer to a question that
had piqued the American mind for thirty-three years: Who
fired the shot that snuffed out the life of George Armstrong
Custer? It was not Sitting Bull, as the dime dreadfuls had led
many to believe. Nor was it Hawk, Brave Bear, Flat Hip,
Spotted Calf, Two Moon, or White Bull, all of whom had been
credited with the deed at one time or another. It was not the
redoubtable Rain-in-the-Face. It was, the assembled chiefs
finally agreed, Brave Bear of the Southern Cheyenne. A mon-
etary reward from Mr. Wanamaker had elicited the information. Chief Brave Bear was relieved to learn that Chief
Wanamaker was only curious, and did not intend to come out
from New York and shoot him.

At the council, Dixon had not spared the film. The result-
ing still and motion pictures drew great acclaim, their major
theme being feather-bonneted Indians riding into sunsets. In
1913 Dixon's book deriving from the event, *The Vanishing
Race,* was printed by a well-known Eastern publisher. "We are

exchanging salutations with the uncalendared ages of the red man," the book began. "We have come to the day of audit. Annihilation is not a cheerful word, but it is coined from the alphabet of Indian life and heralds the infinite pathos of a vanishing race. We are at the end of historical origins. The impression is profound."

The old man smelled of woodsmoke and whiskey. He was tall, obese, had small feet, a puffy face dished in toward tiny piggish eyes; his hair, gray, was done up in the traditional Crow fashion of two long braids and a thick forelock brushed up and back in resemblance of a wave. White Man Runs Him had been one of General Custer's scouts. He had participated in the Last Great Indian Council and had represented the Crow tribe at the ground breaking for the memorial in New York. Now he scuffed along, weaving slightly, pausing to clear his throat and spit. Across his chest he cradled a carbine with a brass receiver, whose muzzle described wide, careless arcs. Dixon and Booth followed him; farther behind came McLaughlin, Annie, and Fry.

The battlefield glowed under thin clouds and a drizzling rain. Coulees separated the naked tan ridges. Below, in a cottonwood bottom, the Little Bighorn twisted like a blue-gray intestine between the trees.

"Sioux camp was over there." White Man Runs Him spoke in an indifferent tone; he had given this spiel to hundreds of tourists. He let the muzzle of his rifle droop until it rested on the ground. Using the rifle as a cane, he leaned forward and pointed with his chin. "Sitting Bull and his Hunkpapas was on the end." He tottered, regained his balance. "Custer sent the scouts back. We would have died with him, if he had let us.

"There. They got him over there."

White marble markers toothed the grass, around a taller monument behind an iron fence. Dixon set up his portrait camera. Booth applied a whisk broom to White Man Runs Him's leggings.

"Hey, White Man," Booth said. "Know why the Indians thought Custer was the best-dressed general they'd ever fought against?"

White Man Runs Him groaned. "I heard that so many times it makes me wanna puke," he said. "Cause he was wearin' an Arrow shirt."

Dixon motioned. "Get him around to the right."

"Want the big marker in the background?"

"Yeah. We'll get some with, some without."

"General Custer was a helluva soldier," White Man Runs Him said. "He was a pisspot, but he could drink and ride and shoot." He belched. "Not all at the same time, though."

Booth positioned White Man Runs Him in front of the monument. McLaughlin, Fry, and Annie moved out of the way.

"A pisspot," White Man Runs Him was saying. "I believe he liked horses better than men." He laughed thickly. "Once I watched him tryin' to kill a coyote. Drunk as hell. Like me." White Man Runs Him gave a slow grin at the revelation. "He was ridin' his favorite horse, chasin' this coyote, and he went to shoot and blew his horse's brains out."

Booth straightened. "No bullshit?"

"Bet your ass no bullshit."

Dixon stepped back and lifted the camera's cloth.

Too good to pass up. Instinctively Fry lined up and grabbed the shot—and saw a movement out of the corner of his eye. Annie had turned and was looking at him. He blanched. At that instant a shot rang out.

White Man Runs Him cringed and Booth grimaced and Dixon leaped high in the air. The Indian looked dumbly at his smoking rifle and then at the ground. The slug had cratered the earth beside his moccasin, sending stone chips flying. "Chrriist!" Dixon thundered, rubbing his shin. "Will you *unload* that thing!"

McLaughlin rolled his eyes, motioned for Fry and Annie to follow him down the hill.

The sage gave off a clean, washed scent. A jackrabbit exploded from behind a clump and went zigzagging away, big back legs pumping. Fry stole a glance at Annie. She was watching the jackrabbit, no particular expression on her face. Thank God, she hadn't heard the click. He relaxed. He looked all around. The land, bleak and empty, looked like he had always imagined Outer Mongolia must look. It did not seem a reasonable place for a battle. He had toured Gettysburg with its stake-and-rider fences, farmsteads, orchards, hamlets, and roads, which looked to have some value, making the land worth fighting over. But this dull, rumpled rug . . .

"The Crows were always at odds with the rest of the tribes," McLaughlin said. "About as popular as scabs and strikebreakers. The Sioux hate 'em like poison."

"Not quite," Annie said.

"Well, there is animosity, wouldn't you say?"

"Some."

The Major stopped. "You know why Sitting Bull is remembered? Rain-in-the-Face? Crazy Horse? Because of their names. Think about it. Suppose Sitting Bull had been Kutepi—Shot At—why, no one would have noticed. Fish, Snot, Bobtail, all perfectly good Sioux names. Gall, who commanded the Indians here at the Little Bighorn—lousy press name."

"I thought Sitting Bull led the Indians," Fry said.

"That's what everyone thinks. He was the spiritual leader, the flame they gathered about. But he didn't lead them, he didn't even fight. I once asked Low Dog what role Sitting Bull had played in the battle, and he replied, 'If someone had loaned him a heart, he might have fought.'" McLaughlin, shivering, buttoned his coat. His face was chalky. The drizzle shone on his cheeks like sweat.

"Hunkpapa. Sitting Bull was a Hunkpapa." McLaughlin tossed his head at Annie. "She's a Hunkmama."

"Oh, Father."

"Hunkpapa. Means a border or an edge. At all the big councils, that's where the Hunkpapas would camp, right on the edge, so they could greet the enemy first." He swept an arm. "When Reno attacked and the rifle balls started ripping through the tipis, Sitting Bull gathered up his wives and children and lit out for the hills." He gestured south toward Wyoming, where clouds cloaked an iron range. His voice was feverish and louder than usual. "He was in such a hurry that he left one of his sons behind. I have this on the authority of several Indians who were there. After the battle, they sent out riders and overtook him ten miles from camp. Later, he explained it away by saying that his capture would have meant the loss of his medicine to the Sioux."

Farther up the hill, Dixon could be seen repositioning White Man Runs Him. There was an angry shout, and a brown bottle went flying through the air.

"Custer walked into a buzz saw," McLaughlin said. "The battle was short. Fifteen minutes. Nobody has the foggiest notion who plugged him. Then the cutting and hacking began." He stopped to lean against a stone marker, holding onto its top, his breathing shallow and quick. Annie went to him, a worried look on her face. "In Gall's camp one time," he said, "I found a child playing with a necklace of bones looked like no bones I'd ever seen. Asked his father what they were. 'Trigger fingers,' he said. 'Custer men.'"

McLaughlin was trembling. His features looked sharp and pinched. "A coward! A liar! An egotist! A fraud! All the faults of the red man and none of the virtues."

"Father, are you all right?" Annie said.

Dark circles lay below McLaughlin's eyes, which were unnaturally bright. "Malaria. Little souvenir I picked up a few years back, down among the Osage." He gave a croaking laugh. "Imagine. Suppose his name had been Porcupine Dung."

After dinner that evening—Signet stood on a siding at the ramshackle station called simply Crow Agency—McLaughlin went to bed. He wouldn't let Annie tend to him. A social was being held at the boarding school, and she, Fry, and Booth had been invited. They sat in the dining hall with several dozen young Indians and heard a homily delivered by a Crow preacher fresh out of Baptist seminary. A skinny, badly complected man with brilliantined hair, he spoke of the "swift invisible arrows" that could extinguish mortal life: the speeding train, the runaway horse, the cramps while swimming, the fall from a ladder, diphtheria, consumption, la grippe, the tiniest splinter left untreated.

"You never know when your time is at hand. Friends, at this very moment Satan may be contending for your soul." He bent and picked up a cardboard box. He popped open the flaps, reached inside, and brought out a chicken, a small red one of the kind Fry remembered his grandmother keeping. The chicken squawked and struggled, then settled as the preacher held it against his chest.

"The thread of life is thin," the preacher said, and instantly Fry knew what he was going to do. He felt for the string in his pocket, but the light was too dim, and Booth much too close.

"The end can be near." The preacher gripped the chicken's feet in one hand. "Yet we may never have a clue." He closed his other hand around the chicken's head.

"I don't believe it," Annie murmured. "It's worse than Catholicism."

"What the hell?" Booth said as youths in the audience laughed, and children covered their faces with their hands.

"Life is but a flicker of flame, a weak candle." Sweat beaded

the preacher's long upper lip. "The barest breath of wind"—
he let the chicken's body dangle, still holding onto its head—
"can snuff it out."

He spun the chicken. Wound the body around the station-
ary head, one, two, three times. Children shrieked at the tops
of their lungs.

The chicken thrashed its wings and the preacher dropped
it on the floor, where it leaped and bounced like a bead of
water on a skillet.

"How will it be, my friends, if you don't come to Christ? For
the everlasting . . . *forgiveness* . . . of your sin-blackened souls?!"

Thus ended the homily. Chaperones and matrons led the
applause. After the chicken was collected, after a group of
grade-schoolers performed a skit, after the gymnastics club
gave a tumbling exhibition, refreshments were served.

Spooning from a dish of tutti-frutti ice cream, Fry found
himself in the minister's clutches. The man made small talk
and, as Fry had known he would, zeroed in for the kill.

"Have you accepted Jesus?"

As usual, Fry waffled. "I belong to a church," he said.
Which he did, though he hadn't attended in years.

"Have you repented your sins and accepted Christ as your
Lord and savior?"

"Well . . ." Fry spotted a red feather on the preacher's suit
sleeve, a freckle of blood on the bleached white cuff.

"Repent, brother. I can lead you to the Lord."

Fry looked for an escape. Booth, towering over the students, was bringing Annie a glass of punch. Fry excused
himself and went over. The preacher, not about to be shaken
so easily, followed. He shook hands with Annie and Booth
and reintroduced himself. "Peter Cloud."

"Perfect name for a prospective angel," Booth said.

"I've a long path to follow," the young man smiled, "and
many temptations to overcome, before I join the heavenly
host."

"I've decided not to join," Booth said. "The dues are too high and the company's too exclusive." He toasted the young minister with his punch glass.

"Miss?" The preacher turned to Annie. "Have you accepted Christ as Lord?"

"I was raised Catholic," she said, "though you might say I've lapsed."

"You could convert," the man said quickly.

"I'm leaning in another direction," she said. "*Re*vert might be a better way to put it."

"What do you mean?"

"I think Indians are asked to give up too much of themselves. You're a Baptist. Benny here, he's a—what are you, Benny?"

"An opportunist."

And how, Fry thought.

"Ansel . . . ?"

He couldn't think of anything witty. "Lutheran."

"And I'm Catholic. But also Sioux. We have our own religion."

"Pagan beliefs do not constitute a true religion."

"You have little room to talk, after that display," Annie said.

He spread his hands, smiled. "In seminary they taught us to use visual aids."

"Anyway," she said, "a person's religion is her own business."

"Then you believe in an Indian religion?"

"I believe that Indian ways are important. They shouldn't just be thrown away."

The preacher wagged his head. "You should feel fortunate, Miss, no, *blessed*, to be on the earth now, when you can receive God's glory. When you can go to heaven and not have to burn in hell for all eternity, like your grandparents no doubt are burning, maybe even your parents too." He paused, seeing from her face that he had gone too far but plunging ahead anyway. "Tell me. Your mother and father. Have they accepted the Lord? Or are they savages yet?"

She stared at him, frozen. Inside, ice changed to fire and she wanted to throw her drink in his face. But something stayed her hand—maybe a memory of the smallness, the loss of dignity she had felt after flinging the eraser at the matron, and cracking the whip at the liveryman, or maybe just the realization that the preacher was so young and untried and foolish.

She turned away, as Booth interposed his bulk between her and the man. He wagged a finger in the minister's face. "Go 'way—go feed the birds or something. Shoo." For emphasis he placed a large hand on the man's chest.

The preacher backed up. "The Lord have mercy on your souls."

Fry stood, feeling drab and lacking, as Booth squired Annie away.

He bounced around for the rest of the evening: first the rail car (the Major's door was shut, his light off), then the deserted agency, the darkened town. He looked in the windows of shuttered stores. Lamplight glowed in the small frame homes. He found himself wondering where they had gone. He returned quickly to Signet and felt unaccountably relieved to find Annie's room light on, Booth playing gin rummy with Giannetti in the observation room. They played for over an hour, Booth wisecracking and telling off-color jokes, Giannetti playing attentively and carefully, although it was Booth who finally won; then they picked up the cards and went to bed.

For something to do, Fry got out a shipper's map of the Great Plains. He traced his finger around the brown contours of mountains, over blank expanses of prairies, across little blue squiggles that were rivers: all gridded over with black lines, squares, and hard angles that signified the whites' brief tenure on the land.

He wished McLaughlin would call him in right now, tell the rest of the story. How had Sitting Bull died? Had it just happened, a flare-up, sudden wild shots—or had it been set up? He recoiled from the thought: The Major is no murderer, he can't be, you get to know a man being around him this long. But it had all happened twenty-three years ago, and the man now might not be the man then. So he wanted to know.

He folded the map and turned off the light. Dropping caution this once, breaking a standing personal rule, he undressed right there in the common room, shucking off suit and vest, depositing the camera immediately in his trunk. As he did it—ten seconds, less—he felt totally, brutally exposed.

He stood in his underwear, one bare foot planted on the trunk's lid. And grinned. Things were going swell. He had seen the latest clips. Good work, it reproduced well, and the paycheck had been a hefty one. Kravitz's letter was ecstatic: The pictures were still causing a great to-do in the Eastern press, could he please send more of them? The *Dispatch* wanted a spread of candids for the Wednesday paper, in addition to the Sunday one. As it was, he'd been scraping the bottom of the barrel, sending some shots he'd held back for one reason or another, old ones from Oklahoma, some from California and the Northwest. He figured it was good to mix them up, so it wouldn't appear the photographer had actually attached himself to the Expedition. He'd even sent a few more of Dixon and Booth. No doubt it would stir things up, but he was growing bolder, figuring they'd never put two and two together, they paid him such little mind.

A few weeks back he had done something crazy. He had taken a page of candids up into coach. The train had been ascending the Columbia gorge—the river broad as the Susquehanna, flowing between naked dry hills—and he had taken a window seat and informed the conductor that he was from the private car; the man wedged a chit into the seat back in front. At The Dalles a man got on and sat next to Fry; he showed the conductor a railway pass.

The man, an engineer, nodded out the window, where wind whipped the river's alluvium into thick ocher clouds. "One inch of sand, and the road becomes impassable," he said. His voice had a westerner's twang. He pointed out some Chinese laborers who had just cleared the track with shovels. "There are more up-to-date methods of countering the sand. Panels can be erected, and deflecting fence. The most promising technique is to spray heated crude petroleum, producing a thick film that holds the grains in place."

Fry shook open the newspaper, made a show of sitting up straight. "Will you look at this," he said.

The engineer wrapped the bows of wire-framed spectacles behind his ears and peered at the photographs.

A woman in an open coat over a fancy ruffled gown, smiling suggestively back over her shoulder as she led a man by the hand up an outside fire escape.

An old Navaho lighting a cigarette, Billy Trimble standing behind the counter, all but invisible in the shadows.

A hobo leaning back against a brick wall, shabby, destitute, whipped by life. A tourist woman haggling at an Indian pottery stand. A Temperance quartet with their sheet music and animated faces.

"Look at that old girl," the engineer chuckled, pointing at one of the singers. "Face would stop a clock." He held the paper in the light. "Progressive photographs. The wave of the future. Although you'll notice the photographer has not had the courage to reveal his name."

After the man got off, Fry moved up to the next coach. A drummer pronounced the photographs "swellegant"; a minister said he liked the pictures, but he also liked the view, the seat cushions, the dining-car meals. Fry made bold to approach a woman traveling alone. She was buxom, corseted to a minuscule waist. Wrinkles ramified from the corners of her eyes. Her blonde hair, worn in the new marcel wave, was rooted brown and going thin on top. Looking at the pictures, she pressed her leg against his. "Ooh, Indians! I just love Indians. Did you see 'Broncho Billy's Indian Maiden'?" The photographs? "Dreadful—the poor people have had no warning." She laughed shrilly. "No chance to suck their tummies in! No chance to fix their hair!" She leaned so close that her cheek grazed Fry's, and, blushing furiously, he rose and retreated to the private car.

The next day, back in coach again, his seatmate was a young Indian in a fashionable jacket and houndstooth cap, who snapped his chewing gum loudly—Fry identified it from the bouquet as Wrigley's Doublemint.

"What do you do for a living?" Fry asked.

"Kidnap babies."

Fry's eyebrows jumped.

"Just kidding. I write dime novels, only in my stories the Indians always win." The young man grinned, masticating furiously. "You?"

"I'm a stenographer." Suddenly he felt a strong urge to share his secret with this stranger. He looked around—a dozen bored-looking passengers, of course nobody from the private car. "Also a photographer—"

"Stenographer, photographer, pornographer, all the same thing." The Indian offered Fry his gum pack, and Fry took a stick. "What kinda pitchers?"

Fry opened the paper and placed it in the man's lap.

The Indian studied the photographs for a long, snap-ridden moment. "Yours?"

Fry nodded.

The Indian made a show of scrutinizing the pictures, holding up the paper, turning his head this way and that.

"What do you think?" Fry asked.

The Indian tore off the corner of the page and wadded his gum in it. This annoyed Fry greatly.

"I said, what do you think?"

The young man stripped a fresh stick of its wrapper and buckled it into his mouth. "You're in the right business," he said.

25

The days grew shorter; often the wind blew cold. The aspens shone gold in the foothills, and the plains were bleak and brown. The expedition passed mile 10,000 between Havre and Poplar, Montana.

In a week they gave ceremonies on three reservations. After the first, the Indians were sure they had been made citizens. It took McLaughlin the better part of an hour to straighten them out. At the next reservation they got all huffed up, thinking it was land the visitors wanted, not just some photographs and a couple of *X*'s on a parchment. At the third ceremony, a rift opened between Dixon and McLaughlin.

Partly it was the malaria, which had weakened McLaughlin and made him edgy and glum; partly it was the bogus uniform Dixon showed up in, a khaki outfit complete with jodhpur breeches, a tie tucked between two buttons of the shirt, and an officer's hat. Dixon strode onto the stand whapping the side of his leg with a swagger stick, in front of the assembled Assiniboine and Yankton Sioux on Fort Peck Reservation. A quiet rage rose within McLaughlin—now the Indians would surely think this a government expedition. The Major edged next to Fry, said in a quiet, icy tone, "Goddamn him to hell."

"Those noble red men," thundered Dixon, "those noble chiefs who raised this flag in New York, they told me they'd never had a flag, never before felt a part of this country.

Why," Dixon raised his arms grandly, "time was when you *were* the country! You owned the vales and the hills, the mountains and the rivers. Your crime was simply that you owned the land. The white man came and wanted the land, so he stole it!"

McLaughlin winced. Fine words to feed the bitterness. Fine words to harden people's hearts against change, against anything that might improve their lot.

Dixon clambered onto a table and urged the Indian interpreter up with him. He took the flag and draped it over and around the man's shoulders, until all that remained uncovered was the interpreter's head. Booth made a photograph. The flag looked like a giant red, white, and blue, striped and starry amoeba engulfing its prey. The interpreter grinned and blinked. The banner began to stir as the Indian leaders pulled on the ropes, the colors unwrapping themselves and climbing the pole.

Dixon's hand made a broad arc and settled over his heart. "My friends, on behalf of Rodman Wanamaker I present to you this flag. It is your flag; it does not belong to the Government or to the reservation. It is the Indians' flag, floating free on Indian land."

When McLaughlin spoke, there was shoulder to his tone. "Despite what you have just heard, do not forget that the Government is the best friend you have. And whilst many things have transpired upon Indian reservations that I wish had not taken place, still I must say that the Indians, as a whole, have been treated fairly, honestly, and justly by the Government. At no other time in history has a conquered people been treated with such magnanimity by their conquerors."

Dixon rose again. "There is a strong implication in the remarks just made that I am guilty of casting aspersions upon the United States Government, which I utterly, absolutely disclaim." He referred to a long line of broken treaties and trusts. "The white man can never get out from under his disgraceful treatment of the Indian." The Indians grinned and applauded. "Every wise and truthful man will say I speak the truth." Whistling, vigorous nods, more handclaps.

Dixon fairly shouted. "I am commissioned by the President of the United States" (a bald-faced lie), "and by the Secretary of the Interior" (another lie), "and by the Commissioner of Indian Affairs, and am a representative of the Government as I stand here today" (all, all lies), "and I say to you that the white man and the Government are seeking to redeem themselves, as evidence of which we have this Expedition!"

"Take this down," McLaughlin hissed at Fry. "Get every word right!" He could not let it rest, and rose again, asserting that the Government was indeed the best friend the Indians had, and the people snarled and hooted and shouted him down.

In the car, the air was brittle with politeness. McLaughlin took to his bed. He suffered alternating fevers and chills; every four hours Annie would bring him ten grains of quinine dissolved in water. The quinine made his ears ring and his head ache.

The next evening Annie came into the observation room, where Fry was typing. She said, "He'd like to see you. He wants you to take some dictation."

"How is he?"

She shrugged. "I think a little better."

He went and knocked on McLaughlin's door; was invited to enter. Annie slipped in with him and took a seat by the window.

McLaughlin's face was drawn. The blankets were pulled up to his chin. He looked at Annie, then back at Fry, and said—so suddenly and baldly that Fry wondered if he were delirious— "Buffalo Bill, Buffalo Bill, never missed and never will."

A sardonic glint in the gray eyes. The tangled white eyebrows were active and quick.

"Completely inconceivable and therefore totally believable," McLaughlin said. "I turned my hand and read the telegram once again: 'Confidential, Headquarters, Division of the Missouri, November twenty-fourth, eighteen ninety. Colonel Cody is hereby authorized to secure the person of Sitting Bull and deliver him to the nearest commanding officer United States troops.'

"Buffalo Bill," McLaughlin said, "was going to capture the dreaded Sitting Bull.

"The great scout, you ask my opinion, cut a less than manly figure. Black sombrero, ruffled shirt, black suit with sequins that caught the sun as he walked. The scout was a sot. The scout had a fat ass."

He winced slightly, shook his head.

"No, strike that." He paused. "The locals gathered to stare at Buffalo Bill. Ed Swabb, the wolfer—who, I would have warranted, was running guns and whiskey to the Sioux—a hulking bearded man in a greasy buffalo coat, his face lit with awe." McLaughlin curled his lip. "Now, Swabb was real. And Mort Dancereau, his sidekick—an illiterate half-breed, tip of his nose bitten off in a brawl—he was real too. A big crowd of people, including Hansen the barber—one night that very winter he got drunk and passed out in the ditch and froze solid from the waist down, leading to gross gangrene, serial amputation, finally death—well, Hansen stood there staring, and even my own policemen, all of them real people, all of them gulled by this creature of imagination and device."

His laugh was dry, and it cracked before his mirth was expended. "Who 'always shoots and shoots to kill. And the company pays his buffalo bill.'"

A shiver crossed McLaughlin's shoulders, and he clutched the blankets tighter. "If you would," he said, inclining his head toward the foot of the bed. Another blanket lay folded there. Annie shook it out and laid it over McLaughlin, whose pale hands drew it up to his chin.

"I laid the orders on my desk, along with a copy of the telegram I had just fired off to Washington: 'William F. Cody, Buffalo Bill, has arrived with commission from General Miles to arrest Sitting Bull. Such a step at present is unnecessary and unwise, a few Indians still dancing but does not mean mischief. I have matters well in hand, when proper time arrives can arrest Sitting Bull by Indian police without bloodshed. Request General Miles's order to Cody be rescinded, and request immediate answer.'

"An answer," McLaughlin said, "that I was still waiting for.

"No question at all, the fool would have been killed." Again McLaughlin shook his head. "Strike that as well." He pursed his lips. "Had Cody attempted the capture of Sitting Bull, he surely would have lost his life, depriving us all of a royal good fellow and a most excellent showman. And the whole thing would have blown up into war.

"Drum, the post commander, tried to stop him. At the officers' club he sent forth his junior officers in relays. Cody drank them under the table, every one." McLaughlin shivered again, the tremors running from his shoulders up his neck and into his face. "He had some friends with him, and a reporter, and a couple of drivers from the livery, who were apparently the only sane ones because they were sweating bullets. When he saw me coming he raised a white-gloved hand. 'Major!' he said. He reached back and peeled the canvas away from the wagon bed.

"Candy canes, jawbreakers, licorice, lollipops, bags and boxes of sweets. 'We travel heavily armed,' Cody told me. He turned back to the reporter.

"'Of all bad Indians, Sitting Bull is the worst.'" McLaughlin had adopted a breathy, theatrical tone. "'If there is no disturbance, he will start one. He is now poised to flee to the Badlands where a thousand armed fanatical Ghost Dancers await him.' The reporter scribbled like mad. 'Should he be allowed to join the hostiles, the stage will be set for an uprising both bloody and protracted.' Cody waved to the crowd. 'I am off on the most dangerous assignment of my career!' And they cheered him. They actually cheered him! 'Hip hip, hooray!'"

His lips were blue, his jaw quivering. "I laid my hand on the wagon wheel. 'There is no need for you to risk your life and the lives of these men.'

"'Now, Major,' Cody told me, 'Little Willie and Ol' Sit go back a long way. True, he's as dangerous as a coiled snake, but even the deadliest python can be charmed.'

"'Cut the blarney.' The reporter looked up, and I let him have it. 'The press has blown this Ghost Dancing business out of all proportion. A few disgruntled Indians, pay them no mind and it will all fizzle as soon as the snow flies.'"

McLaughlin huffed. "Of course the reporter would not write down what I said.

"'The camp is dangerous,' I went on. 'They may shoot before they recognize you.' At this, one of Cody's friends, a miserable little man in a bowler hat, piped up: 'If they dare, we'll fill 'em as full of lead as Joplin and Galena.' The little man grinned triumphantly. 'This is *Buffalo Bill*, mister.'"

McLaughlin continued in a quieter tone. "As luck would have it, Buffalo Bill chanced onto Louie Primeau coming north. Primeau had just been told that the Ghost Dancers planned to kill him for being a meddling half-breed and the agent's toady. And now Buffalo Bill was going to waltz in there and get his head blown off. So Primeau made up a story. Said he'd just come from Sitting Bull's camp. Primeau said that Sitting Bull was heading toward the agency on Antelope's Road. 'Go look,' he said, 'and you'll see his tracks—a wagon drawn by two horses, one shod and the other not.'

"It was true, the tracks were there. Primeau had met an Indian, not Sitting Bull, driving there the day before. And Buffalo Bill, anxious to effect 'the Surrender of Sitting Bull'—

one of the men with him, the little one in the bowler, planned to write it up for the Beadle & Adams series—well, naturally he hurried back to the agency.

"Where I met him. And handed him a telegram, just arrived, rescinding his orders."

A weak smile lay on McLaughlin's lips. The whites of his eyes were yellow, cracked with small red veins. His smile faded as he patted imaginary pockets under the blankets; he glanced around as if confused, then spied his watch lying on the nightstand. "What time is it?"

Fry checked. "Ten past nine."

McLaughlin said, "My medicine." He waved at Annie, and said to Fry, "I'm very tired, son. We'll take this up again later."

She mixed the quinine and gave it to him. He pinched his nostrils and drank the bitter liquid; then, with a shaking hand, chased it with a glass of milk.

They were alone. A silence lay between them.

"We're going home," he ventured. "It won't be long. We'll see Mother and Charlie and Sib."

She nodded.

"And you'll start fresh."

She wouldn't look up.

"A new job, another chance. Maybe your last chance."

She continued to stare at the backs of her hands.

He said with feeling, "Why do you keep hurting yourself?" His teeth chattered faintly. He clenched his jaws, and said, "You had a good job. A responsible position. You were in line for promotion. Now you're going to a day school in the middle of nowhere and lucky to get even that."

He waited. He loved this girl. He owed her. Owed her, he believed, his very life. Certainly he owed her her father's life, and indirectly her mother's life. He had taken her into his family and treated her as a daughter, had come to see her as a gift from God to replace his beloved Imelda. They looked a bit alike, he reflected, the same direct, independent, often defiant, almost brazen black eyes.

"Daughter," he said.

She looked up. Her expression was anything but brazen.

"Why did it fall apart at Lapwai?"

She said, "Death."

He waited. Her eyes were dark and clear.

"It's followed me around, all my life."

He nodded, knowing the feeling.

"At school I would teach the children and get to know them. They're away from home, away from their mothers and fathers, so naturally I would become sort of a mother to them. When they'd die, a little part of my heart would clot and scab off. And after a while I wouldn't, or couldn't, let them get close." Tears came to her eyes, and she frowned and angrily shook her head.

He reached for her hand, but it was out of reach. He said, "An evaluation like that will plague you your whole career."

Her eyes danced. "Because I wouldn't scrub out mouths. I wouldn't paddle, wouldn't even call for the matron to do those things. What was the point? They were going to die. Curl up in a knot and cough their lungs out. Their eyes go shiny and blank, and they die. I wouldn't administer corporal punishment like a teacher is supposed to. And I told them things I thought they needed to hear."

The same old story. They had gone round and round on this before. He thought, That stubborn streak—she could have gotten it from me.

"I told them, Remember: You're Indians. You're not white people. You're different."

"Annie."

"Because if, by any chance, they ever get away to walk down the street in Lewiston or Bismarck or Denver, they're Indians.

They're different. Not equal." Her tone was controlled now, steady. "Isn't that right?"

Now it was his turn to keep silent.

"When I take that day-school job, things won't change. I'll teach them arithmetic and penmanship and spelling and the Pledge of Allegiance and the Lord's Prayer. I'll teach the little ones to sing 'Jesus Loves Me' and sit still and not swallow the chalk. And I'll teach them to remember that they're Indians."

"It was always the same to me—Indian or white."

She lowered her eyes, as if not quite sure that was so. She said a bit brusquely, "Here," made him lean forward, and fluffed up his pillow. "You're feeling better?"

"Maybe a little. Day by day. It takes time."

He looked at her. She was pretty and smart and too independent for her own good. Twenty-four years old—most girls had married and borne children by then. Now who would have her? A reservation full-blood wouldn't; he'd never feel comfortable with her educated ways. A white man might, the races could mix, he knew it from his life with Louise; but it didn't seem likely she would make that connection, either. And if someone did marry her, would she be happy with him? At least she can take care of herself. At least I've given her that.

"Annie, you don't belong on the reservation." He said it on impulse. "It's not your country any longer. No reason for you to be there. Go east, Minneapolis, Chicago, Washington, the cities are crying for teachers. I'll help you get a job. Find someone, marry. Have a family. Have a life." In her black eyes he caught the tiny white moons of his reflected face; he went on blurting thought. "Fit in, Daughter. Fit in. Live."

But her face had turned to stone.

The twin steel rails led them out onto the frosty morning plain. Ought to be a law, she thought, that the railroads use more ties; put it in the antitrust, make them set the ties closer so you can step on every second one. As it is, they're too close together and too far apart: Your foot is always coming down in loose stone.

Fry went along balancing on the rail, whose polished top caught the morning light. A lean man, guarded, shy.

"What was it like," he asked, "having him as a father?"

She thought for a moment. "Sometimes bad, sometimes good."

"Most things are like that."

"I suppose."

"When I was growing up," Fry said, "my father pretty much directed my life. My path was straight as this rail." He stopped, teetered like a bird on a wire, caught his balance. "School. Then the business course. Move to the big city. Get a job."

"Settle down," she said. "Fit in, live, dissolve."

"Yes. Just like that."

"So?" she said. "You did it."

He frowned slightly. "Maybe I did and maybe I didn't."

They heard a whistle. A train was coming across the plain, black and squat, long horns of smoke above a glaring yellow eye. She got off the track on the station side.

He stood there balancing. "You can feel it coming," he said. "Like somebody dragging a chain across the rails."

The station wasn't far. The passenger train had stopped on the eastbound track; the oncoming freight would pass it on the westbound track. They had gone for a quick walk, a couple of minutes, to get the kinks out.

"We'd better go back," she said.

"There's good and bad in everything, in everybody." He had to speak loudly above the approaching freight. "What I mean is, nothing's ever just black or white."

The freight came closer. The locomotive whistled again. It looked big as a bull. Then big as a house.

"Get down!" she called. And thought, Quit showing off.

He jumped down on the far side of the tracks. The locomotive passed between them, a mass of torrid pounding steel. The ballast groaned as the rails pressed down into it. Two engines, both smoking. Moths were plastered to the lead engine's light, and small broken birds were trapped in its cowcatcher.

Boxcars went clanking past. Between them she could see him looking at her, and she pointed toward the station and began walking that way.

The line of cars clicked and clattered. In one of them, a ragged man stood in an open doorway: His eyes brushed over her. She walked along in the dirt beside the raised barrow of gravel, past rusty spikes, tangled wire, clinkers, a flattened glove, broken glass.

He's on the wrong side. He'll miss it. Father will be so mad.

After the boxcars, a file of grimy tankers.

She went quickly to the conductor.

"Can you hold the train?"

He stared.

"Just for a minute."

He had a walrus mustache and a high-crowned, flat-brimmed hat. His eyes squinted at her.

"Please," she said, swallowing her pride. "My friend got caught on the wrong side."

The conductor popped his big gold watch. "We've got a schedule." He peered between the cars. Fry stood in the intermittent shadows of the tankers.

"The asshole." The man looked at her, as if he must exact a price.

It made her mad, him talking like that.

"The goddamn"—he smirked, enjoying her discomfort—"gaping asshole." He checked his watch again, peering down his nose at it. Snapped it shut. "Sorry, honey," he said. "James J. Hill don't run his railroad on Indian time." He turned and strode toward the front, circling his upraised hand to signal the engineer. He looked back, brass buttons gleaming, a portly, satisfied man, and swung himself up.

Signet bumped ahead an inch—then stopped, in the fluxional moment before departure. She went partway up the steps, gripped the railing, turned and peered at the freight. The caboose trundled past: The air seemed to shimmer in its wake. The Pullman had begun to roll when Fry came jogging across the track. The car picked up speed. Fry ducked his head and pumped his legs. His footfalls on the platform were drowned by the many screeches and clanks of the moving cars. He raised his eyes to hers. Sprinted harder, reached out, caught her hand, and swung himself up onto the steps. His body pressed lightly against hers. She felt a wiry strength through his hand, which she did not abandon until she was sure he was safely aboard. She felt, also, a hard, foreign something in the center of his torso—she flushed and almost giggled, but it was too high for *that*. Then he was pulling back, laughing and shaking his head and panting his thanks.

The sky was deep blue with tiny stipples of cloud, as if someone had shot them up there with a scattergun. The light was low and slanting: getting around to winter again. On all sides, grass, nothing but grass. The train mounted a curve and she could see far ahead, see the shining rails straighten and converge. Crooked poles with green-glass insulators carried twin wires along the track; they marched all the way to the horizon to vanish with the rails. The train completed the curve, and she was confronted again with the absolutes of sky, clouds, and grass.

To everyone else it had seemed ironic and cruel that she should have been the one to find Fidelity. To her it was the most natural thing in the world. The woman was her mother. Small wonder she should have excused herself from the supper table, gone out the door into the still-wicked sun, kicked her shoes off, and run down to the river.

The agency was quiet, dead. Ninety-five, maybe a hundred in the shade. A dry breeze sifted. In a field, magpies stood panting, their wings upraised. The river would be cool, she would hitch up her dress and wade, or shuck it there on the bank and swim, under the cottonwoods in the little backwater where Mr. Archambault kept his rowboat, which he'd used that time to tow the sturgeon in, and when they slit it open there were eggs inside, hundreds of them, round and glossy as pearls. Muskrats lived in the backwater, and frogs, and ducks—little fluffy ones that followed their mottled brown mother into the cattails whenever Annie approached.

Today the ducks were nowhere to be seen. There was only the rickety wagon and, in a patch of shade, the horse grazing the sparse grass: the paint mare, unharnessed and staked out.

The backwater was still. The body did not bob. It came in like a log when she pulled on a heel. The skirt was hitched up around the middle so that the buttocks showed. The buttocks and the backs of the legs were smooth and brown. The feet were wrinkled and strangely white, some of the toes missing: just bones left, curling down like possum tails—she supposed that the turtles had nibbled them. She pulled the ankles into the shallows, crossed them, and heaved one leg over the other so that the body turned in the water, in waltz time, arms like eels. The skin around the pudenda was thinly haired, puckered and off-white. The face, under a swirl of hair, had white blotches all over it. The teeth were good Indian teeth, straight and strong and white. So someone else had died; she wondered if she would be given sweets.

She found a heavy sodden branch to lay across her mother's ankles so that the river, if it rose, should not carry Fidelity away. She worked for maybe an hour to drag the branch down the bank and place it across Fidelity's swollen ankles. Then she got into Mr. Archambault's rowboat and untied it, and when the current refused to reach into the backwater and take her, she found a pole and pushed, pushed until the body was a small drab lump on the bank, and the cottonwoods, where the screech owls lived, began shifting steadily to hide it from view. She lay in the boat, hearing the current sanding the hull; almost immediately in the heavy, pressing heat she fell asleep. When she woke it was night. The stars were bright, in skewed patterns. She slept again. Some time the next day the boat hung up at Mobridge, where the whiskery man looked in and said, "Well holy hell, you must be the little squaw they're huntin'," and turned her in for the reward. And she felt, in a way, that she had drifted ever since.

26

"They went in the dead of night, toward morning, when the heart lags and the capacity for action is low.

"They set forth from Bull Head's cabin, riding two by two, the horses' hooves striking sparks on the road. No moon or stars. The white kerchiefs that Louise had made for them rose and fell like moths."

The words arrived like stones dropped in a well. There was no eye contact between them. Fry did not feel like a recording device, he felt like a priest in a house that might soon be in mourning.

"They had not taken the wagon, as instructed: Just saddle up his big horse, Bull Head said, get him on it and ride away.

"The riders entered the wide bed of the Grand. The horses' hooves crushed the strange petrifactions that lay in the dry, sandy places. Shards of petrified wood and turtle shells and little skulls slid down off the banks into the black water. Hinhaska, the white owl, laughed from the trees like a heyoka. The police splashed up the bank and stopped. In the camp, no fires were flickering. No dogs barked. A fine sleet came ticking against the hat brims. Bull Head's voice was calm: Red Bear and White Bird will saddle the gray horse. Little Eagle, High Eagle, Red Tomahawk, Shoots Walking, Shave Head—you come into the cabin with me. Bull Head looked to his troop. Hopo, he said. They put their heels in their horses' ribs. The animals walked, then trotted, then stretched out their legs and ran.

"Bull Head hammered his rifle butt on the door. A voice from within said, 'Hau, timahel hiyuwo.' Bull Head kicked the door open and they flooded in. A match spurted and kissed a wick. Sitting Bull sat up and his wife covered her nakedness. The many pairs of moccasins hissed on the floor. Little Eagle and High Eagle pulled him out of bed, and Bull Head said, 'You are under arrest,' and Shave Head said, 'Brother, we have come for you,' and Red Tomahawk said, 'If you fight us, you are dead.'

"They thrust articles of clothing at him. Sitting Bull sat back on the bed. 'I'm going with you,' he said, 'but I must have my best clothes.'

"On the wall was a painting of Sitting Bull wearing a head-dress and holding a rifle, which an admiring white woman had painted. Medicine bundles hung on rawhide strings. A young child lifted its head and whimpered. One of Sitting Bull's wives started scolding the policemen, while the other began a mournful keening. High Eagle tried to force a moccasin onto Sitting Bull's foot while Shoots Walking pulled a shirt over his head. 'You needn't dress me,' Sitting Bull said. 'You needn't honor me this way.'

"Outside, the sleet had stopped. Some of them worked at saddling the big gray circus horse, while others stood holding their fellows' riderless mounts, which danced and neighed back and forth at the Ghost Dancers' horses. Dogs barked. The white kerchiefs of the police let them see each other — and be seen. The dancers started coming, in ones and twos and threes. Gun steel flashed. They cried out angrily, 'What are you doing in this camp? This is a Hunkpapa camp!'

"One of the wives leaned through the doorway and cried, 'They have come for him!'"

Now McLaughlin turned toward Fry. The words came gushing out.

"When Sitting Bull reached the door frame he tried to block himself in it. They kicked and shoved him through. Bull Head held an arm, his rifle pointed at Sitting Bull's ribs. Shave Head gripped the other arm. Behind, Red Tomahawk pressed a pistol into Sitting Bull's neck. A dirty ribbon of light lay along the horizon. The police looked black in their dark uniforms, with the white kerchiefs and the silver stars. The crowd pressed in, making them give ground.

"'Kill them, shoot the old Metal Breasts and the young ones will run away!'

"'Let him go!'

"'Get out of here!'

"'You are killing your own medicine man!'

"Catch-the-Bear came stalking down the line, blanket falling off his shoulder, looking each Metal Breast in the face. Catch-the-Bear was chief of Sitting Bull's guard. He nurtured an old grudge against Bull Head. On he came, hunting. Little Assiniboine, Sitting Bull's blood brother, spoke words of reason. 'Let us break camp and move to the agency,' he called out to Sitting Bull. 'Brother, you take your family and I'll take mine. If you must die there, I'll die with you.' The police tried to move Sitting Bull toward the gray horse, but the crowd would not let them. Red Bear and White Bird brought the gray closer. Buffalo Bill had given it to Sitting Bull, a trick horse. The dirty light had grown more general. It made the sage bushes look like people. It made the people look like rocks. One of Sitting Bull's wives sang, 'Sitting Bull, you have always been a brave man, what is going to happen now?' She sang it over and over again.

"In the cabin door, black in the light from behind, Sitting Bull's son appeared. Crow Foot's shadow was long and grotesque. His voice was resonant like his father's, and full of scorn. 'You have always called yourself a brave chief, and now you give yourself up to Indians in blue coats!'

"Sitting Bull stiffened and began to thrash. *'Hopo, hopo!'* someone shouted. Catch-the-Bear pressed his rifle's trigger and Lieutenant Bull Head fell. In falling, Bull Head shot his own gun, the ball slanting upward through Sitting Bull's body. In the same moment Red Tomahawk shot Sitting Bull in the head."

He sat propped up in bed, sunlight warming him through the window. The train had stopped in an unknown town with a ramshackle grain elevator, shabby stores, and clapboard houses whittled by wind and sun and dust. Outside, not far off, a man was singing. The voice was untrained, but strong and pure, carrying a tune McLaughlin did not know; the singer could be heard above the sounds of the train, though the words could not be made out, only the clear notes floating through the air.

His face was pale, he felt weak as a kitten, but the fever had climbed to a final pitch, and broken, and the chills that had afflicted him had not come back. He looked around for Fry or Annie, but the room was empty. He whispered to himself, "The big gray circus horse sat on his haunches like a dog. Bullets sang all around. The horse must have thought he was back in the ring. He raised one hoof and pawed at the air. He lowered that hoof and raised the other one. The police and the Ghost Dancers believed that the spirit of Sitting Bull had entered the body of the horse. By some miracle the horse wasn't hit. The police retreated to the cabin and the corral. They were well schooled, and acquitted themselves quite favorably under fire, although in the cabin they committed a shameful act. They found Crow Foot hiding under a bed, drove him out the door, and shot him."

There was an empty glass in his hand with dried milk on the rim. He looked at it and set it on the table.

"The troops, F and G of the Eighth, appeared on the lip of the valley, which was filled with smoke. They set up the Hotchkiss gun, and fired one shell. It landed near the corral and exploded. The Ghost Dancers fled.

"The troops secured the camp, saw to the wounded, built fires, and cooked breakfast. After a while, a man in a ghost shirt came out of the trees by the river. He lowered his lance and rode toward the soldiers, who shot at him with their rifles. He wheeled his horse and rode across in front of them, singing, 'Father, you said we were going to live.' Then he went into the trees, and was gone."

Annie knocked softly and came into the room. She brightened when she saw that his head was up and he was giving attention to the world.

He looked at her, and through a mist of tears he managed a smile. I had to do it, he thought. Forgive me, daughter. I could have done no other.

27

In Minot, North Dakota, Booth went into the bar of the Mercantile Hotel, ordered a beer, and struck up a conversation with the man standing next to him. Each expressed concern over recent events in Europe. "There will be a war," the man predicted. He identified himself as a grain broker. "It will be very good for business."

Several beers later, Booth stepped into the street. Electric lamps buzzed above the quiet town. The breeze blew the cigar smoke off his jacket. He strolled with his hands in his pockets, whistling. At the station he had to wait as a freight rumbled past. The engine shook the sidewalk planks and rattled trackside windows; Booth felt the heat from the firebox pass over his face, as if the sun had shone through a hole in the clouds. Cattle cars shuttled past, a long string of them, crammed with bawling, shuffling beasts. "Whoopie ti yi yo," Booth said, touching the brim of his hat.

When the track cleared he crossed over and walked the far platform. A ball of paper sat next to a hole rusted through the base of a trash can. He kicked the paper, and the breeze took it and rolled it along. It stopped on the edge of the platform, where he bent and picked it up. He uncrumpled the paper, spread it. A photograph, its emulsion cracked in a spiderweb of lines. He almost threw it away before noticing that the image was round. He strained for details, then hurried back and rummaged through the bin and found another crumpled-up paper. He strode to Signet and took the steps two at a time.

Dixon was in his stateroom. Booth burst in. "Here's your candid photographer!" He flattened the photographs on Dixon's desk: Booth from behind, in conversation with a handsome Cayuse woman whom Dixon later had photographed, entitling his portrait, "Flower of the Wigwam." Dixon standing on the observation deck of Signet, reaching out a hand to see if it was raining . . . the picture taken from *inside* the private car.

"Giannetti?"

Booth shook his head. "He's in the darkroom too much. Although maybe the wop printed 'em."

"Then who . . . ?"

"McLaughlin or Fry."

"Not McLaughlin—that's preposterous."

Booth winked. "He's got this fetish. Likes to take pictures of people when they don't know it. Gives him a feeling of power."

"Power he's already got." Dixon's face was astonished. "Fry?"

Booth grinned. "None other. Small Fry. Oh, yeah, it'll be something, watching him swing."

Dixon sat back, still holding the photos. "Say nothing to Giannetti. He may not be involved."

"Want me to grab Fry and frisk him?"

"Not yet. Do that and he doesn't have a camera, and we'll never catch him. Wait, and watch. If you get a chance, search his luggage. At some point we'll know. And then we'll make our move. In public. The candid photographer will be exposed." Dixon shook his head. "Most embarrassing to the Bureau of Indian Affairs. Most embarrassing to Inspector McLaughlin."

They met the combined Gros Ventre, Arikara, and Mandan tribes in Elbowoods, North Dakota, on September 27.

Afterwards they laid over in Bismarck. Booth was cha-
grined. He hadn't caught Fry photographing, hadn't caught
him doing anything suspicious at all. Nor had he met his self-
imposed deadline for getting into Annie Owns the Fire's
bloomers. Not because he hadn't tried. He had dined her and
attempted to wine her (she said she never drank), taken her
on long walks in private places, bought her candy, brushed
against her every chance he could get. Once, in a screaming fit
of horniness, he even tapped on her door in the middle of the
night (she hadn't answered). So she hadn't spurned him yet,
but she hadn't encouraged him, either.

Booth had never been one to walk away from a challenge.
Something stood in your way, you bowled it over. Something
fled, you kept walking after it, not too fast, not too slow, you
just kept walking purposefully, steadily, until finally it
stopped. Sooner or later he would get her. Because she was so
fine.

He would get Fry too. The little weasel kept a padlock on
his trunk. He didn't carry around a book (his notepad was too
small, ditto his fountain pen), or a cane, or a parcel, or a pistol.
(One company made a camera that looked like a revolver:
You pointed it, then pulled the trigger to release the shutter.
Imagine the expression you'd get—now that would be a can-
did shot!) So, thought Booth, maybe he just sneaks it out and
palms it. Or like Giannetti said, wears it under his coat.
Though where could he put it? Didn't seem to be any bulge.
And how skinny could a guy be?

At the post office they picked up mail. The clipping service
had forwarded a fresh copy of the Washington *Dispatch* with
eight new candids to be pored over. The Interstate Fair in
Spokane, where they had knocked off ten tribes, ten flags
flying on the line—the candids showed people eating cotton
candy, shelling peanuts, having fun. A nigger, all eyes and
teeth, spread against a wall, getting frisked by a couple of
cops. Then some hollow-faced Indian kids in smocks. And a

picture of some hick photographer taking a picture of whoever it was taking all of these other pictures—it *had* to be Fry—the man waving the slide and saying something, dumb look on his face, bunch of Indians gathered around looking suspicious: It was one hell of a shot. Maybe there was something to this candid photography after all.

Booth had a date with Annie that night, if you could call it that. She wanted to go to the Carnegie Library and look at the books, see if there were any she could take to the reservation to use in her teaching. Booth shaved with scented soap, brushed his teeth, and gargled. He wetted his comb and straightened the part in the center of his head. Not too many chances after this. He whistled a few bars of his college fight song.

"Annie, you're one fine and lovely filly. Annie, the hell with this book business, let's go hop in the sack."

He knocked on her door.

She came out fresh and pretty as could be. This is the night, he told himself. She looked at him with her serious black eyes. She wore a pleated skirt, a starched ivory-colored shirtwaist with a black tie. Her hair was pinned in a pompadour, under a black hat. You look like a Gibson girl, he thought. A Gibson squaw. Wanna fuck?

The night air was cool. The library was down a lamplit street lined with box elders that had lost most of their leaves; the leaves scraped along in the gutter with the wind. A red brick building, concrete steps mounting to a pillared entry. He caught her in the shadows and laughingly tried to plant a kiss at the base of her neck; she smiled a little but pulled away. The librarian was an old maid with frameless eyeglasses and a frosty tone. "The books may be used here in the library, Miss. Burleigh County residents *only* are eligible for loaning cards." Annie went through the stacks anyway, browsed in the history section, checked for a couple of titles in literature. When she reached for books on the top shelf, he relished her long limbs and lifting breasts.

She tried again with the lady at the desk. "I'm sorry, Miss. Those are the rules. We can't just flout them, now can we? Perhaps there's a library in the county of your residence."

"Come on," she said to Booth.

Outside, he took her arm in his. He liked the way the librarian had looked at him, as if he were some kind of reprobate, to be taking up with an Indian. He smiled and gave Annie's arm a squeeze. Steered her left at one corner, right at the next, seeking out a dark side street. He got them down near the tracks. He turned her into a field, stopped, took both her shoulders in his hands, and kissed her.

She didn't return the kiss. He drew back but could barely see her face. He pulled her to him and reached around behind her, cupping her buttocks, drawing her hips into his. He felt the points of her breasts; her hat fell back off her head.

He probed with his tongue. Still no response. It beat all. He felt himself swollen, jamming against her front. He ran one hand up her flank, up her side under the coat, and sought out a breast. There. Now she was moving. Struggling, trying to get away.

Won't do you any good. His weight bore her down. He opened her lips with his teeth, tasting blood. Her hands pressed against his shoulders. With one hand he kneaded her breast. With the other hand he explored beneath her skirt. She was under him, struggling, then subsiding, then rocking up against him, and he relaxed and smiled and drew back to have a nice look.

That quick she rolled and broke away. He grunted and had about grabbed her back when he saw them, two men coming across the field. He hesitated, just long enough for her to gain her feet and start walking.

"Annie," he said, getting up. She kept on walking, stumbling through the weeds. The men came nearer, it looked like uniforms, better wait. They came on up. *Shit*, a couple of trainmen carrying suitcases. One of the men smirked at him. "Lose your girlfriend?" he said.

Booth gauged the distance from his fist to the man's chin. Then he shrugged.

"Don't worry, buddy," the man said. "Plenty more where that come from."

The other man took a pack of cigarettes out of his coat, shook one out for himself, and offered one to Booth. Booth took it and accepted a light. The first trainman said, "Come on and have a drink."

In a saloon around the corner they bought him a boiler-maker. He inquired as to the local talent and was directed to a yellow two-story house with scrollwork under the eaves, where he had another drink and bought a brass check for fifty cents, entitling him to ten minutes with a boarder.

McLaughlin sat at his desk in the stateroom. He had just finished reading the Commissioner's latest letter, a nagging shrill tirade. Thanks to the candid photographs, Cribbs was feeling the heat again, the do-gooders had all ganged up on him, talk of a Congressional inquiry, of course the Bureau could be doing a better job, just name one federal agency that couldn't, the difficulty of administering the various tribes, problems of logistics, budgetary restraints—the bitching went on and on. He put the letter down and had a look at the candids in the latest copy of that Washington rag. He smiled at a boy trying to fit his mouth around a swirl of cotton candy; looked just like Tom, that time they'd gone to Bismarck for the state fair. The Indian children, frail and wasted by consumption, sobered him. Also a picture of some listless young Indian men lounging in front of a barbershop. Then the one where the candid photographer had been looking down the barrel, so to speak, of the other fellow's camera. He thought it an astonishing photograph: the cautious frowns of the Indian onlookers, the bored look on the commercial photographer's face, the head-and-shoulders shadow of the mysterious snap-shooter intruding into the frame. He recalled a commercial photographer like that—where was it, back on the Blackfoot res? Now if you really wanted to know, you'd wire back to Browning and get Art Hay to look up that photographer and ask to see his plates.

He decided he didn't really want to know.

He put away Cribbs's letter, picked up a second letter, and stood, feeling stiff and puny but finally with some life in his bones. He left the stateroom and went down the hall. Fry, as usual, was ensconced at his desk.

"Ansel," McLaughlin said, raising the letter. "Buffalo Bill is back on the plains."

Fry's face lit up. "Where?"

"Standing Rock. Here, read about it. He's formed a motion picture company, gotten General Miles out of mothballs, and the War Department has loaned him three troops of cavalry. Supposed to be making a film called 'Buffalo Bill's Indian Wars.'"

"On Standing Rock?"

"First they were at Pine Ridge, doing the Battle of Wounded Knee. Now it's the capture of Sitting Bull."

She hadn't expected it, certainly not that quickly. She hadn't wanted it, hadn't particularly liked the man, although there was something about him, his boyish face and exuberance, combined with confidence and that ever-present masculine strength.

Standing in front of the mirror, brushing out her hair, her hands trembled so that she had to lay the brush down. She placed her palms on the bureau and took a deep, painful breath. Her lips were bruised, her back ached, and she'd lost her hat—for some reason that made her the maddest. And there was nothing she could do. She could hardly go to the police, he hadn't raped her, and even if he had, what then? You can't rape an Indian wench. Likely he'd tasted it on the reservations; plenty were willing, why not this one? She could go to Father McLaughlin, but it would put him on the spot: He would confront Dixon, Dixon would no doubt back Booth, and this tense butting of egos would grind even harder.

That night, after she heard him return, she went and knocked at Booth's door.

He had just climbed into bed. He got up naked, opened the door a crack, blinked at the light, and saw who it was. A sequence of expressions passed over his face—surprise, anger, puzzlement, hope, and then—his eyebrows sliding back and his teeth baring—lust. She stood there in a chemise. Her hair was let down, her arms spread one on either side of the door, so that the passageway light placed her body in silhouette.

"I'll be damned," he said huskily, opening the door and reaching to take her.

She shoved the gun barrel in his belly and advanced, and he went stumbling back on his heels until he hit the wall, cracking a pane with his elbow, the window latch gouging his back.

"Jesus," he whimpered.

She leaned, driving the muzzle into him. The hammer on the rifle was cocked back. She held the buttstock clamped between her elbow and side like a soldier doing bayonet drill. The gun sight disappeared into his flesh.

"I understand," he pleaded. *"Jesus God, I understand."*

His hands quivered on the ends of arms that knocked and twitched. His face was wide and gray, and his baby blue eyes begged above his apple cheeks. He gasped, his features knotting in a grimace.

She heard him spattering on the floor. The anger had all burned out of her. She felt weak and weary and sad. She drew the muzzle back, turned, and left.

28

The superintendent's wife led the parade, riding on a motorcycle, American flags on the handlebars and bunting woven through the spokes. She wore goggles and a hat tied to her head with a scarf. In a cloud of exhaust and with the engine blatting, she proceeded in barely controlled S-curves down the broad street. Among the spectators were people from the reaches of the reservation who had never seen an automobile, let alone a motorcycle, and when she approached, they danced back with shrill cries; the braver among them feigned indifference, at peril to life and limb.

Behind her, McLaughlin strolled arm in arm with his old friend, the tribal elder John Grass, dressed in a gray suit, hobbling along with a cane. Dixon and the superintendent followed; then Fry, Booth, and Giannetti, in a wagon with the Edison; then a stout white man in a plaid shirt and a black hat, who hurled a silver baton high into the air and, when it came tumbling down, caught it about every second chance. Horns blaring and drums thumping, the Standing Rock Reservation Marching Band brought up the rear.

McLaughlin was saddened by the garbage-strewn lawns, the houses in need of paint, the broken fences and sagging gates. After the Army had left years ago, the Missouri shifted in its bed so that boats—the few that still plied the river—no longer stopped at the town; clearly Fort Yates was in decline. He took heart, however, at the great crowd lining the street, and recognized many faces, and was hailed with shouts and cheers.

The marchers accordioned into a dusty lot next to the cemetery, where the expedition members and dignitaries mounted a wooden stand. The spectators, a thousand or more, filled the field. The vast majority were Indians, many wearing bright blanket capes or buckskins, surplices of porcupine quills, beaded pouches and peace medals, dark dresses spangled with polished elk teeth, great trailing bonnets of snowy, black-tipped eagle feathers. The Edison drew its wondering murmurs; the flagpole was a towering stepped staff with a bright ball on top, brought over from the decommissioned fort, and much was made of its great height, one hundred feet, which was nevertheless sixty-five feet shorter than the promised memorial in the harbor of New York. The huge flag climbed the pole in increments, as people threw back their heads and gaped.

Dixon: "The Great Spirit smiles on us today. The wonderful plains and hills of Dakota stretch away from where Old Glory now waves. There is music in the swish of the wind through the prairie grass, there is solemnity in the mighty flow of the river, there is great glory in the cerulean sky. . . ."

Fry, his pen scraping, searched for faces in the near crowd, but Annie's was not among them. He was still basking in the memory of yesterday. The two of them had been alone in the observation room. She had seemed moody and tense, but the longer they talked the more relaxed she became. She picked up the *Dispatch*—the latest one, he hadn't filed it yet—and looked at the candids. "I know these children," she said excitedly, pointing at the picture from Lapwai. "That's Bobby Fox. About once a week I had to scold him for dipping some little girl's pigtail in the inkwell. Catherine Murphy's a Mohave—absolutely addicted to animal crackers. And Tim White Dog, Chippewa, he's a real marble shooter, he's won about all the aggies in the whole school." She was wearing her hair up, and fine black sprays of it stood on the back of her neck. Her upper lip, Fry noticed, was swollen—had she bumped herself? "At Lapwai," she said, growing sober, "only one child in five goes home." She gazed at the page. "'An expert operating in the West.' I wonder who it could be."

How he longed to tell her—but bit his tongue. Impossible, he couldn't take the chance. He'd been jumpy lately, had a feeling that somehow, somebody knew. He had even considered taking the camera off for a while.

She held the page for him. "Here," she said, "this woman walking past the tree. Do you see how the tree is moving?"

He looked, puzzled. "It's outside the field of focus."

"No, I think it's in motion."

"Maybe the wind?"

"It's moving by itself," she said. "Like the people. That's one of the good things about these pictures, they show how everything's alive. This tree, like it's bending over to whisper something in her ear." She smiled, touched his forearm lightly. Had she any idea how that *jolted* him? "An old man once told me that the world is not made up of things that are living and things that are dead. Everything, he said, is living; nothing is dead. Rocks, mountains, old logs, spider webs"—she laughed—"hubcaps from Hupmobiles.

"That's Indian religion. I don't pretend to understand it. But I think this photographer feels it. He knows not to look at things too close. He knows that if you look off to one side, sometimes you can see more than if you just look straight ahead."

They had spent the rest of the afternoon together: she talking of Lapwai and the strain of teaching there, he going on about Washington, the cosmopolitan city where you could hear ten different languages on the street, go to a different play or concert or art exhibit each night. He was concerned about her teaching in a sanitarium. Wasn't it dangerous?

"Certainly," she had said. "Father made me go to the Mayo Clinic, all the way to Minneapolis, twice a year for a tuberculin test. Negative, always negative. Which made me wonder, why them"—she had touched the paper lightly—"and not me?"

There was a break in the ceremony as the Indians signed the Declaration of Allegiance: eight old men in suits and ties and feather headdresses, one of them Red Tomahawk, the policeman who long ago had shot Sitting Bull. Then Dixon beamed at McLaughlin. "The Missouri River over there flows wonderfully deep," he said. "It goes first to one bank and then to the other and cuts a new path for its course. Major McLaughlin's work for the Indian is like the flow of that river, strong and deep; but he has never gone from one bank to the other. The current of his service flows straight, and sweeps on to the Gulf."

The applause was loud and long. McLaughlin spoke through the interpreter. "My friends, I am happy to be with you today. I was your agent for fourteen years at a very trying time. But during that excitement twenty-three years ago, I had the satisfaction of knowing that nine out of ten, and ninety out of a hundred, and nine hundred out of every thousand of you remained loyal to the flag. And when I look out over your faces today, I see that my efforts were not in vain."

Afterwards, Fry went among the people. He looked for Annie but did not find her. He made a couple of photographs and was stalking for a third when he chanced to look to one side—and saw Booth staring. The burly photographer turned and began fiddling with his camera. Fry stood stock-still. Booth didn't normally work the crowd. He let go of the string and casually removed his hand from his pocket. Booth took a couple of steps and faded into the throng.

Sounds impinged on his consciousness—a bell ringing, men laughing, the cadence of yet another Indian tongue. Suddenly he remembered going into his trunk a couple of mornings ago and finding it sitting an inch away from the wall—and he was always particular about shoving it flush. He glimpsed Booth's head above the crowd, pointedly (or so it seemed) looking in the opposite direction.

He put picture-taking out of his mind and started walking. Strangers' faces, coppery and dark, men and women, boys and girls. Then he saw her, alone, entering the cemetery.

The graves had markers for Antelopes and Magpie Eagles and Kills Crows. Its crosses were of wood and rusting jointed pipe. On some of the graves, withered flowers sat in Mason jars. Doves cooed from arborvitae trees, then flashed out of the deep green branches on whistling, peach-colored wings. The drums began to thump as the parade started back to town.

She stood in front of a red stone obelisk that soared above the crosses. While he watched, she lowered her head and crossed herself. He thought of photographing her, and was instantly ashamed. He considered leaving, but didn't. After a while he went up.

"Annie."

"Oh. Ansel."

He stood beside her and read the inscription on the obelisk. *These were killed at Grand River, Standing Rock Indian Reservation, December 15, 1890 . . .*

"They say it was the biggest funeral the town ever had," she said.

. . . in battle with hostile Indians while arresting the noted chief Sitting Bull . . .

"A priest and a minister both. Soldiers fired volleys over the graves."

. . . who was also killed in the fight. Forty-three policemen were opposed by 160 armed fanatical Ghost Dancers.

United States Indian Police.
Lieutenant Bull Head.
Sergeant Shave Head.
Sergeant Little Eagle.
Private Warriors Fear Him.
Private Broken Arm.
Private Hawk Man.
Private Owns the Fire.

He caught his breath. The doves came whistling back.

"Annie," he said. "Your father?"

She nodded. "My mother's in here too, over in the corner." Her eyes, dry, were black in the late-day light. "Come with me," she said.

She led him not to her mother's grave, but out of the cemetery. It was a short walk to the post graveyard. "When the army left," she said, "they took everything with them, even their dead." Tan grass tufted the bare, vacant lot. A weathered picket fence protected the sole remaining grave, whose grass was thick and green. The flat wooden slab had been whittled at for souvenirs, and the paint had all but weathered away, but the stenciled letters still could be read:

SITTING BULL

DIED

DECEMBER 1890

"They claim his body was mutilated," Annie said. "I asked Father about it once. He said the face was smashed because Holy Medicine beat it with a yoke. Holy Medicine was Private Broken Arm's brother; I think he was also an uncle of mine. Anyway, he's been dead for years. Holy Medicine was a Ghost Dancer, the one who sewed all their shirts. He underwent a sudden loss of religion when his brother got killed."

"What does it mean, Annie?" he said. "Why do people hate each other?"

"I don't think people hate," she said. "They just get caught in the middle. When the world moves, they get crushed."

They walked slowly down the hill toward the McLaughlins' house, a big white turreted house, with shrubbery and flower beds, a porch with a green glider, a stained-glass fanlight above the door. The evening was coming on. He looked at her, serene and lovely and strong. At the doorstep she gave him a smile of incredible brightness that made his heart lift.

In his room, he opened his suitcase. He took off the camera and buried it under his shirts, along with the changing bag and plates. He flopped down in a chair. That bastard Booth. Why should he be watching me? He clenched his jaws. He hated it, having his gear so unprotected, but there had been no choice: He'd been forced to leave his trunk back in Bismarck on Signet, because it was so big. He refused to be without his camera for the trip to see Buffalo Bill but the suitcase didn't seem secure.

Upstairs, in the room where she had slept as a child, Annie stood at the window. The Missouri was darkening under faint shoals of mist. Beyond the water the land humped, then flattened and ran.

Such a shy, unprepossessing man. At first glance so formal, so stiff, sissified in that old suit; destined, probably, to be an old bachelor, what the ranchers called a buck nun. She frowned slightly, shook her head. Then you get to talking with him. You listen to his words—even more, to the way he says them—and there's depth. Nervous about something, yes, but doing a pretty fair job of covering up. And he cares about people. A stenographer, a background man, always on the fringe, observing, recording.

She lit the reading lamp, adjusted the wick, replaced the

chimney and globe. She opened her handbag and took out the photograph she had clipped from the newspaper magazine.

Candid Photography from the American West. It was a beautiful, heart-wrenching photograph. The children were in their smocks, so it must have been the evening quiet time. They were studying, or at least Catherine was, bent over a book. Bobby looked as if he was about to reach out and take a poke at Tim, and Tim was squinting and leaning back, getting ready to defend himself or launch an attack of his own. So different from the official class portrait, the annual ritual on the steps of the school—the photographer signaling, and she, behind and to the right of her class (the full complement that would dwindle all too soon), would lift her chin, square her shoulders, purse her lips, turn their corners slightly upward in a frozen semblance of a smile.

Still looking at the photograph, she unpinned her hair. She began brushing it, working the bristles through the long straight strands.

It had to be him. The day on the hill at the Little Bighorn, when they had stood watching the Crow scout, White Man Runs Him. And that time he'd almost missed the train—she closed her eyes, remembering. He had taken her hand, and she'd felt a surprising current of strength through it. Then his body had brushed hers. And on his torso she'd felt a hidden hardness, a clothing-covered bump. A camera? If so, why hadn't Father figured it out? Having lost count of the strokes, she let the hand holding the brush fall to her side. If she asked him, would he tell her? Probably not.

In the morning Mrs. McLaughlin served up a big breakfast of pancakes, ham and eggs, and hashed potatoes. The tablecloth was linen and the silver was neatly ranked. Louise

McLaughlin was a demure, retiring woman who looked more Indian than white; in her demeanor, her quiet deference to her husband, she reminded Fry of an imported Oriental wife. The major's son Sibley sat at the table, a dark and nervous man in his middle years, with a stutter that blackened his face while seizing his tongue. The family would wait mildly until Sibley, at last fighting free of his impediment, went sailing ahead with his speech as if nothing had bogged it.

After the meal McLaughlin went off to have a wagon loaded with tents and bedding, sheepherders' stoves and victuals, Dixon's and Booth's camera equipment. The expedition would proceed to Sitting Bull's camp, while Annie would head for the Antelope Creek School—actually not far from the camp, about five miles up Grand River.

She asked Fry along to the livery, where, from her savings, she bought a buckboard and a span of matched bays. She drove to the agency commissary, where he helped her load flour, sugar, salt, cornmeal, dried beans, coffee and tea, boxes of canned goods, apples in crates, salt pork, baking powder, soap, candles, kerosene, wicks, mantles, matches, a whole case of cod-liver oil. He held up a bottle, made a face. "They love it," she said. "The rancider, the better." Her eyes were charged with light. They bumped heads bending for a crate, straightened with a laugh.

"Let's have lunch," Fry suggested.

There was only one place in town, a boarding house with long plank tables covered with red-and-white oilcloth. When they went in, three white men looked up, local farmhands, their faces dusted with wheat chaff, mouths churning beneath sullen eyes.

"What I'd like," Annie said, "is a picnic. Mrs. Dennison will make up two box lunches if you ask."

They took the food over by the agency office and sat on a bench beneath a bare cottonwood whose shadow lay upon theirs. He was very aware of her: the smell of her hair, the way her shoulderblades lifted against her coat, the whisper of her skirt when she walked. She leaned over to get some food, and her hand brushed his. He felt a surge of attraction so intense it built up in waves behind his eyeballs. Then his heart fell. So little time. Tomorrow she was leaving, and he would never see her again.

Across from the bench stood a short brick pedestal, on top of it a smooth rounded stone about two feet high. "That's the Standing Rock," Annie said.

"Really? I expected a tall spire or a cliff."

"You won't find any spires or cliffs around here. Just these strange little rocks. They're called concretions." She took a bite of chicken. "Actually, that lump of rock is a Sioux woman. You see, she had a terrible mean tongue, and kept whipping her poor husband with it until finally the Great Spirit decided to step in." She giggled. "Poof! Turned that hussy into stone. That's her, with her child on her back."

"She's pretty short," Fry said.

"And awfully quiet."

"Like you."

"And you. We're two of a kind. We don't talk unless something needs saying."

"Maybe we don't talk, even *when* something needs saying."

"Such as?"

He ducked his head, dropped a chicken bone in the sack. "Some ceremony, wasn't it? The people love Major McLaughlin."

"He's a good man. They respect him."

"I like him."

"He was a good father to me. The thing that's best about him, the thing that makes the Indians love him, is that he never tells a lie. Never." She smoothed a fold in her skirt. "He isn't perfect. If you don't do things his way, don't abide by his rules, you're in deep trouble. But he's always honest—you might say honest to a fault."

"Annie, what do you think about this whole hullabaloo—the Expedition of Citizenship, the ceremony, the Indian Memorial?"

"I don't suppose it does much harm," she said. "Although I don't like the idea of a monument." She lifted her chin toward the Standing Rock. "They make a statue of a person, and there it is, it's funny, or heroic, or romantic, but it's just a rock. And then everyone forgets about the thing it's supposed to represent."

"I don't trust it, either," Fry said. "Too grand. Too designed for publicity, for effect."

She nodded. "What can you do about it?"

He looked at her. Something in her tone suggested the question was real: that the "you" signified not some nameless, theoretical person, but Ansel Edwin Fry, a gray man with a camera under his coat. A man with a good dozen photographs that caution had kept him from sending: Dixon with his flag tricks, Dixon tossing nickels in the air, Dixon urging Indians to kiss the flag. And while the pictures Booth took of these scenes looked dramatic and stirring, Fry's own images painted them as so much hokum: Dixon gesturing, the Indians looking sarcastic or bemused—and that one shot, he'd waited a long time until Dixon had finally done it again, had paid an Indian, actually passed money to the man, bribed him into signing the Declaration of Allegiance. He had enough photos, Fry guessed, to sink this expedition. And now he sat, a bump on a log, the moment slipping away, until finally Annie said, "Well," and brushed the crumbs off her skirt.

The sun was lowering and the air growing cool. She packed up the remains of the lunch and stood, the shadow of a tree limb across her face. He saw her eyes and the upthrust cheekbones. "Thank you," she said.

"My pleasure."

They walked toward the McLaughlins' house.

"I'm so excited, Ansel," she said. "I can't wait to get out there and start teaching. Teach them facts and figures, how to write, what the capital of Venezuela is."

"Maracaibo?"

She grinned. "Caracas. I want to teach them how to feed themselves properly, how to stay healthy and clean—and above all, how to be themselves. How to be Sioux people, and still fit into this country, this world.

"And I want to learn from them! Growing up here"—she looked at the McLaughlins' house—"I learned one set of ways. Now I want to learn a new set of ways."

"I envy you," he said.

"Don't. A lot of it will be bitter. It's like it is on most of the reservations, almost no medical care. Somebody gets appendicitis—" She opened and closed her hands helplessly. "Well, they'll probably die. A heart attack, a bad accident, an ectopic pregnancy—the same."

He wanted to say, "What about you, you'll be just as far from a doctor?" But "ectopic pregnancy"—what *was* it?—scared him off.

"And you," she said. "What will you do?"

"Finish up with the Expedition and go back to the stenographers' pool, I guess." At the thought of it, he flinched. He leaned against the fence and looked down at flowers fading in the bed. "It's not as dull as it sounds." He raised his face; she was looking at him. He could not hold her gaze. "It's getting late," he said.

"And I have packing to do. Winter clothes—Ansel, it can go to sixty below. Your spit, just like Jack London wrote in 'To Build a Fire,' it freezes with a crack before it hits the ground."

"Do you spit very much?" The joke was weak, foolish.

"Not a lot. In spite of what some may think, I'm a lady."

McLaughlin opened the door. He was in his shirtsleeves, and he looked out, coughed into his hand, and closed the door again. Fry and Annie smiled at each other, and he followed her up the walk.

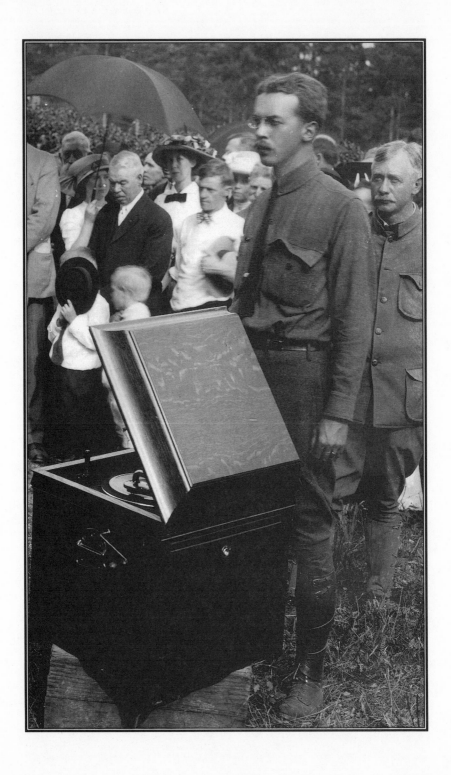

29

The sun came up red, dawdled in the river cottonwoods, rose and donned a white coat to be about the business of the day. After breakfast McLaughlin collected Fry, and Fry got his steno pad, and the two men climbed the cemetery hill. Below, the town lay cupped in tan fall grass; to the south were the streets and parade ground of the old fort, and farther in that direction stood a line of low hills.

"The wagons came from the hills." McLaughlin felt altogether recovered from his bout with malaria. His tone was crisp and his sentences composed and certain. "The first wagon bore a ghastly load. It carried the dead. They had put him on the bottom and stacked the policemen on top, and he was black with their blood.

"The next wagon held his wives and children. The women were wailing, having hacked at their hair and gashed their arms and breasts. Then came the surviving policemen, also in a wagon because the Ghost Dancers had stampeded their horses during the fight.

"We laid the wounded in the school hospital. Shave Head called for his wife; he wanted the priest to marry them in a Christian ceremony. She was sent for, but before she could arrive, he died.

"Bull Head turned to me and said, 'Father, did I do my duty?' I told him, 'Yes. We will always remember you.' 'It is well,' he said. He turned his face to the wall and passed away."

They stopped at Sitting Bull's grave. McLaughlin gripped a

fence picket in each hand. "There was no other way," he said. He looked at Fry. His eyes were without remorse. "*They* must arrest him. *They*. Not Cody, not the Army, *the Sioux*."

The Major stared at the wooden slab. The earth seemed to rush at him from all sides, shoot up through his legs, explode the memory in his head. The sweet-smelling pine coffin, the body staining the canvas, lumpy as a sturgeon in a net; the grave diggers, post prisoners, pressing down on the rigid arms, wedging the sack into the box, then sitting on the lid, smoking cigarettes and joking while the carpenter turned the screws down. They lowered the coffin on ropes and sent the dirt thudding in. The sergeant ordered the prisoners into the grave to tramp down the fill. They threw in more dirt, eight feet of it, to keep him forever still.

With a grim smile McLaughlin turned to Fry. "Some said I had sold the body for a thousand dollars. That the skin would be tanned and put on exhibition. That I had plotted murder all along. The Eastern press was full of such absurdities, and screamed for my recall. But I had been vindicated. My Indians had cast out their medicine man."

Down the hill, Fry fidgeted, kept edging ahead.

"Hold your horses," McLaughlin said. "She won't have left yet."

Fry felt his cheeks burn. He glanced at McLaughlin, who wore a poker face.

She was hooking up the team when they arrived. She looked Fry full in the face, and all the doors of her eyes were open. He, confused and wondering, looked down. Studied some little broken rocks. Shouted at himself, Good God! and lifted his face by effort of will. But by then McLaughlin had taken her in his arms.

"Daughter," McLaughlin said, "be careful out there. First thing you must do is get in a supply of wood, twenty cords at the least. Pay one of the farmers to do it, but no more than a dollar a cord."

"Yes, Father."

"I love you, Daughter. I always will."

"And I love you."

They embraced. Fry, looking on, felt an outsider. The Major let her go and went up the walk to the house.

"Goodbye, Ansel." She stood straight, her grave eyes holding his. She offered her hand. "I'll remember you."

He wanted to wrap his arms around her but hadn't the nerve. He shook her hand, which seemed somehow also a great intimacy. Heart hammering, he broke the handshake. "I'll remember you too."

"You must write."

"I promise."

"And take care of Father."

"I will."

Mrs. McLaughlin came out, and Fry turned and walked down the street. When he stopped to look, Annie was in the wagon, backing it, then starting up, the McLaughlins waving. He watched until the wagon was a speck.

South of Fort Yates the land flattened and stretched, with a curve to it like warped cardboard. Fences disappeared. Herds of horses cropped the short grass; seeing the wagon, they would trot forward and look, then whirl and run like the wind.

The heavy topless spring wagon had two seats, each wide enough for three passengers. Fry sat in the rear between Dixon and McLaughlin: between a doctor, he reflected glumly, who is not a doctor, and a major who is not a major, going to see a colonel who is not a colonel.

McLaughlin spoke across in front of him. "Doctor Dixon, I'd like to thank you for that glowing introduction at the ceremony. Don't know as I deserve such credit, but I'll not refuse it."

"You're most welcome, Major," Dixon said. "A glorious day, an historic event."

"If I may ask, will you be photographing Cody's actual filming?"

"Not the filming per se, but the Indians in old-time dress, the tipis, warriors, aspects of camp life, et cetera. A splendid opportunity."

McLaughlin said, "I wonder if we don't make too much of the past. 'Buffalo Bill's Indian Wars,' wild redskins in warbonnets. That's over and done with. We should be about the business of pointing the Indians toward the future."

"Ah, but the public must have its Indians," Dixon said. "Crazy Horse, Red Cloud, Chief Joseph, Sitting Bull—the public wants its noble red men."

"Sitting Bull noble? In a pig's eye."

"Many call him the noblest Indian that ever lived."

"Then many are very damned wrong." McLaughlin braced his feet and stiffened his neck. "For years he sowed dissension on this reservation. For years he held his people back. The Sioux helped themselves no end when they removed him."

"The Sioux," Dixon murmured. "I'm sure I read that you ordered his arrest."

"Indeed I did. But the people were behind me."

"It seems," said Dixon, "that tolerance and understanding would have gone a long way toward bringing Sitting Bull onto the white man's road."

"Sir, you were not there. You talk with blanket Indians still living in the past, with today's Indians playacting in their grandparents' feathers and rags, and you conclude that Sitting Bull was a hero. I'll tell you what he was. He was an egomaniac who would stop at nothing to hold onto his power. He got exactly what he deserved."

In the front seat Booth had turned to listen. Fry drew back as the words passed in front of his chest.

"Sitting Bull was a great leader—all the Indians say so."

"A mere medicine man. A charlatan and a fraud."

"I'm suspicious when a man can't find anything good—not one single thing—to say about another man."

"If he had any good in him, he never showed it to me."

They sparred for several minutes, voices rising, until McLaughlin barked at the driver to stop. "We're getting down," he told Fry. "It's enough to share a railcar with this blatherskite, we don't have to ride with him as well."

They climbed down from the rig, and the Major slapped the nearest horse on the rump. The wagon lurched, then settled back to a walk. Soon it passed behind a hill and was lost to sight.

Fry looked around. Low clumps of sage. A pox of prairie dog diggings, the fresh-turned earth dark. A sky so wide it seemed to wrap the landscape. He looked inquiringly at McLaughlin, who grunted, stepped off the road, and stalked away through the sage.

"Some people just can't abide the truth," he muttered. "Damn, but he gives me the royal fantods. Should've told him exactly what I think of his expedition." He stopped and surveyed the terrain. "The Commissioner forwarded a letter from the SAI. So absurd it's undoubtedly true." He walked on, apparently sure of his direction. "There will be a war in Europe—that's obvious, yes, but a war so general that we will be drawn in as well, despite that pacifist in the White House." He stopped, squinted, started off on a slightly altered heading. "Part of what the good doctor is up to is paying back the government that has so kindly allowed him to photograph its wards. He's drumming up allegiance to the flag. But not to promote citizenship. To promote enlistment. Troops of Indian cavalry. Best light cavalry in the world. Troops of whooping Sioux, to scare the bejesus out of Uncle Fritz."

Fry slowed. All the talk about a "vanishing race," and they want them for cannon fodder? McLaughlin angled down a low wash.

Certainly. Bow to the flag. Men have died to keep its folds from trailing in the dust. So the Expedition means nothing. He scrambled to catch up. "Sir," he said. McLaughlin halted, half-turned.

"What will we do?"

McLaughlin stood with eyebrows raised.

"Will we continue with them?"

The blocky shoulders lifted, fell. "What else?"

"This fiasco . . . should be exposed for what it is."

McLaughlin regarded Fry sharply. "We have our orders." He turned and resumed walking.

The wash steepened, with scrubby pines growing in patches. Then the cut widened, and after a few hundred yards fed into a narrow valley. From the floor of the valley, a ragged popping sound rose. They headed toward it.

The rectangular black box stood on long, segmented legs. It made an oil-smooth growling, its handle cranked steadily by the cameraman—wearing britches, puttees, his cap turned backward on his head—who stood half-crouched, peering through the viewfinder. Opposing waves of Indians, one blue-clad and the other dressed in white, met in front of the lens. An upraised war club caught the afternoon light. Rifles popped and smoke drifted. An Indian policeman threw his hands up and crumpled to the grass. From behind the camera, a man shouted "CAVALRY!" through a megaphone while his assistant waved a flag. Horse soldiers broke from the trees and thundered toward the melee, Buffalo Bill in the vanguard. His rifle flashed like a raindrop. His white horse made a sudden turn, stopped, and another pop was added to the tumult of sound: A Ghost Dancer about to clout a policeman spun and fell. "Yes! Yes!" cried the director, a short man with chestnut-dyed hair, standing on a chair.

"INDIANS," the megaphone yelled, "RETREAT!" The Ghost Dancers whirled and ran, yipping like dogs.

"Cut! Cut!" The director jumped down from the chair, slapping at the air as if beset by bees. "Tell 'em—Christ!—once they're dead, they can't just lift up their heads and look!"

As the interpreter explained this to the extras, Cody's horse walked through their midst. "All right," the director said wearily, gauging the light, "time for one more take."

"EVERYBODY BACK TO HIS STATION."

Buffalo Bill's horse kept walking. It trudged past Fry, standing with the spectators. Cody sat slumped in the saddle. His white hat was encircled by a braided gold band. He wore white cavalry gauntlets, a buckskin suit, an immense knife in a sheath. His rifle, across the pommel, shone with inlaid gold.

The spectators called out to him, but Buffalo Bill did not lift his head. His eyes were shut in a suet face. His horse carried him in among the tents, where cooking fires burned and the high, breathless babble of a calliope could be heard. The chestnut-haired director swore and kicked over his chair.

By dinnertime Cody had revived, and he greeted McLaughlin like an old friend. The Major, a head shorter, snapped, "Why are you leading the cavalry? You know very well that never took place."

Cody rolled his eyes and shook his head. "This is the story they wrote. I lead the soldiers into camp, but by then it's too late. Sitting Bull has already been shot. I reach my old adversary just as he breathes his last."

"Not a grain of truth to it!" McLaughlin's eyes blazed. "We kept you away from the camp—you never got there at all!"

Cody nodded mildly. "That wouldn't be a story," he said. "If you had my debts . . ." His eyes fell upon Fry. "Here, who's this fine young gent?"

"My stenographer," McLaughlin growled.

"Ansel Fry, sir." Fry put out his hand and the great man took it: Fry could barely feel a grip through the heavy gauntlet. Cody's eyes possessed a distant gaze, no doubt permanently calibrated for searching out hostiles on the shimmering plain. "Fry, Fry," Cody said to the air above Fry's head. "Kin to the Charlie Fry, runs cattle out of Laramie?"

"No, sir."

"Ahh," Buffalo Bill said, baptizing him with whiskey breath. He released Fry's hand, nodded amicably to the Major, and passed on to a table steaming with beef.

That night they sat across the circle from Cody and his entourage. The Plainsman wore a plucked otter coat and a fur cap. His flunkies gathered around him, laughing at his jokes. Dixon and Booth were there—pointedly ignoring McLaughlin —and two dozen Sioux men. Off to one side, three Indians began beating on a drum. A pipe made its way around; when it reached Fry he drew three puffs, remembering from *King of the Bordermen* that three was the sacred number and to puff more or fewer times was a breach of etiquette. He was surprised to see several Indians puff once or twice or not at all.

When the pipe had gone full circle, the Indians threw off their blankets and began to dance: two pats on the ground with one foot, two with the other—a light pat followed by a heavier one—bending and twisting their bodies, snaking their arms to the rhythm of the drum. Each Indian seemingly danced by himself, threading his way in and out among his fellows. When the drumming ceased, the dancers would sit back down and resume their blankets; one man would then rise and make a speech—McLaughlin translated some of it— bragging of hunts, horse thieving, deeds of war.

When a young man got up, Fry wondered what he would boast about. The straight rows of wheat he had planted? The "A" in industrial arts? What would he, Ansel Fry, say, if forced to it? *I took forbidden pictures. I drew a bead on the truth. I stole souls.*

The young man dropped his blanket to reveal a Ghost Dance shirt painted with suns, moons, and stars. He spoke with fervor, his hands slashing. "What's he saying?" Fry whispered.

"He's talking about the film," McLaughlin said. "He says it didn't happen this way at all. Sitting Bull was a great chief, a leader of his nation. The police murdered him, deliberately and in cold blood."

McLaughlin plucked a grass stem, sucked on it. "His father was there and told him all about it. The young man is wearing his father's shirt. He says it's a sacrilege to make this film over the graves of those who were killed."

Fry saw Cody lean out of the firelight and tip a flask. There was joking and glee in his portion of the circle; plainly Buffalo Bill and his friends did not understand what was being said. After a while the young man talked himself out and sat down. The drumming began again.

30

Before dawn, while McLaughlin still slept, Fry left the tent. In a thicket by the river he put on the camera. The evening before, when they had walked into camp, the tent had already been pitched; he had found his suitcase sitting on a cot, the changing bag and plates still inside, apparently undisturbed. He had felt relieved, although not fully at ease: The bag had ridden in with Booth and Dixon, it was possible they had searched it.

Sleep had not come easily. Whenever he closed his eyes, he had seen Annie's face. Their goodbye had been all wrong. He ached to see her again. She was only five miles away. He would walk, or get a horse—rent it, borrow it, buy it if he had to—and go.

But first he had work to do.

He knelt by the stream and splashed water onto his face. Low clouds in the east banked the sun like a glowing coal. He rose and straightened the vest. All was in order. The suit felt barely adequate against the chill—it could snow any day, the Major said.

He saw her strong cheekbones and glistening hair; her dark eyes that penetrated, and admitted penetration. Their frankness disturbed him. Why? Wasn't it frankness that he himself pursued? He had never felt such a sudden, full burst of passion for a woman. She had no falseness about her, no coyness, no shame. A woman without shame . . . And why should a woman, or a man, feel ashamed about life—about love? Love. Did he feel it for her? Did she for him?

The day came with a needling wind. The film company had hired the carousel, and hardly had the breakfast fires been kindled than the Indians were pestering the man to start it up. The calliope snorted and tooted, and the skewered horses began circling the engine, each enameled, toothy rictus chasing the tail in front. Whenever the machine halted, a new set of riders, young and old, male and female, would mount. He closed his eyes as he tripped the shutter: laughing child on a horse's back, knuckles pale against the shaft.

The sky grew grayer, the sun faded to a pearl. The filming was just under way. He found Cody, with two attendents helping him onto his horse. *Click.* Cody took a deep breath and adjusted his hat. They handed up his rifle, a box of blank shells. *Buffalo Bill, Buffalo Bill.* He snicked them one by one into the loading port—God but the rifle could hold a number—then smoothly levered one to the breech. He raised the gun in one hand and pulled the trigger. The shot smoked straight into the air. *Never missed, never will:* As he made the second picture, Fry half-expected an Indian or a buffalo to come tumbling out of the clouds.

He turned. Booth stood partly screened by a tent; he nodded cheerfully, stepped over the rope, lit a cigarette and fanned the match. He pointed the cigarette at Cody. "When I was a kid—Jeez, how I wanted to see Buffalo Bill. He was my hero. I waited for years. Finally the Wild West came to town, but I had the scarlet fever and the health officer nailed a sign on the door. Quarantine!" He chuckled, coming closer.

Fry took a step back. "That was sure tough luck, Booth. Hey, I've got to go find McLaughlin. See you later." He turned and hurried away.

In among the tents, he slowed. Something had collected at his core, something viscous and thick, rising to choke off his wind. Booth knew, he was sure of it. They had gone through his suitcase. Why hadn't they confronted him yet? He wracked his brain. Did they mean to catch him red-handed? Well, he wouldn't be trapped. He'd box up the camera, ship it and the changing bag and the plates back to Kravitz, call it quits—if he had to, pitch the whole lot in the river. There was nothing they could prove.

But could he face the world without his camera? In the night he'd had a dream, and now it came flooding back. He was lying on a bed, naked. He looked down and saw a hole in the center of his chest, a small hole centered between the nipples, a glass eye rimmed with steel. He tried to touch it but couldn't, his hands were pinned at his sides. He was no longer wearing the camera. It was wearing him. The camera had become his heart. To lose it was to die.

He trembled as the rest of the dream came back. Banks of hanging lamps glared in his face. The leering Booth, in a pale gown, fastened a strap across his hips and another across his neck. Then Booth fixed a gauze mask over his mouth and nose, took an eyedropper, held it above the mask, and began the drip-drip-drip. He surged against the straps. Smelling the sweet ether, he tried to hold his breath. Dixon appeared, wearing surgical gloves, raising a scalpel, a real doctor after all. He realized they were going to take his heart. He screamed and kicked, lashing his head. He looked about wildly for help. Kravitz had turned his back. The Major was nowhere to be seen.

Slowly he surfaced from his fear. He strode through the camp. Somebody should have a saddle horse to rent. Get out of here. Ditch the camera—go to her.

"Ansel!"

He looked up. She sat on the wagon seat, the wind tugging at her hair. "Annie!" He gave her a hand down.

She landed lightly. They stood holding hands for a moment. Then she laughed and said, "You should see my school! Mouse nests everywhere. In the stove, in the woodbox, even in the teacher's desk. I was cleaning for hours yesterday. And you know, as soon as I lit a fire in the stove, they started showing up."

"Who?"

"My pupils, of course. So far, six. And they know of eight more."

"That's wonderful! Annie—I'm glad you came."

She gave him her black eyes. This time he did not drop his gaze. They linked arms and walked, and when her skirt brushed his leg, or he caught the scent of her hair, his heart filled.

"Now you can see the famous Buffalo Bill," he said. "Although Major McLaughlin says the film is not accurate."

Stopping, she looked around the valley. The bottom was thick with tall tan grass. Trees lined the river, and brush snaked up the draws. The hills facing south were drier and paler than the hills facing north.

"This is a strange place for me," she said.

He waited.

"I was just a baby when it happened. When I was growing up, there were families who wouldn't let their children play with me because of what the police had done." She thought for a moment. "Maybe that's why I'm happy to be home. I have a chance to repay a debt to my people. I've stopped drifting."

They stepped through the pale sage and the last purple asters and the strawy grama grass. They followed a trail through a patch of wild plums whose lower branches had been picked clean. They reached a clearing where a small oak tree stood. In its scraggly branches, tied there by red yarn, four eagle feathers twisted in the wind. Beneath the oak was a bronze historical marker with the entitling phrase, *Sitting*

Bull's Tragic Death. The legend describing the arrest had, as its last sentence, *An unnecessary and tragic end of a notable, if misguided, Indian leader.* Someone had tried to scratch off the words *if misguided,* but the efforts had only served to polish the heavy raised letters, so that they stood out brightly against the tarnished plaque.

"They say my father died in the first shooting," Annie said. "I hope so. I hope he didn't kill any of his people." She looked at the eagle feathers, white with black tips, small plumes of down billowing at the bases of the shafts. "I've often thought about Sitting Bull. I think I understand how he felt.

"He loved his people. He knew their way of life was coming to an end. He wanted them to adopt the good things that the whites were bringing, but he didn't want them to stop being themselves. He saw his power and respect slipping away, so of course he fought against it. He was just one small person, even though they made him big. Then the world moved, and he was crushed."

"The Major says he did the only thing he could have done, under the circumstances."

She nodded. "He was another small person."

"Can a person do what's right," Fry said, "without getting crushed?"

Her eyes were friendly and shrewd. "She has to try," she said. "They taught us in school, 'Kill the Indian and save the child.' I won't do that. I'll let my children speak Lakota. For that, I could lose my job. If they fire me, I'll go on teaching on my own. I'll teach them the white ways, but I'll also tell them to go home to their parents and grandparents and learn the red ways, because they are needed still. We need to keep them, for ourselves and for the white people when they're ready."

At that moment Fry knew he loved her. "Yes," he said, "a person can make a difference, doing what he thinks is right. But that doesn't mean he won't get crushed."

. . .

The cabin's logs were clumsily squared, weathered a pale gray. One small window and a rusty roof. Could it be the same one? No—no bullet holes. Just an old cabin they were using for the film. The real one, McLaughlin now remembered, had been numbered and taken apart, then loaded onto a flatcar, and shipped to Chicago for the World's Fair.

A dark hand was laid against the wall next to his. Turning, he saw an old man in a faded blue uniform. The face was familiar. "Alvin! Alvin Silent!" Pleased with his quick recall, McLaughlin shook the Indian's hand. "Hello, my friend."

"Hello, Major."

McLaughlin regarded the man's face. Once smooth and full, it was now deeply creased; the eyes were sunk away in pits, and bones and veins strained outward against the skin.

"How are you? How is your wife?" McLaughlin asked.

"She still lives with me," Silent said.

"Your family? I remember a boy."

"He died. A boar pig trampled him."

"I'm sorry. You had, I think, a daughter as well."

"She's gone away, we don't know where."

McLaughlin nodded, lowering his head. He saw Silent's feet, casked in black shoes; he could not recall which one they had amputated after the fight. He scratched his nails against a log in the wall, the gray fibers flaking off and dancing away on the wind. "I've never forgotten the loyalty of my police," he said. "I've never forgotten that day."

"I've never forgotten that day, either. And it has never forgotten me." Silent lowered his tone. "Major, can you spare a dollar?"

"What for?"

Silent rubbed his hollow temple with a knuckle. "We killed Sitting Bull for you. I think you knew—did you?—if we went in there, we would kill him. Because they wouldn't let him go, and he wouldn't go himself, he was such a brave man. After what everyone said, that surprised us."

McLaughlin turned and fronted the man. Silent's eyes were dull, his upper lip stretched thin over his teeth. The skull behind that face was fighting its way out. "You don't look well," McLaughlin said.

"I have terminal."

"What?"

"Terminal. They say a wasting disease, the liver. Medicine man won't touch me."

McLaughlin remembered a diffident lad, handsome, full of grace. *Inilaon:* silent. "No," he said, "I did not know. If Bull Head had taken the wagon as instructed, no one would have been hurt."

"The day we killed him," Silent said, "something called my wife outside. She went out to the henhouse, but the chickens was all right. She went and looked at the cow, it was all right too." He raised his face. "She saw him go by. She saw Sitting Bull go by, up in the air, and she fell down and cried out, but he didn't come down. He just got smaller and smaller until he went away."

"Do you really believe that?" McLaughlin said.

Silent looked at him. "A dollar, Major. Give me a dollar, please."

"Do you believe that a dead man can go flying through the air?"

Silent grunted. "The priest says Jesus could fly." His face relaxed, recalling for McLaughlin the fine, graceful man he had once been. A smirk shredded that mask. "A dollar," he said.

"For food?"

"Yes, for food."

"No. You want it for drink. That's what has ruined your liver."

"Anyway, give it to me."

"No. I'm sorry," McLaughlin said. "I'm truly sorry."

. . .

Annie and Fry reached the cabin. "We have one like this," she said, "on my father's allotment."

We could live there, Fry thought. Or at your school. You could teach them. I could . . . He drew a blank. He looked up and saw McLaughlin standing next to the cabin with an old Indian. He sensed immediately that something was wrong. Annie laid a hand on his arm.

They walked quickly. As they drew near, he felt the pressure of her hand, stopping him.

"You *knew*." The Indian, in a policeman's uniform, stared at McLaughlin. They stood too close for a friendly conversation. Neither man realized they were being watched.

"I most certainly did not." The Major's tone was final. "I did not know there would be trouble. I had no idea that people would be killed."

The words came clearly to Fry and Annie. She continued to hold his arm. She was watching intently.

"If you had known," the Indian said, "would you still have sent us?"

McLaughlin was silent. He stood as immobile as the little lump of rock, the Standing Rock, on the pedestal at his agency. His shoulders slumped. He lowered his face.

The Indian stood opposing his old agent.

McLaughlin straightened. He shook a finger in the man's face. "If you had followed my orders, there would have been no shooting, no casualties, you would have brought him in, I would have talked some sense into him, made him see the absurdity, the utter absurdity . . ."

Fry's arm moved away from Annie's hand. Her glance flickered to his face. He reached into his pocket. Found the string. One frame left, it would be his last. The two old men, the stark hills, the weathered cabin, his heart opening, their images entering—as he let go of the string, the air surged out of his lungs as thick arms pinned him from behind. He heard a shout—Booth's—and saw Dixon trotting over. He felt his feet leave the ground. He bent his body at the waist, then slammed his head back and heard a bellow of pain. The horizon tipped. He felt blows. As the fine bright flakes rushed in from the edges of his vision, he saw Annie's eyes filled with fear.

Branches slapped his face as he blundered ahead. He stopped and shut his eyes, blinking back tears. A knot throbbed at the back of his head, another above his ear. He clawed at the front of his coat: The camera was indeed gone. They had dragged him before McLaughlin, opened his coat, opened his vest, lifted the ribbon over his head. How strange the disk had looked, blue-black and bloodless, an atrophied, disembodied organ. McLaughlin had shaken his head, turned and walked away.

The brush tore at his hands and face. He reached the river, gray and dull. The wind rose, ruffling the sage, keening in the trees. He stopped in a clearing and stood, his sides heaving, like a blown horse. He looked up. In a small gnarled oak, eagle feathers danced on a string.

The river, the wind, filled his ears. The sky was growing dark. A few snowflakes, the season's first, dusted his shoulders. He stood shivering.

She came through the brush holding her skirt, parting the branches with her hand. She stopped an arm's length away. "I tracked you down."

Coming closer, she laid a hand where the camera had been. He felt the cloth all slack, like old skin.

She waited until he raised his face. "I knew," she said. "It had to be someone on the Expedition—and it couldn't have been anyone else."

He nodded dumbly.

"Ansel, the pictures are *good.*" Her dark eyes burned into

his. "If they don't like them, it's because they don't like themselves."

She understood, then. He felt the surge, as when he had taken a picture, the clean, free feeling coursing through every fiber of his being: This is right, this is true, this is good.

She brought her face close and kissed him.

He felt her lashes on his eyelids. He wrapped his arms around her. Her body pressed against his. He kissed her deeply, filling his lungs with her breath.

31

The train chugged across the snow-salted land, the telegraph poles clipping past, a rhythmic hypnotic blink that interrupted the blue light streaming in through the pane. The track curved, and smoke from the engine came clouding back, brown-black, thinning, growing gray and paler still, swirling away to nothingness against the tan-and-white land.

Photographs lay on the desk—men, women, children, Indians, whites: his pictures, and also somehow belonging to the people in them. People caught off guard, full of vitality, full of life. Photographs that cut across race and culture and time.

The images grew shadowy and blurred.

Yes, they were two of a kind. He remembered Billy Trimble's simple Navaho dream: a house with the door facing sunrise, and we'll live there, look at the stars, smell the rain and the wind.

Three days, and he'd thought of little else: Could they coalesce? A teacher, a photographer, each with a mission in life. He tasted salt and blood; his vision brightened, swam. She has her place, on the lonely plain. My place is lonely too—reaching out to a wider world.

He wished he had taken a picture of her. But she had given him so much more.

The door opened briskly on its plunger. McLaughlin strode in, took a chair, and indicated the one across from him. Fry remained standing. McLaughlin's eyes narrowed and he cleared his throat. "I have reviewed your behavior on Standing Rock Reservation and, apparently, throughout the rest of the trip, and I find no other way of interpreting it than as a breach of trust." The formal tone softened. "I put my trust in you, Son. You let me down."

Fry looked at the eyes, gray and icy beneath the snowy brows. "The Indians trust you," he said, "because you tell no lies. My photographs tell no lies."

"Those pictures?"

"Yes."

"Even though you relied on subterfuge to get them?"

"There is no other way."

McLaughlin waved a hand in irritation. "The fact of the matter is that you, an employee of the Indian Bureau, have engaged in acts reflecting badly upon the organization." He paused. "Must admit I'm a little disappointed in myself"—he looked away momentarily, and Fry found his tone difficult to interpret—"for not detecting your activities sooner." The Major said, peremptorily, "You will return to Washington immediately. The Commissioner wishes to interview you. I assume he will terminate your employment with the Indian Bureau." The gray eyes seemed to thaw a little. "I'll send him a wire. A young man doesn't always see the consequences of his actions. And I'll tell you this, you can make a start at clearing your name by taking this camera"—he laid the disk on the table—"and getting rid of it. Throw it away." He checked his watch. "Eagle Butte, South Dakota. We stop within the hour. You may remove your belongings from the car then." He stood and left the room.

The train pulled in, halted, and backed onto the siding. The stationmaster put on heavy gloves and went between Signet and the next-to-last car, pulled the pin, and chocked the private Pullman's wheels. When he signaled to the engineer, the locomotive began edging ahead, drawing the other coaches into the depot.

Fry opened the door. He carried down his suitcase, then dragged his trunk clunking down the steps.

People were boarding the train, handlers heaved mail sacks, a dolly piled with crates went squealing past. Signet stood sober and green, the windows along its side reflecting light. Behind one of those bright squares the Major would be watching, waiting for him to find a trash bin and jettison this part of his life.

Big clock in a brass housing—the long hand gave a sudden jerk and moved up three minutes. He carried the trunk, then the suitcase, in under the platform roof. A door screeched and slammed. People waved to others on the train. The conductor called out "Bo-o-o-oard," looked around the platform, and circled his hand. The pops lifted, and steam gushed from the stack.

Onto the deck of the final coach he went, set down his suitcase, went back for the trunk. Sweating, he got it up the steps.

He straightened. McLaughlin had climbed down out of Signet. He stood with his hands on his hips, a block of a man in a dark suit and perfect white hair. "Fry!" he shouted. His voice was drowned by the whistle. The engine coughed as the rods shot back and forth, turning the great shining wheels. The Major took two stiff steps. He raised a hand. "Fry . . . luck!"

Fry watched as McLaughlin, the Pullman, the station, all went gliding backward, obscured in the tumbling smoke.

The wind sang in the railing, the awning struts. The car swayed and the rails began to click. Gradually, the town receded. He touched the faint bulge beneath his coat.

He would go see Kravitz and give him the photos—all of them. Then he would turn and journey west. He had promised.

Epilogue

The Rodman Wanamaker Expedition of Citizenship to the North American Indian concluded in December 1913 with a ceremony on the Staten Island site where ground had first been broken for the Indian memorial ten months earlier. James McLaughlin was not present. He and Dr. Joseph Kossuth Dixon had fallen out over the photographer's staging of photographic subjects and over the bombastic flag ceremonies that confused the Indians into believing they had been made citizens. "Hot air artist" is how he described Dixon. In his official report, McLaughlin wrote: "I wish to state forcibly that, in my opinion, the Expedition had no beneficial effects whatever, either on Indians or whites. . . . The most I can say for [it] is that it has been harmless."

At the Panama-Pacific Exposition of 1915, in San Francisco, former president Theodore Roosevelt opened the exhibit of expeditionary photographs, and Joseph Dixon lectured three times a day for five months to more than a million citizens. Prints were sold from the three Wanamaker expeditions, perhaps the first photographic print sales on record. Dixon's illustrated book, *The Vanishing Race,* was also selling briskly; it has been reprinted several times over the years, with critics favorably comparing his photographs to the famous Indian portraits of Edward S. Curtis.

In time, the pictorial materials gathered at Rodman Wanamaker's behest were forgotten, the collection consigned to an attic of a Wanamaker store. Eventually portions were transferred to the American Museum of Natural History in New York, to Indiana University, and to the National Archives in Washington.

Many of the glass plate negatives and prints survived; the fifty miles of nitrate film footage—highly unstable and self-inflammable—did not. Nor did the proposed memorial complex of libraries, art gallery, museum, and, of course, the bronze statue of the noble red man overlooking New York harbor. The plans were set aside at the outbreak of the First World War and never seriously revived.

Dr. Dixon remained in the Wanamakers' employ and continued his vague campaigns on behalf of the Indians. After the war, he traveled to France and photographed battlefields where Indians had fought, and military cemeteries where they were buried. He gathered information on Indians' valor in battle and took pictures of wounded survivors. A book, *From Tepees to Trenches*, was incomplete at the time of his death in 1926.

McLaughlin was instrumental in persuading Franklin Lane, Secretary of the Interior under President Wilson, to speed the granting of citizenship to qualified Indians. McLaughlin designed tokens of citizenship that were presented in 1916 and 1917. These consisted of a purse ("The wise man saves his money, so that when the sun does not smile and the grass does not grow, he will not starve," observed the presenter), a leather bag, a button. McLaughlin attended a 1917 ceremony on Standing Rock Reservation conferring citizenship; a photograph shows Indians shooting a symbolic "Last Arrow" and accepting the plow. McLaughlin died six years later in Washington at age eighty-one, still working for the Indian Bureau. He was buried in McLaughlin, South Dakota, a town he helped found.

The Wanamaker Expedition did indeed encounter Buffalo Bill making a film on a Dakota reservation. His movie, *Buffalo Bill's Indian Wars*, has been variously described as an historically correct exposé suppressed by the government, and a mockery of the Indian's tragic destruction. It was never publicly shown; no copy of the film is known to exist.